Praise for the
Low Country Dog Walker Series

"Brimming with Southern charm."
—Breda Arnold, NetGalley Reviewer

"Plenty of clues, red herrings and humor, with a bit of sweet romance to round it out."
—Amary Chaptman, NetGalley Top Reviewer on *Dog-Gone Dead*

"*Dog-Gone Dead* is dog-gone good. An enjoyable series with likeable characters, nice setting and the ending was a bit of a surprise."
—Nancy Baker, Goodreads Reviewer

Books by Jackie Layton

The Low Country Dog Walker Series

Bite the Dust

Dog-Gone Dead

Bag of Bones

Bag of Bones

A Low Country Dog Walker Mystery

by

Jackie Layton

Have fun with Andi & Grace!
Jackie Layton

B

Bell Bridge Books

Bell Bridge Books
PO BOX 300921
Memphis, TN 38130
Print ISBN: 978-1-61194-992-6

Bell Bridge Books is an Imprint of BelleBooks, Inc.

We at BelleBooks enjoy hearing from readers.
Visit our websites
BelleBooks.com
BellBridgeBooks.com
ImaJinnBooks.com

10 9 8 7 6 5 4 3 2 1

Cover design: Debra Dixon
Interior design: Hank Smith
Photo/Art credits:
Money bag (manipulated) © Maxim Popov | Dreamstime.com
Seagull (manipulated) © Adrenalinapura | Dreamstime.com

:Lbbh:01:

Dedication

I dedicate this book to my children. I was blessed with two wonderful sons, Bill and Scott. I've loved every minute of being their mom. Each is married, and I am so thankful to the women who married them, Amanda and Kellianne. I want to include my amazing grandchildren Brooke, Allie, Cameron, and Baby Layton who is coming later this year. My kids have all listened to my dreams of becoming a published author, and I appreciate their love and encouragement.

Chapter One

FOR YEARS I'D been Andi Grace Scott, lover of Cokes, coffee, and chocolate. Fast food was my favorite kind of supper. I knew how to prepare simple meals like hot dogs or grilled cheese sandwiches. I could even toss a salad. But fast food had kept me alive.

Now? My feet pounded on the beach near the water where the sand was firm. Perspiration beaded my hairline despite the briskness. I had become a runner. *Me.* A runner.

How had Marc Williams, the oh-so-handsome attorney, persuaded me to take up running? The man had a way of convincing me to make healthy choices, so I shouldn't complain. This was a better cardio workout than walking dogs and solving murders—not that I planned to investigate any more murders. From now on my attention would be firmly focused on the beauty around me.

Orange, purple, and gray streaks stretched across the horizon. Puddles mirrored the white clouds floating in the morning sky. A recreational boat zoomed by. If they'd been out fishing all night, they would've needed to bundle up. The wind had a cool bite on this first Monday morning in March.

I breathed in through my nose and out my mouth and tried to ignore the stitch in my side. The muscles in my calves tightened. Maybe ignoring the pain would keep the leg cramps at bay.

If I complained, Marc would argue I should've drunk more water and stretched longer. As an attorney, the man knew how to state his case. He'd be right, of course. My pre-run time had been spent savoring my first cup of coffee. I'd never give up my morning cup of java.

Sand stuck to my damp legs, but I kept running.

Marc slowed his pace to match mine, and his dog Chubb ran at his side. "You're doing great, Andi Grace."

"How'd you talk me into running so early?" I tried for annoyed, but the morning's beauty made it impossible to be grumpy. The company wasn't bad either.

"It's good for our metabolisms." Marc grinned.

I gulped for air but didn't stop because I didn't want to disappoint Marc. My German shepherd, Sunny, ran at my side with her ears perked up like little radars. Her head turned from side to side, watching for danger or unexpected surprises like a wandering ghost crab or a cannonball jellyfish. "What's your day look like?"

"I've got a contract dispute this morning and two new clients this afternoon. How about you?" His words flowed with ease, and he didn't appear a bit winded.

"Can't talk." Pain stabbed below my ribs, and I slowed while clutching my side.

"Okay, I'll talk. Since your old boyfriend, Danny, decided to run for state representative, he's been a doozy to deal with." Marc's fists clenched at chest level instead of their normal relaxed position and gentle swing. "Do you suppose he heard we started dating and is gunning for me for personal reasons?"

"Danny Nichols doesn't care one bit about me." I huffed. Interesting to see Marc frustrated by Danny.

"He and his family decided to drop their fight with you over Peter's will. It's possible he cares more than you suspect."

A solid black cat sitting on a beach house's wooden walkway scratched behind his ear. I tensed, expecting chaos, but the dogs were focused on the water and sand and never noticed the feline.

Chubb chased the water as it came onto land and rolled back to sea. The golden retriever was almost a year old. He was lots of fun and smart as a tack, but he hadn't matured. Chubb made me laugh, while Sunny made me feel loved and protected. My German shepherd had appeared at my house over twelve years earlier and had never left me. Her maturity and loyalty were stellar. I loved both dogs. In fact, I'd never met a dog I didn't like.

Sunny barked and sprinted to the large rock barrier ahead of us. So much for maturity. I pointed. "Marc, did you see her run to the beach groin? She never runs off without permission."

"Yeah, she's supposed to exert a positive influence on Chubb." He laughed.

"I know." Uneasiness settled over my shoulders. The air grew still. Another odd thing for a March morning on the coast of South Carolina.

"Maybe she's reliving her youth. Hanging out with Chubb might not be a good thing for her. He often leaves me on a whim."

I shifted into a jog until I reached the rigid rock structure a few hundred yards away. The rocks had been engineered to trap sand and prevent beach erosion. But instead of sand, the structure had prevented something larger from drifting away.

Sunny stood over a woman's body. Layers of clothes. All wet. No movement. My feet halted their movement. My lungs froze. No. This couldn't be happening again, but the coloring and texture of the woman's skin warned me she wasn't alive. "It's the cat lady." My words came out in a whisper, my mouth suddenly dry.

"Aw, man." Marc yanked off his ball cap and ran a hand through his thick blond hair. "Tabby Malkin was one of my first clients at the law firm. I know people around here think she's strange, but she's—she was—a real sweetheart. Even though I was a stranger to her, she trusted me to handle her affairs." Marc removed his phone from the pocket of his mid-thigh running shorts. "I'll call the sheriff."

Sunny paced then laid down beside Tabby on the beach.

I stooped to check for the woman's pulse, in case she was alive, then I stopped. Sightless eyes looked skyward, unable to distinguish a white seagull from a brown pelican. What was the last thing she'd seen? One of her beloved cats? Tears welled in my eyes. Locals had nicknamed Tabby *the cat lady* because she walked the beaches and island streets with two bowls, a jug of milk, and cat kibble. If she spied a feral cat, she fed it. The woman hadn't lived in the area for long, but in a small town, it didn't take long to get noticed. I'd never taken time to ask if Tabby was her real name or if she'd started calling herself Tabby because she loved cats. Although maybe her love of cats came because she'd been named Tabby.

There'd be no more opportunities to ask her now. A tear slipped down my face, and I shouldered it away.

My stomach churned at the sight of the poor woman. Was her death a tragic accident or something sinister? I gazed at a fluffy white cloud on the horizon then back to Tabby. I didn't believe her death was an accident.

Tabby's body was sandy and wet but not bloated, making me think she'd been killed on the beach. Moisture in the air might have contributed to some of the wetness, but more likely the tide had washed over her body. Being this far up on the beach had probably prevented the body from washing out to sea.

We stood near the meandering high tide line, where little bits of driftwood, drying seaweed, and scattered shells marked how high the ocean had come on land.

I wrapped my arms around my stomach. There were no obvious gunshot wounds, at least not on the front of her body. What had happened to Tabby? Had she tripped and hit her head on the boulders making up the beach's protective structure?

She wore baggy black sweatpants, a gray T-shirt, and a long-sleeved denim button-up. The shirt was torn at the shoulder. A black high-top Converse sneaker covered one foot, but the other foot was bare.

Chubb barked and jumped over the short end of the rock groin near the sand dune. His long legs aided his quick departure.

Marc cupped his hands around his mouth. "Chubb! Come back."

I sighed. "You better go after him. I'll stay with Tabby."

"Sure you don't mind?"

"Go." It was the only word I could squeeze out.

Marc ran after his dog while holding the phone to his ear.

The stitch in my side eased, but the dead woman hurt my soul. We had something in common. Both of us loved animals. She focused on cats, providing food and milk to the felines on the island while allowing them to be free. Canines claimed my attention. If I found a dog, I always matched him with an owner. Different animals, different methods, but we both loved the abandoned animals around Heyward Beach. My throat grew tight.

I couldn't peer at the woman any longer, so I turned my focus toward Marc and his dog. Chubb stopped along a sand dune and dug with his front paws. Sand flew through the air. Marc backed away and spoke into the phone. The golden retriever continued his mission until Marc snapped the leash on Chubb's harness and led him back to me.

Three cigarette butts floated in a sandy tidal pool a few feet from Tabby's head. I'd never seen the woman smoke, but some people hid the habit.

Sirens wailed from the west while waves pounded the shore.

Sunny stood and approached me, stopping to stand by my side.

I rubbed her back. "Oh, girl, I'm so sorry you had to see Tabby like this." It wasn't the first time I'd come across a dead body, but my German shepherd hadn't been around when I found Peter Roth or Corey Lane. "It sure doesn't get any easier."

Marc and Chubb joined us near the line of rocks where Tabby lay.

Marc raised his eyebrows. With one hand he held the phone, the leash in his other hand. "Are you okay?"

My mouth quivered. "Yeah. Did you ever see Tabby smoke?"

"She wasn't a smoker. After her accident in Dallas, she became obsessive about her health."

Whoop. Whoop. Tires screeched and the siren ended.

Sheriff Wade Stone and Deputy David Wayne ran to us from the nearest public entrance.

Marc reported their appearance to the emergency operator then disconnected and slid the phone into the pocket of his running shorts.

Chubb threw his head back and howled.

"Quiet, boy." Marc knelt and wrapped his arms around Chubb.

David reached us first, glanced at the corpse, and turned his attention to Marc and me. "Did you touch anything?"

"I've learned my lesson." I raised my hands and stepped back.

The sheriff stopped beside his deputy. "Call the coroner and cordon off the area, David."

"Yes, sir." David stepped away then turned back. "I left a message with the police chief but haven't heard back yet."

Wade nodded. "They're tied up with a gas station robbery. We're in charge for now."

Marc stood and turned his hat backward. "Wade, I've got to be in court this morning. Can we give you our statements soon, or should I try to contact the judge?"

The sheriff dug a little notepad out of his shirt pocket. "Consider this a preliminary interview, but I need to speak to each of you separately. I may have more questions later. Who first?"

"Andi Grace, you go ahead." Marc reached for Sunny's leash and attached it to her harness. Our hands touched, and tingles danced up my arm.

Every day I made decisions about my life and business. For years I'd stood on my own two feet, but when it came to the law, I appreciated Marc's support. The sheriff had grown up in the area and even attended high school with me. Still, I didn't want to give him a reason to arrest me—again.

Wade clicked his pen. "Andi Grace, tell me what happened."

I took a deep breath and silently counted to ten in French as I exhaled. What details could I report? "There's not a lot to tell. Marc and I were running with the dogs, and we found Tabby's body. End of story. Where's your Toughbook?" After two murders in Heyward Beach, I'd learned the sheriff liked to use his small computer when solving crimes.

"At the office. It's too sandy out here to risk destroying the thing. Is there anything else you remember?"

"We passed a few other runners, but they were dressed in athletic gear. Nobody looked suspicious. There was a boat out on the water." I crossed my arms. "I feel like Tabby might have been killed on the beach.

I've been watching crime shows, and her body isn't bloated. Dirty, yes, but not ruined by the salt water. Although I do think the tide reached her body."

Wade shook his head. "You're not investigating Tabby's death, but for kicks, explain your theory to me."

"I didn't spot blood on the stones, and one shoe is missing." I pointed to the structure designed to protect the shore from erosion and to trap sand. Not to ensnare dead bodies. "It'd be easy to imagine she slipped and struck her head on the boulders, but maybe she was killed in the sand. It's possible her body drifted to the groin and stopped there, or she could've been dragged so we'd believe she'd fallen. Depending on when she was killed, the tide would wash away the drag marks and footprints."

"Duly noted. Do you need to tell me anything else?"

I racked my brain but came up empty. "No, that's all."

"Good. I want to make sure we're on the same page. We'll investigate and determine if Tabby Malkin's death was an accident or murder." He pointed his pencil at me. "Are we clear?"

"Yes." I wouldn't argue and try to defend my past actions. "You're the sheriff, and your department plans to solve the murder."

"First, we'll determine how she died." He ran a hand over his face. "I'll talk to Marc now."

I jogged to where Marc stood near the water with the dogs. Sunny and Chubb stood obediently on each side of his body, with eyes fixed on the crime scene. I rubbed each one on the head. "Marc, it's your turn to answer questions. I'll take the dogs."

Marc handed over the leashes. "Stay close."

"Why?" My voice squeaked.

"I know the place will soon be crawling with law enforcement, but stay alert. If Tabby was murdered, the killer could be lurking behind the dunes or on rental property along the beach."

"Okay. We'll be right around here." Aha, so I wasn't the only person suspicious about Tabby's death. I'd much rather it be natural causes, but the churning deep in my belly told me something different.

Chapter Two

AFTER I FINISHED walking the dogs on my morning schedule, I swung by Daily Java. It'd become my favorite coffee shop. Originally a bakery, they still carried baked goods as well as sandwiches, salads, and healthy options like smoothies.

"Good morning, Andi Grace." Erin Lane, the owner and a friend of mine, slid a tray of fluffy golden croissants with chocolate drizzled on them into a display case.

"Morning, Erin. Those look delicious." Erin's husband had been murdered a couple of months earlier, and I'd been the one to find the body. She'd suspected my brother of killing Corey and our friendship took a hit until the real murderer was caught. We were slowly getting back to a comfortable relationship.

"My grandmother's recipe." She wiped her hands on the pretty flowered apron tied around her slim waist.

"No doubt it's a recipe she learned when she spent time in France. How are you doing?"

"I'm making it. My family is around and providing lots of support. I'm also learning to lean on God instead of money and my family's reputation." She gave me a lopsided smile. "Goodness, too much in-formation. Sorry. What can I get you? I just took a fresh batch of cinnamon apple muffins out of the oven. It's a new recipe with natural sweeteners. How about one to go with your coffee?"

"It sounds delicious." I paid, stuffed a tip into the appropriate jar, and moved to a table in the back. After getting settled into a seat, I checked my phone for text messages.

"Andi Grace, hey, how are ya?"

The question startled me, and I flinched. High-heeled pumps clicked on the tile floor, and my gaze drifted up to Hannah Cummings.

She pointed to the empty chair across from me. "May I?"

I smiled and nodded. "Sure. How's your campaign going? Should I just go ahead and address you as State Representative Cummings?"

She slid onto the seat then leaned close and lowered her voice. "I'm glad I'm not running for sheriff or mayor with the high crime rate. Specifically, murders. I heard you found another body this morning."

"Whoa. News travels fast. It's true, but how did you hear?" I broke eye contact at the sight of movement. "Wait. Erin's coming over."

Erin carried a tray with two mugs of coffee and two muffins. "Here you go. Let me know if you can use a refill."

"Thanks, Erin. You know I'll want seconds."

After she left us, Hannah broke open her muffin and slathered butter on it. "I was at the courthouse with Daddy this morning. Sheriff Stone was talking to Marc Williams. That's your boyfriend, right?"

Her southern drawl made me smile. "We haven't put a label on our relationship, but yeah, he was due in court this morning." I stirred cream and sugar into my coffee and avoided eye contact. "Maybe you caught him during a break."

"Oh, I understand. You're dating him, but it's not exclusive."

I stopped stirring and peered at her. "Have you seen Marc dating somebody else?"

Hannah's eyes widened. "No, honey. That's not what I meant."

"Do you want to date Marc?" Why wouldn't she want to go out with him? He was handsome and kind. Smart, talented, and funny.

Hannah's cheeks reddened, and her mouth turned down. "Oh, dear. I'm not interested in Marc. My hands are full with the election, but even if my days were carefree, I'd never move in on a friend's man."

My lack of experience dating was going to ruin my relationship with Marc and my friendship with Hannah if I didn't get a grip. I sank back into my chair and realized Hannah was silent and staring at me. "I'm so sorry. I guess it's hard to believe somebody as terrific as Marc is interested in me."

"My skin is thicker now than a year ago thanks to politics. Because we're friends, I want to encourage you to trust Marc. It's obvious he's crazy about you, and you shouldn't let your fears get in the way."

"You're right." Hannah considered me a friend, not just a business associate. I buttered my muffin and bit into it. Moist apples mixed with just enough cinnamon to be perfect. "Mmm, this is delicious."

"I agree. It's definitely worth the calories."

I grinned and wiped my sticky fingers on the napkin. "Did Wade tell you about Tabby?"

"To be honest, I overheard part of his conversation with Marc. Then Danny Nichols interrupted and there wasn't anything else to hear. Oops—I mean Dan." She wrinkled her nose. "As in *Dan the man*. It's his new slogan. I've never heard one person call him anything except Danny."

"You're right. He grew up here, and it'll be hard for folks to call him Dan." I sipped my java. "My guess is he'll run against you with everything he's got. Why'd you decide to run in our district?"

Her shoulders hiked. "Daddy's a businessman and travels around the low country a lot. Our home was in Georgetown, but my grandparents always invited us to spend the summer at Heyward Beach, and I fell in love with the place at a young age. I even lived here with my grandparents for a couple of years right after college." Her face relaxed, and her lips eased into a smile.

"Why don't you live here now?" I took another bite of the muffin.

"Excellent question. I own a gift shop in Georgetown and run an online business. Until recently I thought living there was the smart business move."

"But?"

Her eyes twinkled. "You inspired me, Andi Grace. I noticed you live on the island, even though you run your B&B and doggie day care in the country at Kennady Plantation. I decided to buy my grandparents' old beach house. Technically, it's located on the creek, but it's on the island."

"Hey, I refer to my home as a beach house even though I'm not oceanfront either. How exciting to know we'll be neighbors. Honestly, in my opinion everyone living between the marsh and the Atlantic Ocean is my neighbor."

"I guess with the shops, it'll be easy to get to know the locals, but it's going to be a tough year with the election."

"You're going to be fine. It's my turn to tell you not to worry." I patted her hand.

Hannah smiled. "Since you've lived here so long, is there anything you can tell me about Dan?"

I choked on my muffin. Gasping for air, tears filled my eyes and my nose ran. So embarrassing.

Hannah thumped my back. "Andi Grace, are you okay? Do you need water?"

I shook my head but continued to hack up a lung. It took a few moments before I could speak. I wiped tears away with the scratchy white paper napkin. "Sorry about that," I wheezed.

"I'm sorry if I said something to upset you."

I waved off her apology. "Danny and I started liking each other in middle school. We dated in high school. He's a couple of years older than I am and went to the University of Georgia. The plan was for me to join him there when I graduated, but the summer between high school and college, my parents died in a car wreck. I'm the oldest of three kids and couldn't let my siblings go into the foster care program."

Hannah's mouth dropped open. "What'd you do?"

"I stayed here and raised them. Danny dumped me. He graduated and went to law school. Worked in Atlanta. Came back to Heyward Beach about the time his uncle died. His uncle, Peter Roth, and I had become friends. Your dad and Peter were friends. Peter left me the plantation, and I believe you know the rest of the story."

"I've heard parts, but thank you for sharing with me."

My phone chirped a thirty-minute warning for an appointment I'd scheduled. "Let me know when you get settled into your new home. Or I can help you move, but right now I've got to run and meet a young couple at Stay and Play. They want me to teach them how to train their puppy."

Hannah sighed. "I'd like to have a dog one day. Maybe after the election."

"I'll be happy to help you find the right dog." I gathered my belongings.

Hannah's eyes sparkled. "Great, but after the election. Hey, thanks for spending time with me this morning. If you think of any tips to help my campaign against *Dan the man*, please let me know."

"You're going to give him a run for his money. If I think of anything to help, I'll be in touch. Have a great day, Hannah." I left her with a wave, paid for a mocha latte to take with me, and drove to the plantation with only a quick stop to pick up Sunny from my house.

According to Hannah, Wade had questioned Marc at the courthouse. Again? It'd only been a couple of hours since we left him at the beach. If they were discussing Tabby's death, they must be suspicious.

I parked in the shade of an oak tree near the dog barn at the plantation. Sunny snoozed in the back of my Suburban, and there was no sign of the couple I was supposed to meet for dog training. Perfect time to start making notes on Tabby's death.

I hopped out and sat in an Adirondack near my SUV while waiting for my clients to arrive. Sunny snoozed by my feet. The older she got, the more she napped. Finding a dead body had probably zapped her energy for the day, and I didn't disturb her rest.

Instead, I used my phone app to research the murder victim we'd found on our run. Information outside of town gossip was needed.

Tabby Malkin had moved to Heyward Beach from Dallas, Texas. Like me, she loved the town. She'd been an emergency room nurse at one of the biggest hospitals in Dallas until she slipped in a puddle of water at the nurses' station. The fall caused a brain injury and ended her career. The hospital paid all of her expenses, and after months of rehab, Tabby moved to the coast.

A minivan pulled around the house, which served as the bed and breakfast. The driver parked next to my vehicle. I got up and tossed my notepad into the passenger seat then grabbed my bag of dog treats before moving to greet the couple. Sunny followed me in slow motion.

Dylan King jogged to me from the barn. "Hey, boss." He stuffed his hands in his front pockets and avoided eye contact.

"I thought you were working with Griffin on the old kitchen renovation." I'd been trying to give Dylan a shot at living an honest life. He'd gotten into trouble in the past, and I couldn't risk him relapsing while working for me. People and dogs depended on me to provide a safe environment when they came onto my property.

"I took an early lunch break. Do you need help before I go back to Griffin?" Dylan stopped fidgeting and met my gaze.

"Would you take Sunny to the play area inside the barn? I need to meet this couple about dog training." I pointed to the van, where a female stood at the back of the vehicle with the door wide open.

A black Labrador retriever jumped out, circled the woman's legs, and the woman fell to the ground with a soft thump.

I turned to face Dylan, hoping the woman wouldn't know I'd seen her fall. "Poor thing."

"Dude. It looks like you've got your work cut out for you." Dylan's eyes twinkled. "I'll get Sunny settled inside then get back to helping Griffin. You should come by and see the place. Soon nobody will know the building was the old kitchen years ago."

I rubbed Sunny's head. "Thanks."

"If you go into the dog barn, I left the TV on in my apartment. Don't freak out if you hear any sounds." Again, he avoided eye contact.

"Okay, but if I ever hear sounds, I'll call or text you first. I respect your privacy." His apartment was in a corner of the barn, a little distance from the dog training areas. I turned on my toe and headed to the woman, who'd barely gotten the lab under control. "Hi, I'm Andi Grace Scott."

"We're having a typical morning. Young dog plus clumsy owner leads to multiple accidents. I'm so ready to start working with you." Her thick red hair was secured in a messy bun, and there was a paw print stain on her jeans.

"I know dog training will help. Is your husband with you?"

"No. He's a pharmacist and had to go into work at the last minute. His partner got strep throat." She struggled with the dog. "I'm Violet Seitz, and this is Yoyo."

I giggled. "Yoyo? Really?"

Violet shrugged. "Yeah, he's all over the place. Up and down. Back and forth. Inside and outside. If Yoyo is in the house, he wants out and vice versa. I'm desperate for help, and Erin at the coffee shop recommended you."

"Training a dog is as much about training you as it is about the pet. Let's begin with sit and come. We'll reward him with affection and treats."

"Sounds good."

"At our next lesson, we'll move on to down, stay, and leave it. Don't get discouraged though, because it'll take a few weeks."

We spent the next hour practicing the commands sit and come. We rewarded Yoyo when he obeyed, and before I knew it, our time was over. I walked Violet to her minivan. "That was a good first lesson. Practice what we discussed, and don't forget, you're in charge."

Violet shook a finger at her lab. "You hear that boy? I'm the boss."

"Same time next week?" I smiled.

Her eyes grew wide. "Uh, how about another lesson this week? I'm off on Thursday."

I pulled out my phone and checked my schedule. "Looks good. Eleven?"

A lock of thick red hair fell forward, and she shouldered it away as she reached down to lift her puppy.

I lunged forward. "Stop, Violet. Yoyo is big enough to get into the van by himself. May I?"

She released the dog and stepped back. "Go for it."

I patted the inside of the van. "Yoyo, come."

He cocked his head.

"Wait a minute." I ran to the dog barn and got Sunny. We hurried to the van. "Maybe if Yoyo watches Sunny, he'll be more secure to try it. Sunny, come." I patted the van's flat-load floor.

My German shepherd hopped into the back of the vehicle.

"Good, girl. Now down." Sunny leapt out, and I tapped the van's floor again. "Yoyo, come."

Nothing.

"Let's try with Sunny again." We repeated the process three more times. Sunny performed the action while Yoyo watched. "One more time. Yoyo, come."

The lab hopped into the vehicle and looked at me expectantly.

"Good, boy." I passed him a treat and pointed to his travel kennel. "Get in the crate. Crate."

He entered the expensive travel kennel and turned in a circle until he faced me.

"Good boy, Yoyo. Here's your treat." I gave him a dog bone and secured the door.

Violet clapped. "You're amazing. I wish he'd obey me."

I smiled at Violet. "He will. Be consistent. Reward him for good behavior. Call his travel and home kennel the same thing."

Her eyes widened. "That makes sense. We'll say crate like you did."

"Part of loving your puppy is to teach him to be obedient."

Yoyo barked.

"Guess that's my cue to go." Violet lowered the hatchback and moved toward the driver's door. "I'll see you Thursday."

I waited with Sunny at my side as Violet drove around the main house and disappeared into the woods lining my driveway. My land sat between River Road and the Waccamaw River. I'd inherited the place the previous year. Instead of living on the plantation, I'd decided to convert it into a bed and breakfast as well as a doggie day care. The main house had been tweaked to work as an inn. Guests stayed in the many rooms and ate breakfast on the first floor.

My best friend, Juliet Reed, ran the bed and breakfast, and we were planning an expansion in hopes we'd turn a profit. Juliet's brother Griffin was a contractor who was renovating the old kitchen into more guest rooms. Dylan had experience in building homes and helped Griffin most days, in addition to assisting with my dog business. At Stay and Play I provided training, day care, and boarding. My next two projects were to add dog grooming and a shelter for strays.

I walked to the kitchen and stopped in front of the door. "Griffin? Dylan?"

Sunny wandered to a shady spot near the brick structure and plopped down.

The building had been transformed many times over the years and even served as an art studio for one of the previous owners. There was also a rumor the old kitchen had been part of the underground railroad for runaway slaves, but I hadn't found evidence to prove the theory. Secret markings and small hidden spaces gave me hope it was true, and we planned not to destroy any clues supporting our theory.

In the distance a siren blipped. River Road was only two lanes, but it wasn't narrow. Still, there were car accidents from time to time.

Griffin's clomping footsteps sounded before he appeared in the yard. "I'm glad you stopped by. We framed the upstairs and were able to create a little reading nook on the landing between the bedrooms. Come on."

I followed him in the main doorway. On the first floor he'd framed out two guest suites and a sitting area, where we'd keep light refreshments. We climbed the stairs and stopped at the second-floor landing.

With his clipboard, Griffin pointed to the space across from us. "Between the shared bathroom and the bigger guest room, there's enough space for a reading nook."

It didn't take much for me to imagine a comfy chair or a cushioned bench with a lamp and small shelf full of books by local authors. "I like it. And if a family rents the entire top floor, it opens this area up as a small gathering place. Very nice."

Dylan joined us from the smaller of the two upper guest rooms. "Closet is framed out."

Griffin flipped through the pages on his clipboard. "Good job. The drywall needs to be hung and mudded. Dylan, are you able to assist with that, or should I hire more men?"

Dylan's eyebrows rose, and he turned his attention to me. "Boss?"

"I'll handle Stay and Play. I might offer my dog walking clients a free day of doggie day care to keep me from running back and forth so much. You can work with Griffin."

"Yes, ma'am. Yes, ma'am."

A flash of blue light caught my attention followed by the sound of tires rattling over gravel in the driveway.

I looked at the guys where we stood in the open area at the top of the steps. "What in the world?"

Dylan shoved past us, ran down the stairs, and raced out the building.

My stomach knotted. "Griffin, do you know what's going on with Dylan?"

He tapped his foot. "He was late to work. Said he had to help a friend. Then he took an early lunch break."

"I hope he hasn't done something stupid." I rubbed the back of my neck.

Griffin gave me a hard look. "Dylan's a good worker and before today, he's never given me any trouble. I think you should trust him."

"Okay, but let me know if he becomes a problem." I followed Griffin down the stairs. "We need to name this building something besides the old kitchen."

Griffin held the door for me. "How about calling it the guest house?"

"Don't you think that's a little prosaic?" I glanced at the much bigger main house. Pulling to the front was a sheriff's SUV.

"That can't be good." Frustration laced Griffin's tone.

"Maybe it's Wade. Marc and I found Tabby Malkin dead on the beach this morning." I walked toward the official vehicle and Sunny joined me.

"You what? Wait, should I call Marc?"

I glanced back at him. "Only if they take me away in handcuffs."

Chapter Three

I REACHED THE front porch of the main house. Wade and Juliet were in deep conversation as I climbed the steps. "Hey, there. What's going on?"

The corners of Juliet's mouth lowered. "Wade just told me you found another body this morning."

"I planned to tell you after the dog training appointment, but I ended up checking on the construction at the old kitchen first." I made a mental note to tell Juliet immediately after I found another dead body. If I ever found a body again, which I hoped wouldn't happen.

Juliet ran her hands up and down her arms as if chilled. "You should've called me."

"Marc and the dogs were with me." I raised both hands in surrender. "I had plenty of protection."

The sheriff cleared his throat. "Ladies, I believe you can finish your conversation later."

I turned to the sheriff. "Wade, why are you here?"

"I need to ask some questions." He wore a gray shirt, black slacks, and a ball cap with the sheriff's logo on it.

My pulse accelerated. "I barely knew Tabby. Y'all can't think I had anything to do with her death."

"Calm down, Andi Grace. I'm actually here to speak to Dylan." He swiped a hand over his face. "My questions are for Dylan. Not you."

"Why?" I'd feared Dylan was up to something. "I doubt he knows Tabby. They've got nothing in common."

"I'm pretty sure you're wrong. Have you met Kylie Black?" He pinched his lips together.

I was clueless. "No. Who is she?"

Juliet placed her hand over her chest. "She's a friend of Dylan's. They met kayaking on the marsh one day."

I touched my friend's arm. "How did you meet her?"

"Kylie showed up with pizza last week and wasn't sure where to find Dylan. She said it was a way to thank him for replacing the tire on her bike. She's the athletic sort."

"She's also Tabby's paid companion." Wade frowned. "That came out wrong. Tabby's daughter, Susan Rochester, hired Kylie Black to be a caretaker for her mother. Tabby had seizures after her accident in Texas. My understanding is Kylie was hired to drive Tabby around and run errands with the woman. Because of the health issues, Susan wanted a full-time caretaker."

Wow. Wade must have been super flustered to share that much information without me pushing. I didn't remember him ever being so gabby about a case. "What's any of this got to do with Dylan?"

"We want to question Kylie and can't find her. One of the neighbors suggested she might be with her *boyfriend*." His eyebrows rose. "Dylan."

"He lives in an apartment in the dog barn. I'll take you." Dylan having a girlfriend was news to me.

Juliet backed toward the front door. "I'm baking a batch of oatmeal cookies for our guests. Why don't you stop by when you're finished, Wade? I'll start a fresh pot of coffee."

Wade smiled and tipped his hat. "I'll be sure to do that."

Whoa. Was Juliet flirting with the sheriff? I whirled and stomped down the steps and around the house toward Stay and Play. Juliet and my brother were supposed to be in a relationship, but Nate was slower than a snail moving through peanut butter, and Juliet was ready to settle down. Had she finally gotten tired of his wishy-washy stalling?

"Where's the fire?" Wade had followed and caught up with me in the yard, with Sunny not far behind.

"Sorry. I've got a lot to do today." Including having a heart-to-heart with my brother. I pointed to the barn. "We converted this to accommodate my dog business. My office is inside, and we built an apartment for Dylan."

"It's admirable how you took the boy under your wing."

I stumbled over a root and regained my footing right before Wade gripped my elbow. "You can't go around giving me compliments without some warning."

Wade laughed and released his hold. "I'll remember next time, or maybe I won't say anything nice again."

"That's more like it." I smiled.

Wade was a good man, and he needed somebody special in his life. Hannah popped to mind, but I wasn't a people matchmaker. Pairing dogs with humans was my strong suit.

"Are you saying Dylan's not in trouble?"

"I only want to ask him about Kylie. She was probably the last person to see Tabby. It's possible she's in danger."

I slid open the barn door and motioned for Wade to follow. We passed the room of kennels for the boarded dogs and walked down the hall past my office to the apartment. I knocked on his door. "Dylan, Sheriff Stone is here to ask you some questions."

Seconds ticked by.

"Let me try." Wade pounded on the door. "This is the sheriff. I'm just here to talk. Nothing else."

Sunny sat, her dark gaze on us while her tail swept back and forth on the cool concrete floor.

Wade crossed his arms. "I don't suspect Dylan of any wrongdoing."

"Maybe you shouldn't have knocked so hard. He's probably terrified." I knocked again. "Hey, you're not in trouble."

The door swung open. Dylan rubbed his belly. "Sorry. I was in the bathroom. Must be the gas station breakfast burrito. Do you need me?"

Wade said, "I'm looking for Kylie Black. Have you seen her today?"

"I don't know where she is. What's going on?" He opened the door wider. "Come in."

I glared at him. He didn't answer Wade's question. I walked into his studio apartment, looking for something suspicious. Bed made. Pillows arranged on it fashionably. No dirty dishes scattered around. Both chairs were pushed in at the small modern kitchen table. Not a crumb to be seen. The place was neat as a pin, heightening my suspicions. Last time I'd been in here, it'd been a lot messier. "I'll sit on the love seat and let y'all sit at the table." Sunny lay at my feet.

Dylan turned off the TV and joined Wade at the table. "Why are you looking for Kylie?"

"I'm sure you know she assisted Tabby Malkin." Wade pulled out his notepad and paper.

"Yes, sir."

"Tabby's dead and Kylie is missing. I need to make sure your friend is safe. If Tabby's death wasn't an accident, Kylie could be in danger. There are questions only your friend can answer about Tabby because they lived together. She may be able to lead us to a motive for Tabby's death."

Dylan's leg bounced. "People around town think Kylie was taking care of Tabby, but the truth is they took care of each other. Is Kylie in trouble?"

Wade shook his head. "No, but she can help the investigation."

"She's gonna be real upset. Tabby treated Kylie like a daughter or niece."

Wade motioned with his finger for Dylan to continue. "Tell me more. I need to get a better feel for the situation."

Silence.

Sunny crossed the room and rubbed against Dylan's bouncing leg. Dylan ran his hand over my German shepherd. "Kylie worked as an aide at the hospital where Tabby was hurt." He stopped, his brow furrowed. "No, she called it a patient care technician."

"What is that?" I didn't spend much time around hospitals to know.

"She only had to learn basic life support and have a high school diploma. I only know she worked with patients and families. A nurse supervised her work. Anyway, that's how she met Tabby. They became friends. After the injury, Kylie visited Tabby every day when her shift was over."

I tried to picture a relationship between the women. "How old is Kylie?"

"Twenty." He stood and paced. "You really don't get it, man."

"Suppose you explain it better to me." Wade pointed to the empty chair.

Dylan took his seat and ran a hand through his hair. "Kylie's parents were the worst. When she was growing up, they beat her all the time and made her work for her own food. She moved out of their house when she was seventeen and lived with some older guy who claimed to love her. It was a ruse. He tried to get her to do drugs, but she refused. He threatened to kill her if she didn't become a prostitute. Turns out he was a sex trafficker. Girls who are hooked on drugs are easier for pimps to control."

I closed my eyes. "How'd she survive?"

"She managed to escape and return home. Things got worse there for the next couple of years. Her parents stole her money. Even though she had a decent job at the hospital, Kylie couldn't make enough to get away from them." Dylan stared at the ground.

Wade stopped taking notes. "Then what?"

"Fast forward to Tabby's injury. Kylie met Susan—that's Tabby's daughter—she's a rich business tycoon in Dallas, and didn't have time to take care of her mom. She offered to pay Kylie to be her mom's caretaker. When Tabby got out of the hospital, she knew she couldn't go back to work. She told her daughter she was gonna move to South

Carolina. She and Susan argued about it, but Susan gave in when Kylie said she'd go with her. Both of them got a fresh start when they got to Heyward Beach. There's no stinking way Kylie would hurt Tabby." Dylan clenched his fists.

Wade's shoulders slumped. "I'm not accusing Kylie of any wrong-doing, but I need to get the facts. We need to make sure the girl is safe. Where is she right this minute?"

"I don't know." His shoulders hiked.

My head hurt. Poor Kylie. All alone in a new town and the one woman who treated her with kindness had been killed.

When Wade left, I faced Dylan in his apartment. "You're holding something back. What aren't you telling us?"

He lifted his hands, palms up. "Why do you think I'm keeping a secret?"

"You evaded Wade's question about Kylie, and you're not answering me. Where is she?"

"I don't know." His face turned red.

Sunny tilted her head and stared at Dylan.

"Your place is never this neat. It makes me think you picked up Kylie this morning. Maybe last night. You let her hide here. While you worked, she cleaned your apartment. Boredom or nervous energy pushed her into action. Safe action, but still she had to do something. I'd react the same way."

"I'm supposed to be working with Griffin." He tried to scoot around me, but I caught his arm and held on. Not tight enough to hurt, but I didn't want him to walk away.

Sunny barked.

"Dylan, trust me." I loosened my grip. "I can help y'all."

"Kylie's scared, and I can't share anything without her permission."

"Okay." I respected his logic. "Find your friend and bring her back here. Together we'll figure this out."

He shook his head. "She's afraid of the sheriff."

"Wade? He's an honest man."

"No." He growled. "All cops and deputies and law enforcement scare her."

I couldn't break the law to protect a potential suspect, but there was a Bible verse about taking care of strangers. *I was hungry and you gave Me something to eat, I was thirsty and you gave Me something to drink, I was a stranger and you took Me in.* After my parents died, I clung to those New Testament words. Did they apply to my situation with Kylie? A warm tingling sensation filled me. "Dylan, she can live with me until we find the truth."

"What about Griffin? He's expecting me to help with the renovation."

"Finding Kylie is your top priority this afternoon. I'll explain the situation to Griffin. Go."

Dylan left, and I knelt beside Sunny and hugged her. "Girl, I hope I made the right decision."

She responded with a lick to my jaw.

"We need to do something productive." I checked my schedule on my phone. "I've got a couple of hours before the next dog walking appointment. Let's go talk to Juliet. No, wait. I can't take you into the kitchen because it's a B&B. Health code and all that jazz." I led Sunny into the empty play area and gave her a fun bone to chew on. "I'll be back."

She blinked slowly.

"Take a nap." I left her in the quiet barn and hustled to the main house, entering through the back door. "Juliet?"

"In here." Her voice had a perky lilt.

I walked past the laundry room and entered the kitchen. "Something smells good."

Juliet washed dishes and glanced my way. "I just pulled out a tray of chocolate chip cookies, and the oatmeal cookies are on the cooling racks on the island."

I reached for an oatmeal cookie since I was trying to get healthy. "What's the deal with you and Wade?"

Juliet's head whipped around. "There's nothing between us."

"You offered him a cookie and coffee." I felt nauseous and sounded like a pouty child. "I'm sorry. Your love life is none of my business."

"Except you're my best friend, and we don't keep secrets from each other." Juliet dried her hands on the nearest towel. "Wade is a friend. You know I'm in love with your brother. Right?"

"I know you care about him, but he's not a fast mover in the romance department." I turned the cookie in my hands.

"Rest assured, I love the man." She nudged me toward a chair in the breakfast area. "Why are you worried about my relationship with Nate?" She sat by me and leaned forward.

I lay the uneaten cookie on the table.

Juliet reached for a napkin and placed my cookie on it. "Well?"

"I want you and Nate to get together so bad."

"We are together. I'm not interested in anybody besides Nate. Do you think I'm giving up on him? That I'll be unfaithful?"

The room grew hot, and I fanned myself with another napkin. "No. I don't think so." An image of my mother leaving the house late at night after an argument with Dad flashed through my mind. The room spun.

"Andi Grace, what's wrong? You're pale."

My vision blurred, and my skin grew clammy. "I don't feel good."

"Are you going to faint?" Juliet pushed my head down between my knees.

I took deep gulps of air. "What's happening? Am I losing my mind?"

She rubbed my back. "Honey, did you eat breakfast?"

I started to raise up, but Juliet nudged me back down. I lost track of time, breathing deep with my eyes closed. The clamminess disappeared, and I pushed myself up. "I'm okay now."

She released me. "It's probably a delayed reaction to the shock of finding another dead body. You need to quit doing that."

"I don't plan these things. Besides, you were with me the last time."

She squeezed my cold hands. "Yeah, and Marc was with you today."

"I'm sorry for the way I reacted." I trusted Juliet. "I'm having a weird day. When I watched you with Wade, it was like I got jealous for Nate." A distant memory tried to break through my foggy mind related to my parents.

"Quit apologizing. We're good. Besides, I'm trying to fix Wade up with Hannah."

Relief zipped through me. "I'd just been thinking they'd be a good couple. She'll make laws, and he'll enforce them. If she runs for president one day, she'll have her own bodyguard."

Juliet laughed. "I never considered that, but if she becomes president, they'll both have Secret Service protection. Although Wade would probably always stay alert for danger."

I nodded. "Yeah, it's probably in his DNA. So you and Nate are good?"

"We're fine. If he decides to propose one day, I'll say yes so fast his head will spin. If he never pops the question, I'll probably go to my grave loving him."

"That's about the saddest thing I've ever heard you say, Juliet." I shook an uneasy feeling. What was he waiting for? Did it have to do with our parents dying so young? Were we too messed up to be good relationship material?

"Hey, I know how you like to fix things, but I'm fine. Nate's worth the wait."

I picked up the cookie. "Sounds like you can write a poem or song about it."

Juliet was willing to wait for a deeper relationship with Nate. Did Marc have the same issues as Nate or did he want something more? How did he really feel about me? We'd gone from strangers to friends to dating. His parents died when he was young, and growing up in foster care had scarred him. He'd had one good placement, but he'd never been adopted. I longed for a deep and meaningful commitment, and my heart had declared Marc was the one. Time would tell if he'd be able to entrust his heart to me.

Dylan walked past the window with a young woman at his side.

"I bet that's Kylie Black. Let's see what she can tell us about Tabby." I hurried to the back door. If the two of them kept walking, I'd follow them. One way or another, I planned to get some answers.

Chapter Four

IT TURNED OUT I didn't have to chase Dylan and Kylie down. We nearly collided at the door, and after mutual apologies, Dylan introduced us to Kylie.

The attractive young woman's wide-eyed gaze bounced from Juliet to me. She crossed her arms over her midsection.

Juliet ushered us to the breakfast nook, and we sat around the table. Kylie's short blond hair needed a good brushing, but it appeared to be clean. Thick eyebrows, brown eyes, and a clear complexion gave her a girl-next-door vibe. Maybe living with Tabby had been a time of healing.

I opened my notebook. "Kylie, thanks for speaking to me. I'd like to ask you a few questions."

"Why?" She frowned.

"I'm not accusing you of anything, but I found Tabby's body and need answers." I worked to keep my voice soothing. "When was the last time you saw her?"

"Around five yesterday." She didn't pause to calculate the time. Instead, her answer came out fast and confident.

"Why are you so sure?"

"On Sundays, we had a routine. Tabby's daughter liked her to rest on the Sabbath. We went to church, came home, and ate a little lunch, then she took a nap. I cleaned the kitchen and looked up online college classes. I'd decided it'd be smart to take a few classes since I don't have a degree."

"Do you mind if I take notes on our conversation?"

She shrugged. "I assumed that's why you opened your notebook."

Touché. I clicked my pen. "What happened when Tabby woke up?"

"We sat outside and discussed her plans for a flower garden."

The coffee maker dinged, and Juliet hopped up. "Does everybody want a cup of coffee?"

We all nodded, and Juliet moved to the kitchen island.

Unsure if their conversation about the yard mattered, I asked about the rest of the day. "What then?"

Kylie shook her head. "It was a normal day. We went for a short walk, she fed the stray cats, she played sudoku, then we ate an early dinner."

Juliet placed a tray in the middle of the table with four steaming mugs, creamer, and sugar.

Kylie added three spoonfuls of sugar and a dab of cream into her drink and stirred. "For the last few weeks, she played sudoku and worked crossword puzzles right after coming in from her walks. It'd become a ritual. She told me something strange was happening at the beach, and she wanted to figure it out."

Besides our love of animals, Tabby and I both enjoyed puzzles. "Did Tabby have a friend she would've shared her concerns with?"

"Not that I'm aware of." Kylie slurped her coffee.

"Do you think she told her daughter?"

Kylie shook her head but didn't make eye contact.

Where'd that leave us? The clock was ticking. Time to alert the authorities. "Kylie, we really need to talk to Sheriff Stone."

"No!" She jumped out of her chair, and it fell backward with a *clunk*.

Dylan stood beside her and touched her shoulder. "Kylie, it'll be all right. We can trust Andi Grace."

"I may not be a college graduate, but I'm smart enough to realize the cops will think I committed the murder. I lived with Tabby and was the last one to see her, but I'd never do anything to hurt her." Her voice grew shrill.

I kept my posture relaxed and remained in my chair. Bay windows gave me a clear view of the backyard full of budding iris and blooming azaleas. "Would you feel better if you had an attorney when you talk to the sheriff?"

"Don't you get it? I can't afford a lawyer. Tabby's death will leave me homeless and penniless. Just when I was getting comfortable with my life here, this happens." She rubbed her forehead. "I'm not trying to sound like a spoiled brat, but her death affects me. I loved Tabby like a grandmother. She always treated me good."

I stopped writing. "You can't think of any motive for you to kill Tabby? That's what the cops will look for."

"I don't have a motive because there's nothing for me to gain by her death. To be brutally honest, if I was going to kill somebody, it would've been my dad for beating me, or my ex-boyfriend for trying to push me into prostitution. I never attacked them. Instead, I ran and hid. I'd never kill anybody on purpose." A note of hysteria laced her voice, which grew louder by the second.

"Kylie, it's going to be okay. Just calm down. I know an attorney who'll take your case for free."

She tipped her head, and her brow wrinkled. "What's the catch?"

"He's a friend. Nothing more." I turned my hands palms up.

"There's always a catch." Kylie turned on Dylan and pointed at him. "I trusted you. I thought you understood my situation."

Dylan reached for her hands. "Andi Grace's friend helped me deal with the law when I was in trouble. I'm living here and working a respectable job. They'll help you, too."

Her eyes narrowed. "Not if you turn me in to the cops."

I interjected, "They're looking for you, Kylie. If you keep hiding, they're going to get suspicious. They have questions, and you may be the only person who can answer them. It's better if you reach out to the sheriff."

Kylie opened her mouth then closed it. Her shoulders sank. "I've never had good luck dealing with the law."

Juliet stood. "It'll be different this time. They need your assistance, and you've got a support team. I'm going to make some sandwiches. We can think clearer on a full stomach."

Kylie slumped into her chair, and Dylan sat beside her, looking at the ground. "These are good people, like Tabby was."

Kylie gripped her mug with both hands but never took the first sip. She shook so hard, coffee spilled over the rim and onto the table. "I don't know why I'm so cold."

"I'll get you a blanket." Dylan left the two of us alone.

"Why don't I call Marc first? He's my attorney friend. We'll wait to call Sheriff Stone when we know Marc's schedule. I truly think the sheriff is looking for clues. I doubt he thinks you're the guilty party."

She didn't meet my gaze. "Tabby was my responsibility. I had a migraine, and she told me to rest. When I woke up, it was dark and there was no sign of her. I figured she was taking care of one of the feral cats. They were her babies, so I searched all of her favorite spots."

"You were out alone in the dark?"

"Yeah. It was around midnight."

"Weren't you scared to wander around the island by yourself?"

"Kinda. But Tabby was teaching me to trust God, so I prayed to stay safe and to find her. I guess God half-listened. I didn't get hurt, but Tabby was murdered."

This didn't seem like the best time for a theological discussion.

"Why do you think she was murdered? Could she have died from a heart attack?"

Kylie wiped the spilled droplets of coffee off the table, and still avoided eye contact. "It's possible. Right after her accident she had seizures, and she wasn't allowed to drive. We knew each other because we both worked at the same hospital, and we became friends. Her daughter worried her mother would have another seizure and nobody would be around to help. So Susan hired me to be Tabby's chauffeur and caretaker."

Seizures scared me more than being chased by a killer. To be responsible for somebody in such a fragile state took a special kind of person. I didn't believe Tabby's death was an accident, but what were Kylie's thoughts? "Do you think she might have had a seizure, fallen, hit her head on the boulders, and died?"

"No. She hasn't had an episode since we moved here." Kylie took another sip of coffee. "I think Tabby was murdered."

My pulse accelerated. "Why?"

"She was worried something bad was happening on our beach. That's what killed her."

Dylan returned with a faded quilt and wrapped it around Kylie's shoulders.

I pushed back from the table. "I'm going to call Marc now. Okay?"

The girl met my gaze. "Sure. Let's get it over with."

Marc surprised me by answering his cell right away. He listened to my story and assured me he could shift some appointments. "I'll be there in twenty minutes."

I prepared a pitcher of sweet tea, while Juliet finished making sandwiches. Once Marc arrived, we sat down to soup and sandwiches. Kylie ignored the food and shared her story with Marc, then we called the sheriff's office.

Deputy David Wayne arrived, and I met him at the door. "Come in. I'll introduce you to Kylie Black, Tabby's caretaker." We walked down the wide hall, and I introduced David to the young lady.

It didn't take him long to realize how terrified Kylie was. He pulled me aside. "Andi Grace, why don't you join us? I think having another woman in the room will make her more comfortable."

"I agree. She seems like a fragile bird with a broken wing." I led David, Marc, and Kylie to the library at the end of the hall. The room was away from the community areas and gave us privacy from guests staying at the B&B.

David pulled out his little notepad. "Sheriff Stone is working on another lead, but we're all involved in this case. Kylie, I'd like you to walk me through the events yesterday."

Her hands shook, and she focused on the floor.

I patted her shoulder. "You're not in trouble. In fact, you may have some information to help us . . . er . . . the sheriff's department, solve Tabby's death. David's a good guy."

Kylie's gaze darted from one person to the next.

Marc said, "Go ahead, Kylie. Tell him what you shared with me."

I smiled at Marc. His calm tone must've put her at ease, because Kylie repeated the details with David that she'd told us.

David tapped the notepad with his pen. "Is that everything?"

She nodded. "Yes, sir."

I said, "David, if you don't mind, I've got another question for Kylie."

"Go ahead."

"Did Tabby write in a diary or journal?"

"I only saw her write lists."

"What kind of lists?" Sometimes getting information out of Kylie was like pulling weeds during a drought.

"Grocery lists and prayer requests. Stuff like that." She wrapped a strand of hair around her finger.

There must be a clue somewhere. What was I missing? I replayed the conversation in my head. "What about the puzzle books? If Tabby was worried about dangerous activities at the beach, do you think she left a clue in those books?"

"Maybe." She twisted the hair faster.

I shifted my attention to David. "What do you think?"

"Seems far-fetched, but it's possible. Let's go check it out. Kylie, can you meet us at Tabby's house?"

"I don't have my own car, and Tabby's is at the beach house." Her shoulders drooped. "How will I get around?"

David said, "I can give you a ride."

Her face grew pale. "No way. I'm not riding in the back of a cop car."

David backed away. "You're not under arrest."

I touched Kylie's arm. "I'll drive you. I actually live on the island and have dog walking appointments later this afternoon. How does that sound?" Only two were scheduled for today. I'd have plenty of time to drive her and still make my rounds.

Marc stood. "If we go now, I can join y'all."

David muttered something. "Circus" was the only word I heard clearly.

"Give me a minute to get Sunny." I hurried to the kitchen. "Juliet, will you stay with Kylie? I'll meet you at the Suburban."

"As long as you don't accuse me of wanting a relationship with David."

I did a double take. "Ha, ha. Very funny."

Marc appeared. "If I get Chubb, can you walk him this afternoon? I've got a feeling it's going to be a late night at the office when we finish all this."

"Sure. I'll meet you at Tabby's place." I paused. "Do you know where she lived?"

"Yeah, I took papers to her once. See you soon." We went out the back door and took off in opposite directions.

I collected Sunny, and we met Kylie at the Suburban. I hugged Juliet. "Thanks."

"Be careful, my friend."

I nodded then followed David to Tabby's house with Kylie riding shotgun. Except for Sunny's panting in the back seat, our ride was quiet.

Marc must've pushed the speed limit because he pulled behind me on the street. We parked and led both dogs to the fenced-in backyard. Chubb barked and raced around the perimeter. Sunny took one lap then lay on the wide composite-planked back deck while the almost year-old golden retriever continued running off his energy.

Kylie opened the back door from the inside, and Marc and I climbed the steps to the back deck and entered.

David stood in Tabby's family room with a variety of puzzle magazines in his gloved hands. He flipped through the pages. "Nothing unusual here. Kylie, does anything appear out of place?"

She walked around the common areas. "It looks just like I left it."

Utilitarian horizontal beadboard on every wall in sight. Basic trim and twelve-foot ceilings gave the room a comfortable and airy feel. "You said Tabby didn't keep a journal."

"Not that I know of, but I didn't question her every move. Maybe she did."

David placed the magazines on the eating table in a neat stack then walked around the open-concept cottage. He inspected the uncluttered kitchen by opening the pantry and all of the drawers and cabinets. From under the sink, he pulled out the garbage can. "Empty."

Kylie nodded. "Yeah, I took the trash out after we ate last night."

"Makes sense. Garbage pickup is Monday mornings on the island." David grimaced. "May I inspect the bedrooms?"

"Yes, sir. That's mine. There's a guest room down the same hall. The master is upstairs. It'd been so long since Tabby had a seizure, she moved up there. She added an office off the kitchen because it made her feel useful."

Useful. Didn't we all want to be productive? "Can I look in there?"

David frowned. "Not until I clear the space. Why don't you three go outside and play with the dogs?" The only thing he didn't do was pat us on the head like troublesome children.

We exited through the kitchen's back doorway and sat in wicker chairs on rollers that had been placed around an old farm table. While everything about the home looked casual, underneath the place screamed money. We scooted the chairs so we could face each other.

Sunny glanced our way but closed her eyes and dozed. Chubb raced up the wood stairs and stopped beside Marc.

Kylie rubbed her arms. "What do y'all think? Is he going to arrest me?"

Marc crossed his legs so his ankle rested on the opposite knee. Colorful sailboats decorated his black socks. He reached down and rubbed his dog. "There's no evidence to show you killed Tabby. I'm not even certain there's sufficient proof she was murdered."

Kylie's eyes grew wide. "I'm certain she was killed, and the motive is connected to what she thought was happening on the beach."

Marc raised his hands. "It's possible she slipped on the protective wall."

Her nostrils flared. "No. Tabby was always careful. She'd had one bad fall at the hospital in Dallas. She felt like the accident stole her life, at least the significant life she led. In Texas she cared for people in pain. In South Carolina she watched over cats. Don't get me wrong, she loved her cats, but it wasn't the same. There's no way she'd be careless and risk having another accident."

"I wonder what happened on the beach to worry Tabby so bad." A spring breeze ruffled my hair. "I believe you, Kylie. Tabby was murdered, and we'll find evidence to support your theory."

"Thanks for having faith in me, but how do you know there's evidence?"

"Oh, honey, there's always evidence. It's only a matter of looking hard to find the clues."

Chapter Five

LONGER DAYS and sunshine warmed my soul, despite the cool breeze blowing off the Atlantic Ocean. Kylie had drawn a map for me, highlighting the areas where Tabby often fed the wild island cats. I zipped my insulated jacket and waited for Marc at the entrance to the pier's building. Both dogs were at my beach house, which would allow us time to retrace Tabby's normal evening steps.

Marc drove into the parking lot with his right hand on the steering wheel and his left holding a phone to his ear. Piles of work probably littered his desk at the small law firm, but it'd do him good to get some fresh air, and it'd do me good to spend time with him.

Sometimes I missed the old Marc who worked on boats in the big shed on his property. However, he was so smart and helped so many people it'd be a shame for him to waste his legal talent.

Marc hopped out of his red truck and headed my way. He'd probably changed out of his suit at the office, because he wore athletic shorts and a navy blue T-shirt. White letters proclaimed *Home is Where the Boat is Docked.* He pulled on a plain gray hoodie as he approached me. The process emphasized his biceps first then his muscular chest. "Hey there. Thanks for waiting for me."

"Anytime, sailor." I moved close and touched his lips with mine. Sweet shivers danced along my shoulders that had nothing to do with the early evening temperature.

"Su-weet." He slipped on his aviator sunglasses. "Any chance we can focus on us instead of Tabby?"

"Uh, can we do both?" I reached for his hand.

He grinned. "Sure. What's your plan of action?"

"According to Kylie, it took a few weeks for the cats to get used to Tabby. She made eye contact and left them food and milk. Once they learned she meant no harm, they approached her, which thrilled her heart. It's doubtful the cats will come to us, but we can leave provisions in the same spots she did and look around."

Marc glanced at his watch. "Five-fifteen. We better get to it before the sun sets. Lead the way."

"I have a map of sorts. Kylie drew one for us." I unfolded the sheet of paper as we walked over the public access boardwalk, past signs warning visitors not to litter and to stay off the sand dunes or pay a hefty fine. "It'll be high tide soon, but we've still got room to walk. Kylie marked a spot under the pier near the dunes with this X."

"The area will need to be above the high tide line, or the cat food will get washed out to sea."

I stopped in the shade of the pier. "The trick will be setting the food in a safe spot without stepping on the dunes."

Marc reached for my bag of plastic bowls. "We'll place one here and pick it up when we leave so it doesn't wash away." He filled the bowl with cat kibble and left it on a dry patch of sand.

I studied the stretch of beach to our right and left. "Nothing seems unusual for March. People are walking their dogs, a man's fishing, and those boys are tossing a football."

Marc pointed to the Atlantic. "There's an outrigger trawler, but it's too far away to see if there's anything hinky happening out there."

I looked in the direction he pointed and smiled. Leave it to Marc to know the real name for a shrimp boat. "Right. Nothing here seems suspicious."

"At least not tonight. Didn't Tabby make her rounds every night?"

"Except for Sundays." I zipped my jacket and pulled the hood up. "Kylie said Tabby was supposed to rest on Sundays. Her daughter's orders."

"Yet, she was killed on a Sunday." He ran his chin covered with five-o'clock shadow.

"True." I rubbed my hands together to warm them. March was always a finicky weather month. One day warm and the next frigid. The sun's rays played with the ocean waves until they sparkled like diamonds. Hot or cold, it was a beautiful day.

Marc stepped out of the shadows of the pier and into the sunshine then glanced my way. "Where to next?"

"North. The second beach access from here." I joined him, and we hustled that way. "Have you heard if the coroner has decided whether Tabby's death was an accident or homicide?"

He shook his head. "Not yet."

I stuffed my hands into my pockets. "Brr. The weatherman said some system from the west is to blame for this cold snap. I can't believe you're wearing shorts."

"It'll get hot soon enough." He carried the plastic bag of cat supplies in one hand and reached toward me with his free one. Our fingers connected and a flush of warmth swept through my body. "Andi Grace, let's get honest here."

My heart raced. Was this the moment he'd declare his love for me? Sunset on Heyward Beach was the perfect setting. "Okay, I'm ready."

He faced me. Only inches separated us. "What's the real reason you're looking into Tabby's death?"

Air whooshed out of my lungs. I'd been thinking romance, and Marc's thoughts were centered on murder and death. Time to regroup, and fast, before Marc read my disappointment. "Kylie needs somebody on her side. I guess it doesn't matter if it's a human in need or a canine. I tend to choose the underdog to help."

"Do you think she's a suspect?"

"It'd be easy to blame her. She's in Heyward Beach all by herself now Tabby's gone. Even if she was in Texas, I don't think she has anybody close enough to defend her. She's vulnerable and weak. I want to protect her."

He gave my hand a nice squeeze. "You always jump in and take care of others."

"Maybe it's a character flaw."

"It's actually a good trait. But if it turns out Tabby was murdered, Wade and David won't be too happy you're sticking your nose into their case." Marc led me toward the public boardwalk.

Three cars were parked in the small area. All normal. I let go of Marc's hand and looked at the piece of paper with the hand-drawn map. "Kylie told me Tabby fed a black cat where the parking area meets the street. Tabby named him Midnight."

Marc lifted his sunglasses, and they stuck on his forehead. "She named the cats?"

"I guess so. It made them more personal." I reached for the bag of provisions and filled a bowl with kibble. "Here, kitty, kitty. Midnight. I've got food." I shook the bowl in hopes the cat would trust me enough to appear.

We waited.

No sign of Midnight or any stray cat.

One side of Marc's mouth lifted enough for his dimple to appear. "Where to next?"

"We're to walk up the street to the intersection of Sullivan Way and Sandpiper. There's an empty lot where a gray and white cat named Socks suns himself. According to Kylie's notes, Tabby gave him a flea collar with a bell on it."

Marc's sunglasses slid down to protect his eyes, and he reached for my hand. "Let's go."

When we got close to our desired location, I spotted the gray and white cat sitting in the middle of the lot, scratching himself behind the ear. He took a few steps, lay on the ground, flipped around, and bounded away. A tinkling bell was the only sound we heard in his wake.

I sighed. "He must be Socks."

"Andi Grace, we're not trying to catch the animals. We're trying to see if there's anything pointing to what led to Tabby's death. What did she think was suspicious?"

I slowed my steps. "You're right. A clue could be anywhere around us." I spun in a circle.

"Exactly. We'll keep our eyes open."

"It's possible she overheard a conversation from one of the screened-in porches."

Marc came to an abrupt stop. His fingers circled my arm. "How could we miss it?"

"What?" I held my breath.

He turned to face me. "It's not shrimp season. May through August is the main season if you want the small brown shrimp." Marc's dimple appeared with his smile, then his brow furrowed. "Why was the outrigger trawler out today?"

My heart leapt. "Keen sense of observation, Counselor. I'll add the question to my notes tonight. Should we keep following the map?"

"Let's roll."

I walked lighter, knowing we had something to investigate. The empty lot was located on Ocean Drive, a two-lane street with a twenty-five-mile-per-hour speed limit. Many of these homes were vacation rentals. Beachfront homes with spectacular ocean views were referred to as first row. Houses across from the beachfront homes were second row. "Every house will be occupied in a few weeks, but it takes a unique person to rent in March."

"Or a person on a budget. It's much cheaper to vacation at Heyward Beach this time of the year."

"True. I enjoy all the seasons on the island." At the corner, I filled the next bowl in my sack and placed it where I thought Socks might find it. "Do you see anything odd?"

Marc removed his sunglasses and stuffed them in the kangaroo pocket of his hoodie. "You can see the ocean from here."

I edged closer to him and turned east. "You're right." The setting sun cast a pink glow on the waves and tide pools. "Nothing looks suspicious to me."

"Hey, now. Just because we didn't see anything fishy, doesn't mean we're giving up." He slid his arm around my shoulders.

I snuggled into his warmth. "You're right. What did she see on her cat excursions that roused her suspicions?"

"We didn't learn much tonight, but we'll try again."

I stepped away from Marc and whipped out my phone to take notes. "On the beach we saw people and a shrimp boat."

"Don't forget the dogs." He gave me a huge smile.

"Of course. Dogs. Tabby knew about the stray cats, but we've only seen one, which you said isn't the important thing. What are we missing?"

Marc paced. "I guess Kylie accompanied Tabby sometimes because she was able to give you a map."

"She used to go with Tabby because of the seizures. It started out as exercise. Once they began to notice all of the stray cats on the island, it became a mission."

"When did Kylie quit going with Tabby?"

I shrugged. "No idea, but I'll find out. I also want to see the puzzle magazines for myself. I don't feel like David took enough time studying them."

"Ahem." David approached us from the street wearing a long-sleeved deputy polo and khaki pants. "Please tell me you're not snooping into my investigation."

Oxygen hitched in my lungs. "Uh, well, wait a second. Are you saying Tabby's death is suspicious?"

"Neither confirming nor denying. What are you two doing here?" The deputy pierced us one at a time with his gaze.

I clenched the bag of cat supplies. "We're putting out food for Tabby's cats. Do you know she named many of them?"

David's eyebrows shot up. "Thought you were a dog person."

I stood straighter. "That's true, but I care about all kinds of strays."

Marc said, "I can vouch for that. Dogs, cats, and people. Take me for instance. I thought I was a happy hermit working in my boat shed fixing old boats and building new ones. Andi Grace dragged me back into the human race, and I'm practicing law again. My way, though."

I patted Marc's arm. "You also stick up for the underdog. Don't try to deny it. You're not much different from me."

David raised his hands. "Your attempts to distract me aren't going to work. It's fine to feed the roaming cats."

I opened my mouth to ask about the coroner's report.

Marc elbowed me in the ribs then turned his attention to the deputy. "Would you like to see our map of the places Tabby fed cats?"

"Yeah, that'd be great." His shoulders relaxed their stiff posture. "Where'd you get this?"

I handed him the sketch we'd been following. "Kylie."

He took multiple pictures of it with his cell phone. "Wonder why she gave it to you and not me?"

I took the map back. "Probably because she knew I wanted to help the cats. People trust me. You have the power to arrest Kylie. I can't, so it's easy to share information with me. You and Wade should let me help."

David backed away and laughed. "We're not going to risk your life with our investigation. Plus, we still don't have the coroner's report."

"If the coroner says she died from a hit to the head, will you be suspicious or chalk it up to the fact she suffered from seizures?"

"Stay out of it, Andi Grace. And Marc, if you don't need another client, tell your *friend* not to interfere with our investigation." He turned and left us standing by ourselves.

It'd be a lie to say his words hadn't rattled me. It'd also be a lie to say I wasn't looking into Tabby's death.

Chapter Six

MARC TOOK MY arm and we retraced the cat-feeding route, leaving David standing alone on Ocean Drive.

The sun sank and the evening grew dark, but there were enough stars making it possible to walk to Tabby's house and speak to Kylie. Marc remained quiet until we reached our destination. A blue Mercedes sat behind a white Volkswagen Jetta in the driveway.

He whistled. "Nice set of wheels."

"Do you think Susan is here?" When Marc didn't reply, I glanced at him. "Susan Rochester is Tabby's rich daughter from Dallas."

He stopped and faced me. "Why do you think it's the daughter's?"

"Rich people drive Mercedes, don't they?"

"Among other vehicles." One side of his mouth quirked up. "What are we going to say if Susan answers the door?"

For a man who'd grown up with grief, Marc sometimes struggled to comfort those dealing with loss. "I can do the talking if you'd like."

He motioned for me to lead the way. "Go ahead."

We walked up the steps to the front porch, and I rang the doorbell of the simple beach house. The unpretentious white home with white wooden rockers on the wide front porch invited a visitor to sit down and share a glass of sweet tea and sweeter conversation.

The lantern-style chrome front porch light flickered on, and Kylie opened the door. "This isn't a good time."

"Who is it?" A feminine voice came from the background. *Tip tap. Tip tap.* Heels clicked on the oak floors. A beautiful woman opened the door wider, forcing Kylie to step to the side. Perfect coif, expensive clothes, and serene expression. No signs of weeping or having flown to the coast earlier. If it was Tabby's daughter, she hid her grief well.

Kylie motioned toward us. "Susan, this is Andi Grace Scott and Marc Williams. They both knew your mother, and they're friends."

"Hi, I'm Susan Rochester." She extended a well-manicured hand with fire-engine red nail polish.

"I'm so sorry for your loss. Marc and I just walked around the island leaving cat food in the places where your mother cared for the wild creatures." I held out the plastic bag for Susan.

Susan crinkled her nose. "My mother had a mind of her own. Come in. Kylie can fix us some tea." She walked through the entry hall to the great room with the grace of a debutante about to be presented at a ball.

Kylie rolled her eyes. "I'll take the cat food. Would y'all like something to drink?"

I entered the house. "Don't go to any trouble. We won't stay long."

Marc snagged my arm. "Should we take off our shoes? This place is immaculate."

I glanced around the wide hall with minimal furniture. "Oh, uh, maybe. We don't want to track sand inside."

Kylie shut the door. "Don't bother. I sweep the floors every night before going to bed. Tabby used to say if you live at the beach you should expect sandy floors."

Yeah, but Tabby was dead and her successful big-city daughter didn't appear to share her mother's relaxed attitude. "Are you sure?"

"Positive."

We followed Kylie to the kitchen, but I stopped at the kitchen counter between the great room and the actual kitchen. Stacks of paper littered the counter that had been neat and organized earlier. Bills, junk mail, and magazines. "What's all this?"

Susan placed a sales flyer on a pile that looked like junk. "I like to keep busy. I'm sorting through Mother's things while I have time."

Kylie opened the refrigerator. "We've got tea, lemonade, water, and Cokes."

Marc gave me an eye signal, but I couldn't interpret it. He edged around Susan and joined Kylie. "I'd love a glass of lemonade. Did you make it yourself?"

"Yes, sir. Tabby taught me how to make real southern lemonade. Not the powdery fake stuff." Her stiff smile made me wonder more about the girl's past.

I tuned out their conversation to focus on Tabby's daughter. Marc could fill me in later if Kylie revealed something important. "Susan, what can I do to help?"

"Is there a recycling center? How about a donation center that accepts clothing?"

"I'd be happy to take these items to be recycled. The library accepts current magazines. If I remove Tabby's name, would it be okay to donate her magazines?"

"As long as you deidentify, darling." Susan dropped pages of scribbling into a white plastic trash bag.

"Of course." I didn't see any of Tabby's clothes laying around. "My church gives clothing to those in need. I can swing by another day to pick up the items you don't want."

"It'll pretty much be everything. My mother and I had completely different tastes. We argued about quite a few things after her accident, including her lack of style." She looked toward the ceiling and took a deep breath. "I never wanted us to live so far apart, but we actually got along better when she moved here."

"Why did Tabby choose Heyward Beach?"

"When the hospital refused to allow Mother to return to work, the spark left her. She got lost in the past. Then one day she remembered how much she loved Heyward Beach."

I smiled. "I understand. To me, this is the best place in the world to live."

"It sounds like you and Mother had a lot in common." She turned her attention to a stack of unopened mail.

"Maybe. How did she decide to move here? Loving the island and moving here are two completely different things." In the same situation, would I have been so brave?

"Once she started thinking about Heyward Beach, living here became an obsession. She brought it up every single day." Susan dropped her wrist to her hip.

"Our small-town life is different than Dallas. She made a lot of friends here." I sat in one of the bar chairs. "Did she need your permission?"

"Not really, but she wasn't functioning at full capacity. Mother needed my help to orchestrate a move. Across the street or clear across the country, she needed assistance. I brought her for a visit, thinking she'd change her mind." She returned to sorting through the papers.

"I guess she didn't."

"Exactly." Susan threw obvious junk mail into the trash bag. "When we returned to Dallas, I gave in only after Kylie agreed to move here with her."

"I'm sure it gave you peace to know somebody was looking out for your mom."

Susan sniffed. "How about you, Andi Grace? Are you close to your mother?"

Pain from my past punched me in the solar plexus. "My parents died over a decade ago. I was still a teenager. We got along well, though."

"Oh, dear. I'm sorry to hear she passed." Susan removed her black pumps, shrinking her close to my height. She led me to the back deck and closed the door firmly behind us. "I'm going to be honest. Brutally so. I don't know what to do about Kylie."

"Won't she move back to Dallas?" Why was the successful business woman confiding in me?

"Kylie has a messy past. Moving here was a way to escape it. I don't know many people in South Carolina, but it seems like I should try to protect her."

"Are you worried about her ex-boyfriend or her family?" I crossed my arms.

Susan stepped close to me and lowered her voice. "Both. How much has Kylie shared with you? Did she mention changing her name?"

"What?" My ears rang.

"Just her last name. It's really Juzang, not Black."

My legs shook. "Poor girl. She must've been terrified to take such a drastic step."

"It's legal. I'm the one who helped her with the paperwork. Samantha Kylie Juzang is now Kylie Black." Susan lifted the lid on the grill and removed a pack of cigarettes and a lighter. In one fluid motion, she lit a cigarette and inhaled deeply. "I kicked the habit years ago, but in times of extreme stress, I give in to the cravings. Mother never approved of me smoking, and I often hid my cigarettes in the grill or a flower pot to avoid a confrontation. I guess old habits die hard."

Not wanting to inhale her smoke, I shifted upwind of Susan. "Tell me more about Kylie."

Susan took another puff and flicked ashes into a little white bowl. "She's of legal age to be on her own. She's a survivor, but without a job, I don't know how she'll live. I can't continue to pay her to do nothing, and moving back to Dallas probably isn't a good move for her. In fact, I believe it'd be disastrous. Mother said Kylie was thriving here, and I can see for myself how much healthier the girl looks."

"Why are you telling me all of this?"

"I need somebody in Heyward Beach I can count on to help Kylie. You two seem to have a connection."

"I haven't known her long." Like barely at all.

"It doesn't matter. It's obvious you like taking care of others, and I can't help Kylie in South Carolina." She stretched her neck to the right.

"Maybe you can do more than you imagine. You seem to care about her." I stared at Susan, who puzzled me. Susan had seen to it her mom was cared for, and now she was concerned about Kylie. Did she hide her kindness thinking it would make her appear weak?

"My husband and I never had children, but for some reason I feel a sense of responsibility toward the girl. Maybe because she treated my mother so kindly." She took another drag on her cigarette. "Can you help her find someplace to work?"

"Maybe." I didn't know Kylie well. Yet. She seemed caring, but what were her skills? Was she honest? Gentle with animals? Trustworthy? Dylan liked her. Maybe I should take a chance on the young girl. "I own a dog walking business. I also board dogs and provide doggie day care. Do you want me to offer her a job?"

Susan leaned against the deck railing. "I'd be obliged. If your payroll can't handle another employee, I can supplement her salary."

How much money did the woman have? "Why would you do that?"

She finished her cigarette and ground it out in the dish. The ocean waves hitting the beach could be heard over a dog barking in the distance. "Like I said, Kylie was good to my mother. I'd like to return the favor."

Her answer resonated with me. "Let me figure out what I can do to help. She'll need a car and place to live." I'd already provided a place for Dylan. Where could I house Kylie?

"Yes, she will. I can give her the Jetta, but I plan to sell the house."

I crossed my arms. "Could she live here until the house sells? It might give her time to build a nest egg before she has to start renting."

Her eyebrows lifted. "Sure. I can even pay her to keep the place clean for showings. Houses sell better if they're lived in."

Susan's compassion toward Kylie amazed me. When Peter Roth was alive, he'd acted kind toward me, and he'd been rich. Tabby had a big heart, so I should accept her daughter's kindness was genuine. "My sister's out of town on spring vacation, but she might help find a place for Kylie to rent when this place sells."

"All right." The woman returned her smoking supplies to their hiding spot in the grill then chuckled. "I guess it's not necessary to hide them anymore, but out of respect for my mother I will."

I nodded. "Susan, do you think your mom died of natural causes?"

"When I first heard she died, I thought she'd eaten shellfish. She's allergic. Then I wondered if she'd had a seizure. Now I don't know what to think." She tossed her hands in the air.

"Did she have any enemies?"

"Not that I'm aware of. We settled with the hospital instead of going to court, so they shouldn't hold a grudge."

"Was there the possibility of a lawsuit?" Marc should be here for this conversation. Instead he was still in the house with Kylie.

"Yes. I threatened the hospital to do the right thing or they'd hear from my attorney."

Interesting. If the hospital wanted to get rid of anybody, it seemed like Susan was the one to gun for. "I'm glad you stood up for Tabby."

"My mother was so energetic and smart before her accident. She was a proud woman. Her life was never the same after the fall, and I blame the hospital for the physical accident as well as the emotional damage from the way they handled the situation." She sighed. "Why would they kill her after they settled? It doesn't make sense. It was probably a terrible accident."

"I hope you're right." In all honesty, I didn't want there to be a killer on the loose.

Susan threw back her shoulders and stood taller. "You take the recycling and see if you can find a job for Kylie. I'll continue to clear out Mother's personal items and list the house with a real estate agent."

I lifted my chin. "Susan, I don't work for you. I'm happy to help, but you're not my boss." Did I sound childish? Maybe. But I suspected the woman would respect me more if I stood up for myself.

Her eyes widened, and she shook her head. "You're right. I apologize."

"I'll grab the recycling on my way out. I'll be in touch when I figure out a job for Kylie." I opened the door to enter the house.

"Andi Grace?"

I turned back to Tabby's daughter.

"Thank you."

"You're welcome. People around town liked your mother. Stop by Daily Java before you leave town. I bet you'll hear some nice stories about her." I left Susan alone on the deck, suspecting she'd pull out another cigarette.

When I entered the kitchen, Marc was placing an empty glass in the kitchen sink. "You ready to go?"

"Yep. I told Susan we'd take the magazines to recycling. May as well take the garbage too." I tied the white bag in a loose knot.

He lifted the eight-inch-stack of magazines. "Kylie, thanks for the lemonade."

She walked us to the front door. "Good night."

I paused on the front porch—how could I have forgotten? "Kylie, how do you feel about dogs?"

Marc chuckled. "Watch out, Kylie. Before you know it, Andi Grace will have you adopting a stray."

"I like animals." Kylie gave us a lopsided smile. "If I had enough money, I'd take in a homeless dog. I enjoyed helping Tabby care for the abandoned cats on the island. It made me feel good. You know what I mean?"

I nodded. Hiring Kylie could work. She seemed nice enough. "If you're interested, I might have a job for you."

Her eyes sparkled, lighting up her entire face. "Oh, yeah. I'm interested."

I couldn't hold back a smile. "Great. Get some rest, and I'll be in touch."

We waved and began walking to the pier parking lot where we'd left our vehicles.

Marc said, "Why are we taking this to recycling?"

"We're not exactly." I stepped from the narrow sidewalk to the empty street so we weren't walking in single file.

"What do you mean?" Marc matched my pace.

"I want to search for clues in Tabby's puzzle books. Kylie said the last couple of weeks when Tabby came home, the first thing she did was get her puzzle books. What if she wrote notes in the margins?" I opened the door of my Suburban and placed the garbage bag on the floorboard.

"And the garbage?" Marc handed me the magazines.

"Susan threw away some handwritten notes. I didn't want to risk losing a clue."

Marc chuckled. "Naturally. I'll follow you home and pick up Chubb." He stuffed his hands in his pockets. "You know, Tabby may have died of natural causes."

"True. But what if she didn't?" I leaned against my SUV. "Oh, yeah. Susan told me Kylie's last name was Juzang, but she had it changed legally."

Marc placed both hands on the vehicle over my shoulders and leaned toward me. "You're determined to solve a mystery no matter what."

He stood mere inches away. Fire danced across my skin. The briny ocean smell combined with the light from the crescent moon made the night romantic. Ooh, la, la.

He closed the gap. His lips touched mine. Lights exploded beneath my closed eyelids.

A horn tooted, ruining the moment.

Marc groaned then pulled back while slipping his arm around my shoulders.

My brother's landscaping truck drew to a stop beside us, and Nate hopped out. "Aren't there laws about public displays of affection?"

Marc laughed.

"Nate, that's rude." I gave him a gentle punch to the arm as heat flooded my face and neck.

He tipped his head to one side. "Juliet asked me to check on you before I went to the plantation."

"How'd you know I was here?"

"The phone tracker. Guess I can report you're safe and sound." He smirked.

Apparently there were some downsides to the tracker app.

Marc said, "I'm going by Andi Grace's to pick up Chubb. I'll make sure the house is free of boogeymen."

"Thanks, man. See you 'round." My brother returned to his truck and left with a squeal of his tires.

I glanced at Marc. "Sorry about that. He's in the habit of protecting his sisters."

"Our timing stinks. Let's go."

"Wait. Have you ever worked a sudoku puzzle?"

"Yeah. I can teach you the basics when we get to your place." He reached for my hand and kissed the inside of my wrist.

If I were a swooning kind of woman, I would've swooned. Instead, I hopped in the driver's seat of my SUV and led the way to my house. Despite my hunger and weariness, I couldn't wait to learn how to work the puzzles. Then I'd be able to figure out if there were any clues in the puzzle book.

Chapter Seven

TUESDAY MORNING I sat in Daily Java studying the sudoku puzzle magazines from Tabby's house. I'd spent most of the night figuring out workable patterns and solving puzzles. The end result was a depleted eraser and very little sleep, but I hoped I could determine if Tabby had left us some hints. I covered a yawn with my fist.

I'd only had two dog walking appointments for college professors who'd left town for spring break. When the local school system had spring vacation, I'd have all kinds of dogs to walk, especially since I'd decided to offer a special rate for boarding dogs that week. Reservations were pouring in at Stay and Play. More work meant it'd be easier to hire Kylie.

I took pictures of the puzzles with my phone, knowing I'd have to turn anything that might be evidence over to the sheriff's department. I studied the other patrons in the coffee shop. Most appeared to be dressed for work and were looking at their phones. I glanced at Tabby's puzzle books. Sudoku was a numbers game. Could numbers relate to Tabby's suspicions of illegal activity on the beach?

I sipped my lavender-honey latte with two shots of espresso. The drink would either wake me up or make my heart explode.

"Hi, Andi Grace. May I sit with you?"

I jerked to attention. "Hannah, I'd love for you to join me."

The tall brunette lowered her briefcase to the empty chair and settled her mug on the table without spilling a drop as she sat. Her hair was pulled back into a sleek ponytail, and she wore a feminine navy suit. "You look tired."

"Yeah, I'm a little sleepy." I lifted my mug and sipped, enjoying the earthy floral aroma almost as much as the taste. "How are you?"

"Fine." Hannah stirred sweetener and cream into her black coffee. "Whatcha working on there?"

I lifted the magazines. "Uh, it seemed like a good time to learn sudoku." Not quite a lie because by learning the game I might find something that would lead me to Tabby's killer.

"I don't know what's going on with you and the puzzle book, but you're a terrible liar." Hannah laughed.

"Hey, I've got the books." I flipped through the pages to show her solved puzzles.

"Something tells me you're trying to solve more than a puzzle. My guess is you're looking into Tabby's murder."

I'd known Hannah was smart, but wow. "I, uh . . ." I slumped. "Maybe you're right."

"There's no way you can suspect my dad, which makes me happy. So let's enjoy our coffee. No more questions about what you're doing. I ordered us each a chocolate-filled croissant. Erin's pulling out a fresh batch soon."

"Oh, thanks." I sipped my drink and avoided commenting on Tabby's murder. "Adding lavender and honey to my latte makes me feel healthy, so I should be able to indulge in a treat. Right?"

Erin appeared with two golden brown croissants on white plates. "Fresh out of the oven. Enjoy." From her apron, she removed silverware wrapped in paper napkins and placed them on the table.

I appreciated her effort to protect the environment, and metal forks were easier for eating my croissant.

We thanked her, and she returned to the front counter to wait on a middle-aged man. He stood with perfect posture, even though he wore jeans and a long-sleeve polo. I didn't recognize him but was glad to see new people in Erin's bakery.

Hannah lifted a flaky bit of the croissant to her mouth and chewed. "Mmm, scrumptious."

"Pretty much anything Erin bakes is delicious."

Hannah wiped her hands on the napkin. "I need to ask you a personal question. Two, actually. I don't want to put you on the spot though, so please feel free to decline to answer."

My heart skipped a beat, and I doubted it had anything to do with the amount of caffeine I'd ingested. "Okay. What?"

"Let's start with the easy one first. Juliet thinks I should go on a date with Sheriff Stone."

My friend hadn't wasted time matchmaking. I grinned. "Wade's a great guy. I think you two would make a nice couple."

"Could we go on a double date? Or meet casually with you and Marc? For ice cream or maybe coffee. It'd be less awkward." Her face reddened.

My stomach churned. Less awkward for who? Marc and I didn't get much alone time. Did I want to expose him to Hannah, who seemed to have no flaws? Beautiful, smart, successful Hannah. No. I couldn't keep comparing the two of us. Marc was interested in me, and I needed get past my fear of losing him.

"Please?" Her gaze met mine.

I took a deep breath. I liked Hannah, and insecurities couldn't take root if we were going to be friends. She was interested in Wade, and Marc cared about me. A double date was doable. "Sure. That's what friends are for. We can cook out at my place and play corn hole, bocce, or even cards if the weather's bad. When do you want this to happen?"

"I don't think I can ask Wade out exactly. My thought was to invite him over to christen my beach house. Something like that. We can incorporate your idea of playing games."

"Great plan. It'll be nice and casual." I held my coffee cup. "And your second request?"

Hannah looked around the coffee shop as if she had a secret of the utmost importance.

Her unease led me to check our surroundings. Three elderly men sat at a table near the front door exuberantly discussing the teams expected to play in March Madness. A young man sat in the back corner with earbuds in, working on his computer. The stranger in the polo had taken his drink and left. Very few people in the coffee shop, but it was the middle of the morning.

"What's on your mind?"

Hannah leaned close. "Danny Nichols is giving me a hard time. He's so moody. He's got one personality when others are around, but he's different when it's the two of us." She fisted her hands on the table. "No, that's not exactly true. He's been rude to me at the courthouse when others are present. Is it possible he's on drugs? Bipolar? Mentally unbalanced?"

"Whoa." I leaned back in my chair. "Drugs?"

"Shh." She waved her hands. "I don't want to start a rumor, but I need to figure out the best way to deal with the man. How do you handle him?"

My thoughts raced. Danny hadn't suffered from mental illness when we dated. "I didn't see him for over a decade. Last summer he moved back to the area to work at his father's law firm, but we don't run in the same circles."

Hannah tapped her finger on the table. "Dad thinks we should hire a detective to investigate my suspicions."

"Danny came back to Heyward Beach at the time his uncle died. His mom's brother. Now that's a woman with issues. She never thought I was good enough for her son, and when he broke up with me, she faded out of my life, too." I shrugged. "Mrs. Nichols doesn't keep her emotions under control."

"Is Danny like his mom?" Hannah sipped her coffee.

"He was angry, almost vicious, when he learned I'd inherited Peter's plantation. He oozed charm with others and venom with me, which takes us back to your questions. Maybe he is addicted to drugs."

She clutched my arm. "He's here."

I turned, not sure whether I'd see Wade or Danny. Too bad it was Danny. "Stay calm. You're running for state representative. You're a successful businesswoman. There's nothing to fear from Dan the man." The sight of Hannah being nervous because of Danny made her seem real, and I liked her even more, although it made me sick to realize Danny affected her in such a negative way.

Hannah sat straighter and lifted her chin. "Thank you, Andi Grace. I needed that. Why does he get me so worked up?"

"Keep eating and focus on me. Maybe he won't approach us." I took another bite of my croissant. Chocolate drizzled down my chin. Before I could wipe it away, Danny stood at our table.

"Ladies, how are you this lovely morning?"

Hannah nodded. "Fine."

I wiped my chin. "We're good. What are you up to, Danny?"

He sneered. "I'm about to beat your boyfriend in court on a ridiculous child support suit."

I bit my tongue. No doubt Marc was fighting for the underdog while Danny represented some sleazy moron who didn't want to take care of his children.

He pointed toward Hannah with his paper cup. "We should have an election debate."

"I'd rather wait until closer to the election." Her expression remained neutral.

"Fine, but you're going down." His arm slung our way. Coffee sloshed out of the lid's drink-through opening and splashed on his hand. He dropped the cup and jumped back. It hit the concrete floor and the lid popped off. Coffee splashed my bare leg and his fancy slacks. He swore under his breath, clear enough for us to hear, but the sports enthusiasts were leaving, and the other guy didn't glance our way.

Hot liquid ran down my leg. I jumped out of my seat and dried my skin.

Erin appeared with clean towels. "Use these. They're softer."

Danny grabbed Erin's arm and ushered her to the outside patio.

Hannah touched my shoulders. "You sit. I'll clean up the mess."

I sat and studied my leg. Tender, but no blisters appeared. Slightly pink.

"Andi Grace, do you need me to take you to the ER?" Hannah paused soaking up the liquid.

"No. I should be okay."

Erin returned. Her face was red, and she ran her hands over the apron. "Andi Grace, I'm so sorry."

"It's not your fault." I pointed to my leg. "No blisters."

"I'll get you some of my special burn cream. Bakers and burns go together." She raised her arms and revealed red scars on her wrists and inner arms.

"Yikes." My stomach flipped at the sight of her scars. "What did Danny say to you outside?"

"He threatened to sue me." She lowered her voice. "I'd swear he'd been drinking except I didn't smell alcohol on him and it's still morning. I'll be right back."

Hannah threw away a gob of soaked paper towels. "If you're okay, I need to run. I've got an appointment with a potential backer."

"You should go. I'll see ya later." Once Hannah left, I closed my eyes. The scene had been such a shock. A gentleman should've apologized. Instead, Danny had gotten angry and threatened Erin. He was a boor. There was nothing honorable about him.

Erin returned with a small white jar. "This should help lessen the sting, and it'll heal faster. I've got insurance if you need to go to the doctor."

"No, I'm really fine, but I will try your cream. Thanks. I lightly applied the white substance. "Erin, do you see Danny often when you're out at restaurants or bars?"

Her face turned pink. "I don't go to bars anymore. I'm a workaholic now. Corey stole money from my business, which forced me into recovery mode. This place gets all of my attention, and it's a good thing." She nodded her head so fast, her ponytail bounced. "If I had too much free time, I'd probably stew over Corey's despicable actions."

"I understand." My twenties had been devoted to work and raising my siblings.

A young woman appeared wearing an apron with the Daily Java imprint. "Here you go."

I lifted a hand. "I didn't order that."

Erin smiled. "It's a mocha latte. On the house. Let us know if you want anything."

"Thanks." I sipped my fresh drink. My journal was in the Suburban, so I jotted notes in the margin of the puzzle book. *Date. Time. What happened?*

Had Tabby used a similar pattern in the puzzle book? Sudoku worked in groups of threes and nines. It was March. Tabby could've written down dates using three digits. February twenty-eight would be written 2-2-8. Times of the day would work except for six hours of the day. Ten, eleven, and twelve o'clock. Morning and night.

I studied a completed sudoku book in a spiral binder, making it easy to turn from one puzzle to the next. The first pages were normal. Near the end of the book, the patterns changed. The numbers didn't add up. Was there a code to Tabby's death in the puzzles? My palms grew damp. In the margin, a blank board had been penciled in with numbers inserted. Each top row in a cube began with a one, two, or three. January, February, and March. My pulse flutter-kicked. If my theory on dates was correct, the second row of the puzzles could signify times. Third rows were empty.

I stared at the page while I finished my coffee. What had Tabby seen on these particular days? If my theory was correct, the times were in the evening because that's when Tabby took her walks. I shivered. Did it make sense or was I losing my mind?

If the top rows were dates, they were a week apart for the first few puzzles. Then the pattern changed. I checked the potential dates on my phone. Mondays. What caused the dates to change from every Monday to random days of the week? Weather?

Susan entered the coffee shop and waved to me before placing her order.

I joined her at the counter as Erin returned her credit card. "Erin, this is Susan Rochester. Tabby's daughter."

"Nice to meet you, but I wish we could've met under nicer circumstances. I'm so sorry for your loss." Erin shook hands with Susan. "Empty words. I'm aware because my husband recently died. If there's anything I can do for you, please don't hesitate to ask. Food for after the funeral or visitation. Anything. Please let me know."

"That's very kind of you. Thanks, Erin." Susan gave her a tight smile. "My mother told me the people here were nice and so did Andi Grace. Seems like they were correct."

The front door swooshed open, and I glanced at the newest customer. Regina Houp entered and stood in line behind us, so I introduced the antique store owner to Susan. It didn't take long for the two businesswomen to start a conversation.

Regina paused long enough to ask Erin for her regular cappuccino and paid her. The women continued their conversation, leaving me out, which was fine. They followed me past empty tables to join me.

I listened to them for a bit and was glad to see them hit it off. "Y'all seem to have a lot in common, and I need to run. Enjoy your coffee." I gathered my belongings and hoofed it to the little parking lot where I'd backed my SUV into a shady place at the far corner of the building. I'd developed a habit of parking in the shade even if I had to walk farther. My spot was about as private as I could get and still be in the parking lot.

Slinking into the driver's seat, I pressed a fist against my mouth. It'd be silly to cry over a run-in with Danny. I looked around and spotted him standing beside a shiny new Lexus. The blue convertible seemed flashy enough to make him happy and serious enough to please his mother. He held a phone to his ear, frowning.

A big red luxury car pulled into the parking lot. Danny's mom was behind the wheel, and she whipped the vehicle into the empty spot next to her son.

I lowered my window and slunk down in my seat, wanting to hear but not be seen by Danny or Mrs. Nichols. There wasn't much traffic, and at least half of the parking places were full. If they looked my way, they might not notice me. If they did, I'd start my Suburban and drive off.

Danny stood taller at the appearance of his mother, almost like a soldier snapping to attention in the presence of a military leader.

Mrs. Nichols—I refused to think of her as Mrs. Leslie—stepped out of her fancy vehicle and pulled a man's suit from the back seat. "Baby, are you okay?"

All right. I could hear them.

Danny ripped the hanger from his mother's grip. "I'm going to be late for court. Thanks for bringing clean clothes." He kissed her cheek, and as he returned to his Lexus, Mrs. Nichols touched her cheek like a smitten schoolgirl. Sickening how much she adored her son, despite his rude behavior. Danny tossed the suit into the back, jumped behind the driver's seat and drove away at a speed worthy of a NASCAR driver.

His mother ran a hand over her black dress, eased into the fancy car, and drove away at a much more sedate pace. Probably headed to her job at the library.

Danny had exhibited both anger and kindness within a few moments of each other. His erratic actions were so different from the guy I'd dated years ago. Back then he'd never done anything to risk upsetting either of his parents. Hannah was right. Danny was messed up, but what was the problem?

Was he abusing drugs? How was I going to find out? More important, could I run my dog business, catch Tabby's killer, and figure out what Danny was up too all at the same time?

A shadow appeared in my side-view mirror.

Cold chills broke out on my arms.

Thud.

My Suburban shook, and I screamed.

Chapter Eight

I LURCHED AWAY from the window. Away from the danger. My heartbeat thrashed in my ears.

"Are you spying on me?" Danny's growl sent chills up my spine. His hair was disheveled, and his necktie hung loosely around his neck.

"No. I just left Daily Java." The words whimpered out of me.

Danny reached through the open window into my SUV, hit the unlock button, and flung open the door.

I scrambled over the console toward the passenger seat and freedom. My fingers reached for the door handle, but he snatched my left ankle, scraping the burn he'd inflicted earlier. He pulled me toward him. The console acted like a large speed bump in a school zone. My ribs rumbled over it with a good bit of pain, but I couldn't give up. With my free leg, I kicked at the monster who used to be my boyfriend. Every nerve in my body screamed for freedom. Then my foot connected with his face.

Yes!

"*Arg!*" Danny howled but managed to grab my other leg with enough force to win the tug-of-war.

Agony flashed up my leg.

"Stop fighting me."

How was I going to get away from the monster? I struggled with all my might, but he was stronger.

He jerked at his loose tie and wrapped it around my ankles. His movements scraped against the tender burn area. My eyes filled with tears, and I screamed.

"Be still," he hissed and slapped the side of my head.

I freed one leg, kicking at him as if I were caught in a rip current. *Move perpendicular to the opposing force.* Survival required action on my part.

Danny pulled both legs but still hadn't gotten them tied back together.

Where were the people? Even Regina would be a welcome sight. I didn't care. I needed help.

Lord, help me get away from Danny.

Face down, I moved my arms through the opening to the back, gripping the seats. Using my arms and hands, I struggled to gain distance from the danger. Danny. I wrestled against the maniac and his herculean strength. "Help!"

"Shut up." He snarled and twisted my leg.

My left ankle popped at the pressure against me. Air whooshed out of my lungs. Black spots danced before my eyes.

Danny latched onto my feet and ripped me out of the car. Inch by painful inch. My head bounced against the hard console, banged into the side of the driver's seat, and crashed onto the asphalt. Bile rose to my throat.

He'd zapped the strength out of me. I fought to remain conscious and struggled to get a full breath.

Danny grabbed me by the back of my shirt with enough power to rip the arm seams. The collar dug into my throat until he spun me around and slung my limp body against the back door. One hand circled my neck and the other clenched my shoulder. "Stay out of my business, Andi Grace." He squeezed my throat.

My feeble attempts to fight back didn't gain my freedom, but I scratched his face, trying to get a good gulp of air. If I died, his DNA would be under my fingernails.

"Hey!" Footsteps pounded the ground, but I couldn't decipher from what direction.

Danny cursed then released me.

I crumpled to the ground. Sandy gravel bit into my cheek, but I didn't care because I could breathe again. Air. Sweet, beautiful air. Thanks be to God. And the person who'd dared come to my rescue.

"Lady, can you hear me?"

The man's features blurred. I blinked, trying to focus on my hero.

"Somebody, call 911. We need an ambulance." His words faded away.

Danny had attacked me, but I was safe with the stranger.

Chapter Nine

MARC HELD MY hand in the curtain-enclosed exam room. He sat in a metal chair beside the bed where I lay. Machines beeped.

"Marc, why do I feel so groggy?"

"You're in the ER. I think they gave you something to take the edge off." He leaned toward me.

I flinched at his movement.

"Easy there. You're safe." Marc continued to hold my hand but inched away.

Whoa. This was Marc. Not Danny. I closed my eyes and pictured Danny's terrifying frown. I tightened my grip on the blanket. "Marc?"

He swallowed loud enough for me to hear. "Nobody can hurt you here."

I opened my eyes. "Sorry."

"You've got nothing to be sorry about." He gave me a lopsided smile. "You've been through a terrible ordeal. I should've expected you to be skittish."

"Why are you here?"

"Nate asked me to check on you. He's out of town working on a plantation, and you know Lacey Jane's in Florida for spring vacation. Your brother is on his way back."

"Tell him to finish working. I'm fine." I shivered and pulled the blanket tighter. "Not great but okay. What's wrong with me?"

Marc rubbed my knuckles with his thumb. "The doctor wants to check on you, and Wade's here to question you. Are you up to it?"

Visions of Danny yanking me out of the Suburban flitted through my mind. The beeping on the monitor increased. I squeezed Marc's hand. "Danny attacked me."

"Let's discuss it with Wade. Then you won't need to tell the story twice."

With an IV connected to the back of my hand, I pulled the white blanket up to my chin. I couldn't get warm enough. "Please don't leave me."

"I'm not going anywhere. Let's buzz the nurse and ask for a warm blanket. She can also let Wade know you're ready to talk." He pushed the red button at my side.

He'd noticed I was cold. Marc was always so sweet and caring. My heart swelled with emotion.

"Aren't you supposed to be in court facing off against Danny?"

He grimaced. "He didn't show. Imagine that. The judge postponed our case, but I never dreamed the reason for his absence was because he was attacking you."

A middle-aged woman with a jet-black ponytail, wearing blue scrubs, entered our room. "Good to see you're alert." She moved to the opposite side of the bed from Marc and felt my wrist. "I still like to check a patient's pulse the old-fashioned way."

"Ma'am, would you inform Sheriff Stone that Andi Grace is ready to talk, and she's cold. Can somebody bring her a warm blanket?"

"You bet. The PA will be with you after a while, but we want you to be as comfortable as possible. I'll be right back and we'll get you warmed up." She slipped through the curtain.

"Thanks, Marc." I sighed. "I feel so helpless."

"You just had the fight of your life. Who knows what Danny intended? If he'd kidnapped you for some reason, it's doubtful we'd have started searching for you until later today. You saved yourself."

"No, there was a man." I tried to remember who, but I couldn't place him.

"I heard that, but you fought Danny."

The nurse returned and cocooned me in soft warmth, forcing me to release Marc's hand. My body began to relax as the chills departed. Her kind smile comforted me as much as her actions. "Better?"

"Much."

She looked at the monitor with the squiggly lines and beeps. "I'll show Sheriff Stone in."

I rested my eyes until the sound of the curtain's movement. "Hi, Wade." I nodded instead of removing my arms from the cocoon of warmth.

"Andi Grace, I promise we're going to get the guy who did this to you." The firm line of his mouth and the anger radiating from his eyes alarmed me.

I glanced at Marc. "Do I look bad?"

He shook his head. "You're beautiful."

Wade's eyes widened, and his expression revealed the truth.

I smiled at Marc. "Thank you, but something tells me you're lying."

His hands remained on the arms of the chair. "You're alive, and you're beautiful to me."

"Ahem." Wade held up a recorder. "Time is crucial. Do you mind if I record our conversation?"

"Go ahead." I nodded, and the room spun.

In spite of the recorder, Wade also pulled a small notepad out of his shirt pocket. "Did you see your assailant?"

I pushed a button on the bedrail until I sat at around forty-five degrees. "Yes. It was Danny Nichols."

Wade's mouth dropped open. "As in the attorney? Your old boy-friend? Dan the man?"

In a small town, we all knew each other's business. "Yes." I reached for the plastic glass of water and drank until it was empty. The icy cool-ness made me feel better.

"Why? Is he still fuming over Peter's will?" Wade tilted his head.

"Maybe, but it's been settled. There's nothing he can do about it. Even if I die, it won't go to him. Nate and Lacey Jane will inherit everything."

"Then what led him to attack you?"

"I'm not exactly sure." The covers slipped down, and I pulled them up to my shoulders.

"Give me your best guess." Wade's jaw tightened.

"I had been at Daily Java. Hannah Cummings joined me. We didn't plan it, but it happened. You know Hannah, right?"

"We've met. How does she figure into the situation?"

"Over coffee, she asked me if Danny had a drug problem. She was very discreet, and nobody could've overheard us. Do you know he's running against Hannah for state representative?" I thought back to the lovely coffee and croissant.

"I'm aware. So you two spoke to Danny before the attack?" Wade held his pencil tight enough his knuckles whitened.

"Yes. I can't remember saying anything to upset him, though." I closed my eyes and replayed the event in my mind. "Danny and Hannah discussed the election and a debate. If he was going to attack anybody, it'd make sense to go after Hannah."

Marc stood and stuffed his hands in his pockets. "Is it possible the stress is making you forget something?"

"No. I'm clear. I refrained from butting into the conversation between Hannah and Danny, but he seemed agitated. He even spilled his coffee on my leg, but it was an accident." I explained the situation.

Wade wrote as I spoke. "Then what?"

"I went to the Suburban a little later." I'd looked at the puzzle books before leaving and drank my latte. "Actually, it was at least fifteen minutes. Danny was standing by his car across the parking lot. His mom brought him a clean suit, then he drove away. I thought he'd gone to the courthouse until he appeared at the window of my Suburban. He accused me of spying on him and tried to drag me out of the car. I did my best to get away, but he was too strong." I reached for Marc's hand. "You're right. I need to get in better shape."

"The goal is to get in shape for health reasons." Marc gripped my fingers. "Not to fight off an attacker."

Wade tapped his notepad. "Were you spying on him?"

"Not exactly, but kinda, because he's been acting so erratic. Please go talk to Hannah. She'll confirm my suspicions."

"Anything else?" Wade poised his pen over the paper.

"Are you going to arrest Danny?" I struggled to breathe normal.

"We'll bring him in for questioning. I believe you, Andi Grace."

"Drug test him. He's acting irrational."

Wade shook his head. "Arresting an attorney is never easy. They know their rights and usually fight every step of the way."

Dr. Jagger entered my room. Cubicle. Roomette? Who knew? "Gentlemen, I'd like to examine Ms. Scott privately." Her small stature didn't take away from her take-charge attitude.

I met Marc's gaze and released his hand. "Will you wait for me? Or call Nate because I changed my mind. I'm not ready to be alone."

"I'll wait."

When they exited, I did my best to smile at Dr. Jagger. "What are you doing here?"

"The PA is a friend and contacted me when she saw you're one of my patients. Tuesday is my day off, so I decided to drop by." She took her time flipping through my chart. "It says a possible sprained ankle."

"It hurts."

Dr. Jagger rehung the chart at the end of the bed and approached me. "May I see it?"

"Do I need to let go of this warm blanket?"

"Good to see you haven't lost your sense of humor."

"I wasn't trying to be funny." I loosened my grip on the warm covers.

Dr. Jagger exposed the bottom of my leg and foot. "Oh, my. How did you get these burns?"

"The same guy who attacked me spilled coffee on me earlier this morning."

"Is that one of those accidently-on-purpose incidents?"

I shrugged. "It seemed innocent, and I didn't think the burn was too bad."

"I'll write a prescription for silver sulfadiazine cream for the burn." She returned to examining me.

When she touched my left ankle, I moaned. "Ow, that's the spot."

"Not surprised it hurts. There's bruising and slight swelling, but according to the X-rays it's not broken."

"Can I walk on it?"

She shook her head. "Try not to. It's definitely sprained. You should rest, use ice packs, and elevate it, and I'll have the nurse wrap it. Tight enough to help but not cause more damage."

"Do you remember I own a dog walking business?" My head sank into the vinyl hospital pillow with a crinkly sound.

"Yes. Hire somebody to help for the next week or so." She patted my shoulder. "From what I hear, you're a lucky lady. Take care of yourself, Andi Grace. My office manager will call and schedule a follow-up appointment for next week."

"Yes, ma'am." I closed my eyes, too tired to argue. As soon as I summoned a smidgen of energy, I planned to contact Kylie about a job. Until then, Dylan could pitch in and cover my schedule.

Chapter Ten

ONCE HOME, I rested on the couch with the evening news on TV. Sunny lay on the floor next to me, and Marc sat in the armchair working on his computer.

The doorbell rang.

Marc checked his watch and placed the laptop on the coffee table. "I ordered Italian from Tony's Pizzeria, but they said it'd be more like an hour." He moved to answer the door.

"Marc, I heard about Andi Grace's accident. Is she okay?" Hannah pushed past him and beelined it to me. "Oh, my. You look terrible. I heard Danny did this to you. I hope it's not my fault." She knelt on the floor beside me.

Marc picked up his laptop. "I'll work on the front porch."

I looked at him and shivered. "Won't you be cold?"

"It's nice out. Are you still cold?"

I wore sweat pants, a T-shirt, and a hoody, but even with the pink and white quilt over me, I felt chilled. "Yeah."

"I wonder if that's normal. If you're not better tomorrow, we should call Dr. Jagger." He lifted an afghan from the back of a chair and draped it over me then left me alone with Hannah.

I reached for her hand. "I hate to ask this, but would you brush my hair? Do something to fix me up. I hate for Marc to see me like this."

"Sure, but I doubt he cares. The man is crazy about you." She stood. "Where's your bathroom?"

I pointed. "Go through my bedroom and you'll find it. My makeup bag and brush are in the vanity's second drawer." My bathroom was tight but worked for me. The fixtures needed updating, but there was always something more important demanding attention and my money.

Hannah returned and sat beside me on the couch. "I'm impressed with how efficient you are with the small space in there. You'll have to help me when I get moved into my place. My master bath is also small, but the location can't be beat."

"That's the way I feel about my home." I sat upright.

Hannah passed me a package of travel face wipes. "I'll brush the tangles out of your hair while you clean your face. Tell me if I hurt you."

I wiped the cool cloth over my face, removing any makeup that had survived the day. A few spots stung. "Ow. I guess Danny scraped my face in the struggle."

Hannah brushed the ends of my blond hair first. "I heard Danny attacked you, which seems odd because he was angry with me."

"I know. Not that I'd wish this on you, but his confrontation at Daily Java was with you."

"Do you think he planned to kidnap you?"

"Honestly, I believe he planned to head to the courthouse. He was standing in the parking lot, and his mother brought him a suit. I tried to hear their conversation from the Suburban. Danny drove away, and I had no clue he was about to pounce on me. He accused me of spying, and he was right."

"It doesn't give him the right to attack you."

I slumped. "You're right."

"Did you see or hear anything important?" She hit a knot in the back of my hair and tugged my head. "Sorry. I'll be gentler."

In one day, I'd survived a burn and an attack, so why had pulling my hair caused tears to spring to my eyes? I blinked them back. "I don't know if this goes with your theory, but at first he seemed irritated with his mom. Then he kissed her cheek before leaving. Maybe he does have a substance abuse problem. Or else he does what it takes to keep his mom happy. I can't figure him out."

"I wonder if Wade has caught him yet." She moved to another section of my hair and began brushing out the tangles.

"I told Wade he should speak to you."

"We met at his office this afternoon, and I described our encounter with Danny. I never would've left you if I'd thought you were in danger." Soon the brush glided through my hair without a single snag. "Perfect. Now for your makeup."

"If you hold the mirror, I can apply it."

"Sure." She lifted the mirror to be the same height as my face.

I drew away. "Ugh. Why didn't you tell me how bad I look?"

"All that matters is you're alive. Why don't you skip the makeup?"

"Just gonna do a bit of damage control." I applied a light coat of foundation and added a swipe of lipstick. "Not great, but I don't look like a ghost anymore."

"Hey, don't you know better than to joke about ghosts in the low country?"

I laughed. "Yeah, and I've had enough bad luck today. After your talk with Wade, do you still want us to get together with y'all?"

A smile broke out. "I'm surer now than ever before. There's something special about that man, and I'm glad Juliet suggested we should get together."

Marc walked into the house with a large paper bag and the laptop under his arm. "Dinner is served. Hannah, we've got plenty if you'd like to join us."

"No thanks." She hugged me. "I'm glad Danny didn't hurt you worse."

"Thanks."

She returned my cosmetics to the bathroom and left with a wave.

Marc said, "You were sleeping, so I ordered spaghetti, manicotti, and lasagna. I figured leftovers would get eaten."

I laughed. "You better believe food won't go to waste at my house." I pushed myself upright. "I feel strong enough to eat in the kitchen."

"Wait a second." He laid his computer in the easy chair then took the food to the kitchen. When he returned, he didn't come too close to me and pointed at the crutches leaning against the bookshelves. "Do you want to use the crutches or lean against me?"

"Come here." I waved him over.

His eyebrows lifted, but he closed the distance between us.

I stood on one foot and held onto his strong arms. "Marc, I'm sorry about drawing back from you at the hospital. I had some kind of weird flashback to Danny. He leaned in my window and unlocked the doors before lunging toward me. I'm not afraid of you."

"Good to know. Can I hug you?"

"I'd love that." I melted into his arms and breathed in his unique woodsy scent. My head rested on his chest, and his steady heartbeat comforted me.

"I haven't been so scared in a long time. When David found me in the courthouse and told me you'd been attacked, I felt like the earth shifted." He kissed the top of my head. "It seemed like an eternity until I laid my eyes on you. Wade met me at the hospital, and if he hadn't vouched for me, I'm not sure they would've let me back to sit with you."

I enjoyed the moment of intimacy with Marc. "I'm surprised Nate hasn't come to see me."

He ran his hand up and down my back. "When Nate called Lacey

Jane, she flipped out. To sum it up, Nate's driving down to Daytona Beach to bring her home instead of coming straight here."

I pulled back. "He's what? That's crazy. I'm fine. Lacey Jane should be able to enjoy her college spring vacation."

Marc raised his hands. "Hey, I'm only the messenger."

I slumped against him. "Sorry. Again."

"It's fine. I'm glad to see your spunk working through the pain. By the way, you look nice." He kissed my forehead. "Let's eat."

After we ate, Marc took Sunny to his home. He planned to leave her and Chubb with Dylan before returning to town. I assured him I'd be fine for a couple of hours and got comfortable on the couch.

Kylie texted me, asking if we could meet and discuss my job offer. Come on over.

The relief I felt when I sent the text surprised me. It'd be good to have somebody with me. Once Danny was arrested, my nerves would lose the jitters. Danny might have physically attacked me, but I couldn't let him instill a fear of being home alone. This was my safe harbor. With determination, I hobbled into the kitchen, with the quilt wrapped around my shoulders, and prepared a pot of decaf coffee.

The doorbell rang. I shrugged off the quilt and reached for the nearby crutches. At the door, I looked through the window to verify it was Kylie before I opened the door. "Hi. Thanks for coming by tonight."

"I was glad to get out of the house. Susan is nice, but she can be intense. I'm sure that's what makes her a good businesswoman, though. Hey, she's giving me Tabby's car. Isn't that nice?" Kylie's tense expression didn't match her words.

"It's very generous. Are you okay?"

She nodded. "Yeah, I just got used to not living in fear. On top of losing Tabby, it's an adjustment having her daughter here."

Let's have a seat in the kitchen. I made us some coffee. Is decaf okay?" I closed the door and dead bolted it.

"That works." She followed me to the next room. "You sit, and I'll pour. Is there creamer in the fridge?"

"Yeah. Pick a flavor you enjoy." I sat in the nearest chair and propped my foot in another seat.

Kylie moved my crutches and handed the quilt to me.

"You're very observant, Kylie."

She set two yellow mugs on the table. "I was a patient care technician. Looking after others comes naturally."

So far, so good. "Right, and I can already discern you're good with people. You said you like dogs, but how do you feel about working with them?"

"Dylan has told me about your business." Kylie pulled out the mocha creamer and returned to the table with it and two spoons. "I love all animals. If you trust me to work with your dogs, I won't let you down."

I poured creamer into my coffee and stirred. "Trust goes both ways."

She pushed short strands of blond hair behind her ear. "What do you mean? I don't think you'll be unfair to me. Dylan talks about how great it is to work for you."

I laid my hands flat on the table. "I know Black isn't your last name."

The girl gripped the mug so hard, I thought it might crack. "I don't want my parents to find me."

"If you're of legal age, what can they do?"

Her eyes widened. "They'll take me back to Texas. I'm twenty. Legal in the eyes of the law, but my parents need my income in order to afford their drug habits."

I ached for this young woman and the horrors she must've endured. "Kylie, we can protect you."

"How? You can't even take care of yourself." Her tone wasn't sarcastic. More like sad or defeated.

"I fought my attacker, and I'm home tonight. He may have hurt me, but he didn't get me." I smiled. "My friends and family will also watch out for you. There's no better place to live than Heyward Beach."

"Tabby thought it was safe here." Her voice was a hoarse whisper.

This was the third murder in less than a year. The kid might be right. Maybe I didn't have a clue. "Kylie, why did Tabby go out alone some-times?"

"She's—she was a grown woman, you know what I mean? The hospital accident took away her independence. I first met her when I was a patient in the emergency room. She took good care of me." Kylie drank her coffee. "One stupid accident stripped away her regular life. Her husband was an attorney. After he talked to the head honchos, the hospital covered her expenses and agreed to pay for extras. You'd think Mr. Malkin was a good guy, defending his wife and all, but he quietly divorced her."

My stomach dropped. Tabby had suffered one loss after another. "Oh, I thought maybe he was dead."

"Nope. Alive and well." She folded her hands together.

"If they're divorced, there's no reason for him to come to the island and kill Tabby."

"None that I can think of." She glanced at the ceiling. "Your boyfriend helped her change her will, so Mr. Malkin has no motive."

Kylie revealed what Marc couldn't tell me. "Is there anybody from Texas that might want to kill her?"

"Hospital gossip said the administration wasn't happy about paying so much for Tabby's care. They should've been mad at the maintenance person who ignored the spill. Or Mr. Malkin. Tabby focused on surviving one day at a time. I used to sit at her side and read the Bible to her. It's how I got to know God."

I leaned back, too exhausted to take notes. "Is there anybody here that didn't like Tabby?"

"I refer to him as Cranky Butt because I don't know his real name. He used to fuss at us for taking care of the feral cats."

"Describe him." There was a local man who'd been forced to retire from his life as a contractor when he fell off a roof. He lived on the mainland but often fished at the beach. The man I knew had a gruff exterior, but deep down he was a decent person.

"Gray hair. Beer belly. Scraggly beard. He complained more than once." Her nostrils flared.

The description she gave me could fit many people. "Did you ever see him fishing?"

"Yeah. We also saw him in the parking areas with his fishing gear. He packs it all on some kind of wagon and pulls it to the beach."

"I bet you're talking about Leroy Peck. He has a rigged-out cart and spends most of his time fishing at the beach, pier, or marsh." I sighed. "He definitely has some anger issues. Anybody else?"

The doorbell rang. "Would you hand me my crutches?"

"I'll answer it. Stay here and finish your coffee." Kylie disappeared before I could argue.

I called out, "Make sure you know who it is before you open the door."

"Yes, ma'am." Seconds ticked by before I heard her open the door and greet whoever had rung the bell.

Heavy footsteps clomped on the floor. Wade followed Kylie into the kitchen. "Andi Grace, I'm sorry to bother you."

"You're not bothering us." I pointed to an empty chair. "Have a seat."

He shook his head. "I can't stay, but I wanted to tell you we arrested Danny for attacking you. He'll probably get released tomorrow, but tonight you should be able to rest easy."

"What a relief. Thanks so much, Wade." His announcement released a coil of tension in my belly. "What about Tabby's death?"

"The coroner ruled it a homicide." He crossed his arms.

Kylie moaned and leaned against the counter.

I met Wade's gaze. "Is Kylie safe?"

He shifted from one foot to the other. "It wouldn't hurt to be extra cautious until we catch the person who did it. Do you have a safe place to stay?"

Kylie's complexion paled. "Tabby's daughter, Susan, is here. I'm staying at the house with her."

"It wouldn't hurt to keep your bedroom door locked if you have doubts about her." He tipped his hat and left us staring at each other in the kitchen.

"Tabby was murdered." Kylie sank into a chair.

Wade called out, "I'm locking this door on my way out."

I smiled. My brother often talked loud enough for us to hear him in just about any room. Maybe it wasn't a Nate thing but a guy thing. "Thanks, Wade."

Kylie leaned close and gripped my hand. "Do you think it's safe for me to spend the night with Susan?"

"She's Tabby's daughter and was in Dallas when the murder occurred."

"Well, yeah, that's what she says, but do we really know the facts?" Her hands trembled.

Kylie's response made me nervous. "Why? Are you suspicious of Susan?"

"I overheard her on the phone this afternoon, telling somebody she'd get the money to them. Then she said money wouldn't be a problem soon."

Interesting. Had Susan fooled me acting all nice and generous toward Kylie? Did she need the inheritance money from her mom? She'd shared they didn't exactly get along, but they lived far apart. Surely Susan wouldn't have killed her mom because she was a nuisance. I shivered. "Kylie, you're welcome to spend the night here if you're scared to be alone with Susan."

"Don't humor me. Believe me. Susan's getting rid of Tabby's personal belongings. What if there's evidence pointing to Susan? It'll be gone before long."

"I do believe you. Stay with me tonight, but let Susan know. Tell her you don't want to leave me alone after my accident. I'm going to call Wade and suggest he get a subpoena to see what all she's throwing out that I don't already have. If Susan is somehow involved in Tabby's murder, we need to look for that kind of evidence."

Kylie stood. "While you call the sheriff, I'll go to your backyard and call Susan."

"Sounds good. Then you can get settled into one of the extra bedrooms." After she walked outside, I called and left a message for Wade. With the aid of my crutches, I hobbled to my office and made copies of the puzzle magazines. There had to be clues in them, but I needed a clear head to figure them out. Wade might be angry I'd taken the magazines, but if so, I'd explain he should be thankful. Thankful I'd saved them before Susan destroyed evidence.

Yeah, that reasoning could backfire in a New York second. But it was the best I could do after the day I'd had. Tomorrow would be better.

Chapter Eleven

PAIN THROBBING in my ankle woke me up. Six o'clock. Instead of getting myself ready to walk the dogs on my morning schedule, I'd send Kylie. There was no way I could walk dogs with my ankle in such bad shape.

My phone vibrated on the bedside table. I elbowed my way to a sitting position and reached for my cell. My brother's picture lit up the screen. "Nate? Why are you calling so early?"

"Our sister refused to spend one more night in Florida knowing you were hurt. We're standing on the front porch and about to come inside. I didn't want to scare you. There's a Jetta and a red Silverado in the driveway. What'd you do, have a slumber party?"

"Kinda. Marc's sleeping on the couch, and Kylie crashed in Lacey Jane's bedroom. I'll meet you in the kitchen in a couple of minutes. Feel free to start a pot of coffee." I stood and reached for my crutches not believing they'd driven through the night.

"Yeah, I'm aware of your OCD." He chuckled.

"What are you talking about?"

"Obsessive coffee disorder."

"Very funny." I couldn't help but smile at his corny comment.

"I thought so." Nate yawned audibly. "We picked up donuts in Charleston and saved some for you. Hope there's enough for this crowd, though."

"Thanks." I disconnected and heard the front door open then the beeps from Nate disarming the alarm.

Lacey Jane pushed into my bedroom before I could make it to the toilet. "I can't believe you didn't call me." She threw her arms around my shoulders and bear-hugged me.

"Ow." My tender ribs didn't appreciate the loving hug, but it did my heart good. "You were on vacation, and I didn't want to ruin it for you. I'm fine."

She gripped my shoulders and eyed me. "I'm not a child. I'm your sister. Family sticks together. Don't you dare leave me out again."

Her words stabbed me in the chest. "You're right. I'm sorry." I sniffed. Morphing into a sniveling mess wasn't part of my life plan. I needed to pull myself together.

Lacey Jane's mouth dropped open.

"What?"

Her eyes sparkled. "I'm savoring the moment. I'm right, and you're sorry."

"Ha, ha. I need to relieve myself. Take my bed if you need to rest. Kylie Black's in your room. I'll introduce you to her."

"I didn't stay awake all night just to sleep as soon as I arrived. I'm here to help you, but a shower would be nice."

Lacey Jane disappeared, and I freshened up. I wanted to look as nice as possible to make everybody believe I was fine. By the time I stepped out of the bathroom, Lacey Jane had returned to my bedroom with her suitcase.

She smiled. "Marc's awake and in the kitchen with Nate. No sign of Kylie. Nate caught me up on Tabby's death and all."

"I figured y'all would discuss it."

"What can I say? It was a long ride." She yawned. "Make sure there's plenty of coffee."

I kissed her cheek. "Thanks for coming home."

"You would've done the same for me. Our family is small, and we've got to stick together."

Lacey Jane must really be freaked out because she was repeating herself. "Good point. See you in the kitchen." I left her alone and hobbled to the kitchen on my crutches. "Did y'all save me a jelly donut?"

Nate pulled creamer from the fridge. "Of course. I know better than to bring donuts home and not have a jelly one for you."

I sat next to Marc, bumping his knee in the process. Tingles danced up my spine. "Did you sleep okay?"

"Your dog snores, but I raised the window and listened to the surf. Nice way to fall asleep." He placed his hand on mine. "It made me rethink why I decided to live inland."

I gazed into his eyes. Was there an underlying message? "Island life's the best."

Nate laid out plates and mugs. "She's always been that way. If our parents couldn't find her, they always looked at the beach first."

I laughed. "There's no telling how many times I got in trouble for wandering to the beach."

Marc's eyes sparkled. "I imagine you were a handful."

Nate filled our mugs. "Oh, boy, dontcha know it. Not sure why nobody tried to kidnap her before now."

My stomach somersaulted. "Nate, that's kinda insensitive."

"Oh, sorry. Blame it on lack of sleep, but you know Mom was kinda the same way. She disappeared for a few days and returned refreshed."

"I didn't realize you noticed." I stirred sugar and creamer into my coffee. I'd been aware of her disappearing to work on her art, and I'd done my best to fill the void for my siblings. It must not have been enough if Nate remembered.

"Good morning, everybody." Kylie entered the kitchen. Her short blond hair was damp, and the only makeup evident was a coat of mascara.

"Have a seat and help yourself to a donut. There are plenty." Nate stepped to the side. He winked at me. "When I said we didn't bring many donuts, I meant we've got a dozen. There are five of us and possibly a sixth person who'll want to eat at your door. Should I run and get more food?"

"A cup of coffee is all I need." Kylie took the seat on the other side of Marc.

"Nate, I think we'll be fine. Thanks for all of this." I smiled at my brother before turning my attention to Kylie. "There are three dogs on my early-morning schedule, and if you're going to work for me, I'd like you to start with them."

"Yes, ma'am." She gave me a little salute.

"Great. You're officially hired. We'll take care of the paperwork later."

Lacey Jane appeared and clapped her hands so loud, we all jumped. "What's the plan today?"

My hand went to my throat. "Divide and conquer."

The doorbell rang, and we all looked toward the family room.

"I'll start by answering the door." Lacey Jane turned on her toe and left the rest of us sitting at the table with a dozen donuts in the middle. "Leave me an iced chocolate one."

Nate kept watch over our sister from the doorway dividing the kitchen from the rest of my home. "She looks relaxed now, but Andi Grace, she was a wreck when I picked her up." He glanced at me. "Scared and angry. She didn't stop fussing at me until we hit the Georgia line."

"I'm sorry you had to deal with Lacey Jane's anger, and I apologized to her."

"Good." He reached for my plate and plopped the jelly-filled donut on it.

"Thanks." I bit into it while the guys each picked a donut. Raspberry jelly squirted down my chin.

Deputy David Wayne followed Lacey Jane into the kitchen. "I saw all the vehicles here and decided to stop by. Looks like a party."

I swiped the jelly from my chin. "Why are you here? Did something bad happen?"

"Wade and another deputy are at Tabby's place with a search warrant." He stood close to my sister.

"Oh, no." Kylie moaned. "Susan will know it's me."

David's facial expression softened. "You're not mentioned at all. We can search your belongings at the house as well if it'd make you feel more at ease with the daughter."

Kylie nodded. "Yes, please."

"Come with me then to Tabby's house."

She went to the back door and picked up her Converse sneakers. Black. Same as Tabby's. "I need to walk some dogs this morning for Andi Grace."

"As long as we don't find anything suspicious belonging to you, it'll be fine."

I made eye contact with the deputy. "David, I have the puzzle magazines. Before I fell asleep last night, I made notes on what I suspected."

His eyes widened. "You tampered with evidence?"

I'd expected this kind of reaction from him. "I saved them from the recycling center. My notes are on paper with references to the magazines. It looks like Tabby jotted down dates and times in the sudoku books. I haven't had time to dig into the crossword puzzles, but it seems logical she left clues in them."

"We have staff who can go through the magazines. Where are they?" He crossed his arms and spread his feet.

"In my office." My words squeaked out.

Nate rose. "Why don't you apologize to my sister then follow me. I'll get what you want."

David frowned. "Apologize? This isn't the first murder investigation she's interfered with."

"After you tell her you're sorry, you might thank her for saving the clues while y'all were deciding if Tabby's death was an accident or murder."

Marc formed a T with his hands. "Time out. We're all on the same team. Arguing won't catch a killer."

I nodded. "You're right. Kylie can go with David. Lacey Jane, will you walk the dogs for me?"

"Sure, Sis."

"Kylie, let us know when you're free to take over. Nate, go to work. Or take a nap. Marc, you probably need to get ready for court. David, do you know more about when Danny will be released from jail?"

His posture relaxed. "We won't know until he appears before the judge. I'll keep you posted."

"Thank you." My morning jolt had cooled, and I added hot coffee to my mug.

The others sprang into action, surprising me. Nobody balked at my bossiness. I didn't care if it was because they felt sorry for me or not. It worked.

The kitchen soon emptied, except for Marc and me. He reached for my hand. "I'm in the office all morning. Call me if you run into trouble."

If I wanted a deeper relationship, I needed to take bold steps. "Can I call just because I miss you?"

A slow smile revealed the dimple that always fascinated me. His gray eyes sparkled. "That'll be the best call of all." He kissed the back of my hand.

Butterflies fluttered in my belly. Wishing there wasn't another murder to solve wouldn't get me anywhere. Once the killer was caught, I'd make a courageous move. Or maybe he'd be the brave one. Until then, I'd surprise Marc with a phone call. Just because.

Chapter Twelve

NO WORD FROM Kylie, so Lacey Jane and I started the mid-morning dog walking appointments. First stop was Larry and Phyllis Mays. Pastor Larry had adopted two puppies, hoping to keep his wife so busy she wouldn't find time to gamble. Phyllis had fallen in love with Captain and Pumpkin.

I parked the Suburban on the street. "Phyllis wants us to give them some extra time to burn off energy. She's hosting a tea at church, which wears her out. I'll go inside and help you."

Lacy Jane pointed. "I see they installed a fence around the back-yard."

"Smart. With a German shepherd and the Australian German shep-herd mix, space is needed for them to run around. I've been trying to talk Phyllis into bringing the puppies out for obedience lessons. She claims they're obedient, but we'll find out soon."

My sister's fingers circled my arm. "I can handle the dogs. Rest your foot."

"The inactivity is killing me. I thought driving would be enough, but I need to actually do something. Let's go." I opened my door and with-drew the crutches. "Good thing I hurt my left ankle."

"You're worse than a child." Lacey Jane retrieved the house keys from my box.

Inside the house, we found the puppies in the laundry room. "Hi there. Are you two ready for a morning romp?" I loved on both dogs.

Lacey Jane elbowed me out of the way. "I've got this. Sit down somewhere and prop your foot on something."

"Thanks for your help." Resting my foot would help me resume normal activities sooner, so I obeyed. Self-control and patience had never been my strong suits. I tended to leap into action, but this time would be different. Giving my burns and ankle time to heal was the smart move.

Lacey Jane's eyebrows popped up. "Nate said you could be on

crutches for a couple of weeks, so I'm relieved you're actually letting me help out."

Prescription bottles lay scattered on the kitchen counter. Shiny yellow capsules with letters and 300 on them had spilled out of the open vial. The labels were marked from different pharmacies, and two of them said gabapentin. On closer inspection, different doctors were listed on the labels. One of the pharmacies was local and the other was mail order. The capsules from the mail-order place had no markings on them. I sat in an oak chair at the oval kitchen table and rested my foot on another seat. "Do you know what gabapentin is?"

Lacey Jane stood at the kitchen counter filling a water bowl. "Seems like I've heard of it. Maybe a pain pill?"

I looked it up on my phone while my sister attached leashes to the harnesses. Captain, with his black, brown, and white coat had a harness with a Captain America emblem. His eyes captivated me. One was blue and the other brown, and the pup was so adorable the superhero image didn't seem to fit. Pumpkin's pink harness stood out against the German shepherd's black fur.

"I'll walk them around the block." She held up her hand when I opened my mouth. "Just like you taught me years ago. Trust me. I know what I'm doing. Shepherds are full of energy and need to be walked."

"I do trust you. When you get back, I'll be able to tell you about gabapentin." I got lost in following the links suggested by my search engine.

Lacey Jane returned thirty minutes later. "I'm in love with Captain. He's so cute."

"Yeah, he is. I just wish Phyllis would let me help her train the dogs."

"Do you want me to let them run around in the back yard?"

I nodded, and after she let them out, Lacey Jane sat across the table from me. "What'd you learn?"

"The drug's original purpose was to treat seizures, but it's mostly prescribed for neuropathic pain these days. Some states have made it a controlled drug because of the potential for abuse. Kentucky, Ohio, and West Virginia, according to this site."

My sister leaned back. "I'm aware our country has an opioid overdose crisis, but gabapentin isn't an opioid."

She made a good point, but I'd been reading about gabapentin's potential to be abused. "Gabapentin isn't a controlled drug in South Carolina, which means the state doesn't track it. I wonder why Phyllis has two doctors prescribing it to her?"

Lacey Jane drummed her fingers on the console. "She has quite a few capsules left."

"True." Is that what was going on with Danny? "Lacey Jane, do you think Danny has a substance abuse problem? Alcohol or drugs?"

She looked out the window. "He does seem moody, and I've seen him drinking at bars." She glanced at me and held up her hands. "I only go to dance, not get drunk."

That surprised me. Heyward Beach was small enough to know another person's business. How had I missed the fact my sister went to bars?

"I can see the questions swirling in your brain." She circled her finger. "I usually go up to Conway or Myrtle Beach with my college friends."

My scalp prickled. "I'm not judging you, but if you ever get drunk, you better call me to come pick you up. No lectures or anything."

"After Mom and Dad's accident, I don't drink unless we have a designated driver. Is this an example of you trusting me?"

"Honestly, I trust you, but I also want to protect you. Sometimes that overrides other instincts." I reached across the table for her hands and squeezed them. "You're smart. I trust you, but please believe I'll always have your back if you need me."

One of the dogs scratched at the back door, but Lacey Jane squeezeed my hands back. "I know. Just like I've got your back today. You should've called me. You know, set a good example for your kid sister."

I laughed. "Touché. You got me there."

We finished with Captain and Pumpkin then took care of the other dogs on my morning schedule. Once we'd finished our morning rounds, I drove to the pier and parked in an empty spot nearby.

"Why are we here? You can't walk on the beach with crutches."

I opened my door. "Maybe not, but I can go on the pier and search for clues. Will you grab my binoculars and camera?"

"Any chance I can talk you out of this?"

"No. Leroy Peck's old truck is over there." I pointed out the battered two-tone muddy pickup with at least one dent along the truck's bed. "According to Kylie, he didn't like Tabby feeding the feral cats."

"So?" She made no move to unbuckle her seat belt.

"It's high tide, so he might be fishing from the pier instead of the beach. Seems like a good time to talk to him about Tabby."

Lacey Jane grumbled but gathered the two items I'd requested and together we walked to the pier building, where you could eat or pay to go onto the large wood structure. After we paid the fee, Lacey Jane opened the door for me. "What's the plan? Are you going to walk up to Mr. Peck and ask if he killed Tabby?"

"Shh. I'm going to take your picture near where he's set up. It'll lead to a casual conversation. If he's not up here, I'll use the binoculars and search the beach."

My sister looked at her T-shirt and faded blue shorts. "I'm not dressed for a photo shoot."

"You look beautiful, sweetie pie."

"The wind's blowing."

I paused and handed her an extra band from around my wrist to hold her hair back. "I always have a spare."

"Gee, thanks." She slid the blue camera strap with dog prints over my neck then fastened her hair back. "Good thing I always carry lipstick with me." She swiped a pinkish color over her lips and smiled at me. "How do I look?"

"Like I said earlier, beautiful." I adjusted the camera and continued along the wood planks. "I think he's the man with the big blue cooler in the fishing cart. On our left, wearing a faded black hoodie."

"I see him. Don't you think it's interesting all of the others who are fishing are on our right? He's all by himself."

"Kylie said he's mean, but my hunch is he's lonely. Let's see what happens." I stopped about six feet away from Mr. Peck and leaned my crutches against the railing.

My sister laid the binoculars near them. "Can you get the waves behind me?"

I gave her a thumbs-up. "Sure. Stand right there." Hopping on one foot, I positioned myself to take pictures that would capture Lacey Jane as well as Mr. Peck. "Good. Good. Oh, hold still. There's a line of pelicans flying south." I snapped away until the birds had passed.

Mr. Peck frowned at us but didn't speak.

"Do you want to see what I've got so far?"

Lacey Jane stood beside me and pretended to look at the photos. "I'm going to ask if he'll pose with me for local color."

I shook my head. "No. I don't want you to get too involved." I kept my voice low.

"There's no telling what I'll have to do as a paralegal. Consider this good training." She approached the man but didn't enter his personal bubble. "Sir, I'm working on a portfolio and wondered if you'd mind posing with me. It'll add local color."

"Ask one of the others." He pointed to other fishermen with his thumb.

She leaned closer to the man and spoke too soft for me to hear.

Mr. Peck secured his fishing pole on the cart and pulled a small shark from his cooler. He turned and faced me, holding the shark high.

Lacey Jane stood next to him. "Go."

I snapped away at different angles as much as my sore ankle allowed. "That should do it."

Lacey Jane shook the man's hand. "Thanks so much."

I joined them. "You're Leroy Peck, right?"

His eyebrows shot up. "That's right. Who are you?"

"I'm Andi Grace Scott. You may have seen me around the area. I'm a dog walker."

He snorted. "Dogs are fine by me. Not like them litter box critters. Keep them as far away from me as possible."

"It sounds like you don't like cats."

"That's right. They're too sneaky."

"Do you know the cat lady? Tabby Malik." At his nod, I pushed on. "Did you hear she was killed?"

"Are you serious?" He squinted at me.

"Yes, sir."

"No, I hadn't heard." He swiped his hand over his stubbled face with the hand not holding a shark.

Lacey Jane elbowed me. "I'll meet you inside."

Strange that she'd leave me alone with Mr. Peck, but what could he do to me with witnesses around? "I heard you two didn't get along because of the cats."

"We've got too many cats on this island as it is. She went around feeding them. Not the natural order of things. If they can't survive on their own, then too bad." He stuffed the shark into the cooler and picked up his fishing pole.

"Are you saying you're relieved she's gone?"

"Look, lady, she and I didn't get along concerning the cats. That's life." He eased his rod behind him then flicked it toward the ocean.

I'd come this far with burns on my leg and an injured ankle, and I wasn't ready to give up. "Have you noticed anything unusual on the beach or island recently?"

"I mind my own business. Not interested in speculation or gossip."

"Aha, you do know of something going on."

"Lady, it's time for you to leave." His gruff voice warned me the time had come to wrap up the conversation.

"One more question before I go. Did you kill Tabby?"

"No." His nostrils flared, and his eyes bulged. "If you know what's good for you, you'll leave me alone."

If his eyes could've spit venom, I probably would've gotten poisoned. Not taking my gaze off the disagreeable man, I backed up. My ankle twisted, and I fell to the deck, gasping at the flashes of pain searing my leg.

Mr. Peck dropped his fishing pole and loomed over me. "You shoulda left when I warned you."

Chapter Thirteen

MR. PECK SNATCHED me up by my shoulders and pushed me against the rail. I wobbled on my right leg. "Stay out of my business."

I lifted my chin. "You don't have to answer my questions, but I'm sure the sheriff will be interested in your relationship with Tabby."

Fishermen and women hurried over, forming a human wall between me and Mr. Peck. Threats and questions flew through the air. Shoving ensued. One burly man pushed Mr. Peck away from me.

"Stop." A deep voice hollered. David ran to where we were all congregated. "Give the lady room to breathe."

Never had I been so glad to see the deputy. I glanced at the others. "Thanks so much."

People muttered replies but didn't walk away.

Lacey Jane was only a few steps behind David. "Are you okay?"

I nodded. "Yeah."

David's hand hovered near his gun. "Andi Grace, do you want to press charges against Mr. Peck?"

"Hey, how do ya know my name?" The man snarled at David.

"You'd be amazed at who and what I know."

"I didn't hurt the lady. She fell. I helped her up."

David's brows lifted. "Do you agree, Andi Grace?"

An ocean breeze chilled me. "That much is true, but he was rude and rough with me. Actually, he threatened me."

Mr. Peck picked up his rod and reel. "Lady, I just want to be left alone to fish and mind my own business. That's all."

David looked at the small crowd. "Do any of you have something else to share? If not, you're free to go back to what you were doing."

I said to the group, "Thanks again for coming to my rescue. I appreciate y'all."

A few fisherfolk mumbled responses or waved at me, and soon it was only David, Lacey Jane, Mr. Peck, and me standing together.

"I won't press charges, but you might want to check his alibi for the morning or night Tabby was killed. He didn't like her."

Mr. Peck huffed. "Lady, we didn't agree on the cats. It doesn't mean I hated her."

I stepped away but was surprised to find myself less afraid of Mr. Peck than Danny.

"You two are free to go." David picked up my crutches that lay about four feet away from me. "Stay out of trouble."

Lacey Jane grabbed the binoculars. "Maybe you should check on us when you're through with Mr. Peck."

I shot her a look. "I need to stop by the pharmacy on my way home."

David tilted his head. "Are you sure he didn't hurt you today?"

"I'm running on adrenaline, but I feel fine. You've got my number if you need us." I waved and used my crutches to make my way off the pier and to my Suburban. "Lacey Jane, why'd you ask David to check on us?"

She shrugged. "I've always had a little crush on him. It seemed like a good excuse to see him again."

I laughed. "So my sister is an opportunist. Good to know."

"I've got nothing else to say about the matter." Her face reddened.

"It's no problem. Do you mind driving?"

"Not at all. Are you sure you're okay?" She followed me to the passenger side and took the camera and crutches, sliding them into the back.

"I'm good, despite feeling like I ran a marathon." Why was I so tired?

"Then why do you want to go to the drug store?"

"I want to ask the pharmacist about gabapentin."

"I guessed as much." Lacey Jane shut my door then rounded the SUV and slid behind the steering wheel. After taking a deep breath, she started the vehicle and pulled out of the parking lot. "Because of privacy laws, they can't tell you anything about Phyllis."

"I've only got a couple of general questions. It won't take long." I closed my eyes and leaned against the headrest.

"You know, I'm really not more interested in my love life than in your safety. Danger follows you, Andi Grace. Or you follow it. Either way, I'll feel safer if David checks on us."

"I know your heart. Family first."

When the vehicle stopped, I opened my eyes. "That was fast."

Lacey Jane lifted a shoulder. "You fell asleep, so I took the long way. I'll get your crutches."

I felt my face for drool. Dry. Good. It didn't take us long to enter the store.

Ethan Seitz, Yoyo's master, stood behind the pharmacy counter. A phone was anchored between his ear and shoulder while he worked on the computer. A tech with jet-black Cleopatra hair offered to help me, but I told her I needed to speak to Ethan about a personal matter.

Lacey Jane left me and explored the gift shop area of the store. Ethan made eye contact with me and held up a finger, signaling me to wait a minute. I nodded and smiled.

Before long, he walked over to the consultation counter where I stood. "Hi, Andi Grace. What happened to you?"

I shared the story of my accident, including the fact it was Danny who attacked me. "I don't like to spread rumors, but he's dangerous. You and Violet need to watch out for him."

"Thanks for the warning, but I suspect it's not the reason you stopped by. Do you need to reschedule Yoyo's training?"

"No, we'll be fine. I really have a question about gabapentin. I've read up on it. Do you know if it's being abused around Heyward Beach?"

He crossed his muscular arms that surely strained the stitches on his lab jacket. "Drug abuse is a problem everywhere, even Heyward Beach. Did the doctor give you a prescription?"

I shook my head. "Ibuprofen is the strongest thing I'm taking. I noticed one of my clients filled gabapentin prescriptions from two different pharmacies and two different doctors."

"It's called doctor shopping and usually focuses on controlled substances, which makes it fraud and a crime. At this time, gabapentin isn't tracked in South Carolina."

"Got it. What about the fact the capsules looked different?" I described the yellow capsules and contrasted them with the others.

Ethan's eyes narrowed. "Not a single marking?"

"Nothing visible." I rested my arms on the counter and leaned toward him. "Do you think they might be counterfeit?"

"I wish the answer was no. Supplements and many vitamins don't have imprints. Could that be what you saw?"

"I wish it was, Ethan." I sighed. "Guess I'll question my client."

"I suggest you contact the authorities. Did you notice what pharmacies filled the prescriptions? Did I?"

"The bottles I found weren't from your store. One was a chain in Myrtle Beach and the other was a mail-order pharmacy. I'm sure you know her, which is probably why she went to a place where she wouldn't be recognized."

His mouth quirked in a humorless smile. "At least I won't be involved in an investigation."

The tech came over and tugged on Ethan's sleeve.

He shrugged. "I've got to get back to work. Tomorrow's my day off, so I'll see you at Yoyo's lesson."

"Thanks for your time." I adjusted my crutches and headed for my vehicle with Lacey Jane at my side. Ethan's answers raised more questions.

Getting distracted by the gabapentin wouldn't solve Tabby's murder. I needed to shift my focus onto finding the killer.

Chapter Fourteen

LATE THAT AFTERNOON, I sat on the couch with my foot propped up on the coffee table and an ice pack resting on it. I studied the crossword puzzles Tabby had worked, making sure the words she'd written down made sense with the clues.

Lacey Jane was outside on the front porch with David, who'd been waiting in a squad car for us when we got home from Beach Pharmacy. He'd been back and forth between working and spending time with us.

My phone buzzed and Marc's picture popped onto my screen.

"Hi, Marc."

"Hold on a second." Muffled sounds told me someone was trying to talk to him. "Sorry about that. Have you rested today?"

"I'm icing my ankle now."

His deep laugh sent shivers up my spine. "Nice and evasive. How about I bring you something for dinner? Mexican? Chinese? Barbecue?"

"Oh, barbecue with macaroni and cheese sounds wonderful." My mouth watered at the thought.

"Are you expecting a crowd like at breakfast?"

"I hope not." The morning had been hectic, but the others surely wouldn't show up again.

"I'll order extra just in case. Do you want me to pick up Sunny and bring her home?"

"If you have time, that'd be perfect." I relaxed into the comfy cushions. "Thanks. I miss her."

"Do you mind if I bring Chubb along?"

"You don't even need to ask. I'm almost out of Cokes, but I can make a pitcher of sweet tea."

"Keep resting. I've got dinner under control and I'll grab some drinks. I'll be there in about an hour."

"Be safe." I hung up and flipped through the crossword pages I'd copied before turning the books over to David. Most looked normal. At last I found one that appeared more legible. This page didn't have evidence that letters had been erased. Very few words intersected.

Boat. Low. Ski. New. Moon. Cash. Tide. Shrimp. Jet. Duffel.

Interesting. Three modes of transportation. I added these words to my notes on the murder.

Lacey Jane and David entered the house. Her face was flushed. "David's officially off duty now. Do you care if he changes clothes in Nate's room?"

"Make yourself at home, David." I loved the fact my siblings still considered the bedrooms here to be their rooms despite the fact they lived other places. The ice pack slipped off my ankle. "You're not looking for evidence, are you?"

"Andi Grace, shame on you." My sister jerked the ice pack off the table.

David laughed. "You're not a suspect in Tabby's death."

"Thank goodness." I laughed with him.

He held an orange and purple duffel. "My only concern is the possibility you'll interfere in the investigation."

"Let's call a truce, you two." Lacey Jane moved to David and nudged him toward the hall. "Nate's room is this way."

I scrambled to gather the puzzle pages and my crutches while nobody watched. I reached my office and stuffed the sheets of paper into a bright blue file folder.

"What are you up to?" Lacey Jane's words startled me.

"You shouldn't sneak up on a person like that." With the aid of my crutches, I breezed past her.

She followed me to the kitchen. "David offered to take us out for burgers."

I reached for my travel mug and took a drink of water. "Marc's going to bring me something to eat later, but you should go with David. He's a nice guy."

"I didn't think you liked him." Lacey Jane put the reusable ice pack in the freezer.

"As long as he doesn't suspect you, Nate, or me of murder, we'll get along fine."

David appeared, wearing sweatpants and an athletic T-shirt. "I just received a text that Danny is out on bail. Wade said the judge read him the riot act for his attack on you. There could even be disciplinary action from the bar association."

"Good." I leaned against the counter. "Anybody who attacks another person should be disciplined. And fined. A big hefty fine."

"I agree. Are you ladies ready to eat?"

Lacey Jane twisted her hands together. "Andi Grace has other plans. Looks like it's only you and me."

He broke out into the biggest smile I'd ever seen on his face. "Cool. I'm ready if you are."

My sister hugged me. "I'll lock and bolt the door and you rest your foot. There's no excuse not to. Dylan's taking care of Sunny, and you don't have any appointments right now."

"You two have fun." I waved them off then hurried to my bathroom and brushed my hair before Marc arrived.

The doorbell rang, and I froze.

It hadn't been an hour yet. I wouldn't give in to fear, but I'd play it smart. A glance out my front bedroom window revealed the blue convertible belonging to Danny. My blood pressure skyrocketed.

My phone rang, and I pulled it out of my pocket. Danny's name flashed on the screen. I answered it. "What do you want?"

"You know what I want." He pounded the door so hard it surprised me the thing didn't crack. "Open the door. I know you're inside."

"You're crazy if you think I'll open the door after you attacked me yesterday." My hands shook.

"Let me explain. I didn't mean to." He panted as if running a race.

On my phone, I tapped the circle to switch to speaker mode. "Go home, Danny." I sent a group text to Marc, Lacey Jane, David, and Wade about the situation. **Danny's at my front door. Help.**

"I'm sorry, Andi Grace." His tone sounded more angry than sorrowful. "Please, let me come inside and explain."

"I don't want to hear your excuses." My house had two doors, and Danny stood at one. I hobbled to the kitchen door, but odds were if I tried to escape in my current condition, he'd overtake me. Hitting the panic button on my alarm system seemed pointless since I'd contacted the sheriff and deputy.

"Andi Grace!" The doorknob rattled, making me glad I'd added sturdy dead bolt locks. He screamed obscenities.

Text messages vibrated my phone. A siren wailed.

"Did you call the cops on me?" He pounded the door again.

"Of course I did. I told you to leave, and you refused. You hurt me yesterday, and I don't plan to let you attack me twice." If I stalled, maybe he'd get arrested again. "What's going on with you? Why would you try to kidnap me? My family's not rich."

He laughed. "Yes, you are. Inheriting Uncle Peter's plantation made you very wealthy, but that's in the past. You know what I'm looking for."

"No, I don't."

The line went dead.

Squealing tires drew me to the family room. Danny sped away, and I sank into the nearest chair. I sent out another group text. **Disaster averted.**

True, but the butterflies swirling in my belly told me he'd return, and the next time I might not be so lucky.

Chapter Fifteen

MARC AND I ATE on the back patio and watched Sunny and Chubb play.

"This was delicious." I wadded my paper napkin into a ball.

Marc patted his trim belly. "It for sure hit the spot. You ready for banana pudding?"

"Maybe later. I'd really like to go for a walk on the beach. It's low tide. You interested?"

"You're supposed to be resting your ankle." He stacked our plates and stood.

"I'll walk slow. The dogs will enjoy the exercise." I gave him my best smile and batted my eyes. "Please?"

He grimaced. "Something tells me you're going whether I agree or not."

"I can drive with my good foot, and the crutches make it so I can walk. So I might go alone."

"Do you plan to search for evidence?"

I ran my hands along the arms of the chair. "I'm going stir crazy. All of this inactivity is getting to me. I imagine Danny's being questioned by Wade, and it's not dark. It seems like a good time to go."

"Fine. Let's put away the leftovers, and I'll join you."

Before long we meandered up the beach. Thanks to me, our progress was slow. Marc led both dogs on their leashes and often paused to give me a steadying hand.

The wind whipped my ponytail, but I didn't care. I inhaled the fresh tangy smell of the Atlantic. "This is my favorite place in the world."

Marc stood beside me. "I know. It's why I agreed to come with you."

The sun began its descent behind us and cast red, orange, and pink slices of color across the sky. White caps sparkled like diamonds as they rose and crashed. A shrimp boat headed south with its outriggers down. Was the vessel heading out for a night of fishing, or had the men finished a day of work? A group of dolphins splashed behind it. "Look, Marc."

"It never gets old, does it?" He grinned.

"Nope." We watched a few more minutes before resuming our walk.

"I don't get what they're trawling for. Shrimp season never starts this early. I need to check it out."

I nodded. "Wonder if Tabby was curious too. No, never mind. We're not going to discuss murder. Let's talk about you. How was your day?"

"Not too bad until I got your text about Danny." He paused while Chubb sniffed at a piece of seaweed.

"He really scared me. If he'd broken down the front door, I wasn't sure how I'd escape him. It's so weird. Since he attacked me, I've felt weak. Like physically weak."

"Should you see the doctor?"

"I've got a follow-up."

"Okay. Good to know, but if you need to see the doc sooner, I can take you."

"I'll keep your offer in mind. Thanks."

He looked around us. There wasn't another soul on the beach. "Do you mind if I unleash them? It'll be good training for Chubb."

"Sounds like a great idea."

He unfastened the leashes and spoke to the dogs while I turned my attention back to the ocean. The song of the surf relaxed me, and the breeze softened like a caress from God.

"Ready?"

"Yeah. Sunset's in about thirty minutes. Let's see how they do."

Sunny trotted between us while Chubb circled us.

"You should've brought him a ball or stick to fetch."

"That would've been smart, but when I left home I didn't think we'd be going for a walk. I've got some at the boat shed, so next time I'll come prepared."

"I've always got plenty of dog toys, so I should've thought about bringing some."

Chubb barked and darted toward the nearest sand dune.

Sunny chased after the golden retriever.

"Isn't that the same dune he ran to the other day?"

"This is the groin where we found Tabby's body, so yeah, I think he's gone to the same place. Chubb, come back." He ran after his puppy.

"Chubb. Sunny. Stop."

Sunny barked again but didn't leave Chubb.

Chubb stopped and dug near the dune.

Marc came to an abrupt halt and watched his dog. I caught up to him, and Sunny returned to stand at my side.

Sand flew through the air, pelting us with particles and tiny shells. Marc didn't intervene.

"Why aren't you stopping him?"

"Watch." Marc pointed. "He found something. Looks like a bag."

"Do you think we should call Wade or David?" I wobbled and clutched Marc's arm to steady myself.

"Easy now." He wrapped his arm around my shoulders. "Until we see the contents, we won't know if it's connected to the murder."

Sunny's ears pointed up.

Chubb alternated digging and pulling on a strap. Sunny joined him, and together they tugged on the blue duffel bag. Leveraging themselves with their legs and using their teeth, they freed the thing and dragged it to us.

Excitement fluttered in my heart. "Marc, see what's in it. If I try to bend down, I might topple."

"If it's connected to Tabby's death, we'll be tampering with evidence."

"It could belong to a high school kid who went surfing or something. The owner's identification might be inside."

"I'll look." Marc pulled down his sleeve and covered his hand before unzipping the bag. "Oh, my goodness. Wait until you see this."

I hobbled closer and peered over his shoulder. Bundles of hundred-dollar bills filled the bag. "Somebody must be frantic wondering where this bag is."

"Time to call Wade." I glanced right and left. "Do you think we're safe?"

"Let's stay alert. I'll watch while you make the call."

I started with the sheriff's number, but he didn't answer, so I left a message then called David.

"Andi Grace, what's wrong?" His voice cracked, and he cleared his throat.

It didn't come as a shock he believed the worst. "Marc and I were walking our dogs on the beach and minding our own business. We weren't interfering in your investigation or anything."

"I won't get mad as long as you hurry up and tell me what's so important." For once he didn't sound frustrated with me.

"Chubb found a duffel bag full of cash near the dune close to where we found Tabby's body." There. I'd spit out the information like he requested.

"On my way. Don't move."

I slipped the phone into the pocket of my jeans. "David's coming."

"I figured he would." He leashed both dogs and held tight.

"Kylie said Tabby feared something bad was going on here. Did I mention I copied pages in the crossword and sudoku magazines? This afternoon I discovered a page where Tabby had words written in the blanks that made no sense when you looked at the clues."

"Interesting. Like what?" He gave each dog a treat.

"Ski, boat, and jet. I remember those because each one is a form of transportation."

"Anything else?"

"Moon and shrimp. I'll show you when we get home."

His shoulders relaxed. "Home. I like the sound of that."

His comment made me feel cozy, and I'd have loved nothing more than to snuggle on the couch with him at that moment. A cool breeze hit me, and I shivered.

"You're cold." Marc pulled off his hoodie and started to pull it over my head. "One arm at a time so you don't fall."

"I can't take your sweatshirt." It was my own fault if I got cold.

"I'm giving it to you." His eyes twinkled.

"Okay, thanks." Ooh la la. Such a gentleman, and I accepted his kind offer. With Marc's assistance, I got into the hoodie without falling on my rear end.

Blue lights flashed, and a sheriff's department truck drove on the beach and stopped near us. David jumped out. "What've we got here?"

"Where's Lacey Jane?"

"I didn't desert her." He met my gaze. "I dropped her at your house. Now why'd you call me?"

I pointed to the duffel bag. "The dogs found it. We only opened it to find out who it belonged to." Marc placed his hand on my shoulder, kindly stopping me from babbling like a brook and getting myself into trouble.

Marc leaned toward David. "Once we saw the money, we didn't keep looking. I opened it with my shirt, so I shouldn't have left fingerprints."

"Was anybody around when you found it?"

"No." I shook my head. "We haven't seen anybody for a while. Just us and the dogs."

Marc said, "Monday morning Chubb tried to dig something up in this area. I didn't let him, and now I'm wondering if the duffel was here then."

David nodded. "Could be. Y'all go on home. I know where to find you if something comes up."

I adjusted the crutches. "Thanks for coming, David. I know you aren't on duty tonight."

"Being a deputy is more than a nine-to-five job. I'm glad I could come help." He looked from us to the bag full of cash. "Keep your eyes open and be careful."

I hobbled to the truck, glad Marc and the dogs were with me, for more reasons than one.

Chapter Sixteen

THE BREEZE WASN'T as strong on my back patio as it'd been on the beach. Sunny and Chubb enjoyed romping around the yard, and Marc and I sat side by side, sipping hot chocolate in insulated mugs.

"Where's your sister?"

"Since we interrupted her dinner with David, she and Kylie decided to go to Scoop It Up for ice cream." The floodlights on the house made it bright enough to see Marc's dimple.

"They're eating ice cream, and we're drinking hot chocolate. Oh, to be young." He laughed.

"You're not old." I elbowed him.

He shook his head. "Thirty-two isn't exactly young."

My shoulders slumped. "I get it. Turning thirty last year hit me harder than I expected."

"Biological clock ticking away?"

"Not really. As the oldest of three kids, I feel like my entire life has been devoted to raising them. Lacey Jane is seven years younger than I am. For years I thought of her as a baby."

He lifted a finger. "Sometimes you still treat her like a small child."

"Ouch." The marshmallows on my hot chocolate shriveled. "When my parents brought Lacey Jane home from the hospital, I was old enough to be a good helper. I even called her my baby." I met his gaze. "Thinking back on that time, it always seemed weird how much my parents allowed me to do for Lacey Jane."

"Maybe three kids were more than they were prepared to handle at the time. Do you want children of your own one day?"

I sighed. "Yeah, but if it doesn't happen, I'll always have Nate and Lacey Jane. I've been their sister, mother, and father. What about you? Do you want kids?"

"Until meeting you, I felt like a lone wolf. If I'm ever blessed with children, I want to be a good father." He cleared his throat. "I thought you were going to show me the puzzles."

I gripped my mug tight. "It's just so nice out here, I hate to ruin the moment."

Marc rocked back on two legs of the patio chair. "I never imagined the day would come when you'd want to take a breather from solving a murder. Do you feel okay?"

"I'm fine." I sipped my drink.

He returned the chair to all four legs on the deck and placed his hand on my forehead. "No fever. That's a good sign."

He'd been rejected so many times growing up in foster care. If our relationship was going to deepen, I needed to make a bold move. I set my drink to the side and reached for his hand. I cradled it to my cheek. "You'll be a great dad to some lucky children one day. Marc, please don't close your heart to love."

"You've taught me a lot, but I'm still learning how to have good friends and how to count on others." His whispered words caressed my neck.

My frantic heartbeat suggested the time had come to dive in the deep end. "You're becoming my best friend."

"Friend?" He pulled his hand away.

I reached for it and held it between both of mine. "Yeah. I think friendships lead to great relationships. Deeper because there's more than physical attraction between two people." Although Marc was very good-looking. His broad shoulders, blond hair, gray eyes, and muscular physique could turn my knees to jelly. All nice qualities to consider when dating, but more was needed for a marriage partner. Marc's kindness, intellect, and ability to remain calm in a crisis gave him depth. "Are you dating anybody besides me?"

"No." He frowned. "Are you?"

"No." I inhaled deeply. "Marc, I'm going to lay my heart out for you. I'd like us to make a commitment not to date others. Like be exclusive. Go steady." Another deep breath. "I'm making a mess out of this. Marc, will you be my boyfriend?"

His eyebrows shot up, and his dimple appeared when he smiled. "Yes."

I ignored my buzzing phone. "If my ankle wasn't injured, I'd do a cartwheel."

Marc leaned close. "A kiss might be more appropriate."

"Counselor, I couldn't agree more." I met him halfway. Our lips touched, and my heart performed the cartwheels my body couldn't.

My phone buzzed again.

Marc ended the kiss. "Do you want to answer your phone?"

"I don't want anybody to interrupt our happy moment."

He laughed. "Sounds like we should kiss again."

Both of our phones rang, and I sighed. "Seems like somebody's trying to get our attention."

Marc gave me a quick kiss before we checked our phones.

"It's Kylie." She was with Lacey Jane, so why wasn't my sister contacting me?

"David's calling me. You stay here. I'll give you some privacy." Marc hustled down the deck stairs. "David, whatcha need?" Chubb ran to his master, and Sunny sauntered over to me.

I swiped my screen. "Hi, Kylie. What's up?"

"Andi Grace, we were hit by a truck!" Her voice wobbled at a hysterical decibel. "You need to come. Lacey Jane's hurt."

Chapter Seventeen

A SUDDEN COLDNESS hit the core of my being. Lacey Jane had been in an accident? They only went to the ice cream shop. "Kylie, where are y'all? How bad is she? What happened?"

Sunny licked my hand hanging limply at my side.

"She's going to be okay. I think. An ambulance is on the way." Kylie's voice still wobbled but at a lower decibel now.

"She's conscious? Let me talk to her."

"Lacey Jane's okay, but a deputy just walked over to her. It's your friend, David. He's talking to her. I guess asking about the accident."

The scattered answers concerned me. "Slow down. Tell me what happened. Where are you now?"

"Near the ice cream shop."

At least I had a location, but Kylie wasn't making a lot of sense.

Marc returned with Chubb. "We need to go see about Lacey Jane."

"Kylie, I'll call you right back. We're on the way." I slipped the phone into the pocket of my jeans and reached for my crutches.

Marc settled the dogs, then we headed to his truck and jumped in. He pulled out of the drive with a squeal. "David said the girls left the ice cream shop and were driving down Charleston Street. A black truck T-boned them and sped away."

"My parents were killed by a hit-and-run driver." Nausea inched its way toward my throat.

"I know, honey." He reached across the console and squeezed my hand. "A witness thinks it might have been intentional."

"Why?" My jaw tightened.

"David will tell us more when we get there."

Heyward Beach was a small town, and we reached the ice cream shop before I could call Kylie back.

Two sheriff department vehicles blocked the street. Blue lights flashed through the darkness, casting an eeriness. Ahead of us was an ambulance. Interior lights showed two EMTs with their backs to us.

"I've got to get to Lacey Jane." I reached for the door handle.

"Let me stop first." Marc parallel-parked his Silverado and turned on his emergency flashers. I slid out, adjusted the crutches, and power-hobbled to the ambulance.

David questioned a man on the sidewalk. When he spotted us, he motioned for Deputy Hanks to let me through. The grouch shouldn't have had to be told. He knew me and was aware Lacey Jane was my sister.

I reached the ambulance, where two young EMTs were speaking to my sister. As much as I wanted to hug her, I didn't want to interrupt if she was getting necessary treatment.

Kylie stood to the side, and I approached her. "Are you hurt?"

She shook her head. "I'll feel the bruises tomorrow, but it's nothing I haven't experienced before."

Her words knocked the breath out of me. Had her parents beat her in addition to stealing her money? I shuddered. "What happened tonight?"

"We decided to surprise you with breakfast and stopped at Donut Dreaming on our way home. I was driving the Jetta. It's destroyed, and I hadn't even transferred the title to my name." She twisted a lock of short blond hair around her finger and held the other arm over her stomach.

"We'll figure out how to fix the Jetta later. Tell me about the accident." I darted my gaze toward the ambulance, where one of the men wrapped Lacey Jane's wrist while the other cleaned a wound on her forehead.

"I pulled out of the parking lot onto Charleston Street. We didn't get far before the truck hit us. It appeared in my peripheral vision. I tried to speed up, which may have saved our lives because he hit the back door. Right behind me. Any slower, and he would've hit my door. My foot was still on the accelerator, and we spun in a circle. My headlights flashed across the driver. He wore a ballcap pulled low, and he wore gloves. I was afraid of dying and you know what went through my mind?"

"What?"

"Why was he wearing gloves on a fairly warm night? Crazy, huh?" Her voice shook.

I ran my hand over her back. "Not crazy at all. Did you notice anything else?"

"A Semper Fi bumper sticker on the back." She shrugged. "That's all. He drove away. When I got the car to stop spinning, I looked at Lacey Jane. She'd hit the side of her head on the window. Shouldn't air bags have deployed?"

"I think they only work if you're hit from the front, but I could be wrong."

Kylie looked toward the ambulance. "Well, I'm really sorry about getting your sister hurt."

"It's not your fault. In fact, I think you did an amazing job saving yourself and Lacey Jane. The accident could've been so much worse." I adjusted my crutches and hugged Kylie.

At first, she resisted my gesture. Her body stiffened. Arms hung down. After a few tense moments, she wrapped her arms around me.

"Andi Grace, you can speak to Lacey Jane now." Marc's voice was calm and reassuring.

Kylie pulled away and stared at the ground. "Go check on your sister."

"I'm going to need you to work tomorrow."

"But I don't have a car."

I balanced on the crutches. "We'll borrow Nate's old truck. Did you tell the deputies what you shared with me?"

"Yeah." She'd gone back to twirling her hair.

"Great. As soon as Lacey Jane is able, we'll go home." I left Kylie and headed to the ambulance.

Marc stayed close to me. "I can't wait to hear what you learned."

"Do you know any marines who drive a black truck with a Semper Fi bumper sticker?"

"Can't say that I do. Why?"

"That's who rammed into the Jetta." Anger bubbled through my veins. Enough was enough. "We better not discover Danny was behind the wheel."

"You need to calm down and focus on Lacey Jane. Let law enforcement worry about catching the driver."

My sister waved from the back of the emergency vehicle. "Did you notice you were the first person on my call list? I didn't make you wait for hours to learn about the accident."

"Nobody likes a smarty pants." I blinked back tears. "But I'll always love you."

"I love you, too. These guys say I can go home now."

"You're okay?"

She nodded. "Nothing but a few cuts."

David came over to us and helped Lacey Jane to the ground from the back of the ambulance. "We've got a lead on the truck that T-boned you. Wade's chasing it down now, and I'm going to stay here and question witnesses. In case this wasn't an accident, do you and Kylie have a safe place to stay tonight?"

Lacey Jane tilted her head. "My roommates are still in Florida."

"No." I shook my head. "You two can stay with me."

David nodded. "Sounds like a good plan. I'll stop by later."

Oh, the questions I had for the deputy. "Will you call first?"

"Absolutely. See you all later." He jogged back to the sidewalk, where a crowd had gathered.

The four of us headed to my house. Once we settled into the family room, Marc took the dogs outside for a walk around the block.

Lacey Jane lay on the couch with an old quilt over her, feet on the far end and her head resting in my lap. I ran my fingers through her light brown hair. Her hair wasn't as thick as mine, and her body was willowy. I wasn't fat, but I was bigger boned. She had brown eyes, and mine were blue. Like my dad's eyes. Nate looked more like our mom, with his red hair, freckled complexion, and green eyes. All three of us were so different, but our loyalty was fierce. If Danny was behind the wreck, I'd go sideways on him.

Kylie paced in a semicircle around the room. "This is all my fault."

"No way." Lacey Jane sat up and elbowed my hip as she positioned her feet on the floor. "It was my idea to get ice cream. Accidents happen all the time."

She stopped in front of the fireplace and fisted her hands. "I don't believe it was an accident."

I sat straighter, not wanting to miss a word. My gut instinct exactly. It was too much to believe it was a coincidence. "Why?"

Marc returned with Sunny and Chubb. "No sign of the black truck. It seems like a normal, quiet night on the island."

Sunny made her way to me with her nails clicking on the wood floor. She wiggled between our legs and propped her head on the cushion between us with ears straight up and raised eyebrows. I patted the couch. "It's okay. Come on."

She hopped up and licked the side of Lacey Jane's chin, avoiding the bandage above her eyes. I stroked Sunny's head, and my sister wrapped her arms around my German shepherd.

I refocused on Kylie. "Will you sit down and tell us what you're thinking?"

Marc said, "Is this girl talk? Should I leave?"

Kylie settled into the easy chair. "You can stay. I was just about to tell them why the driver may have targeted us."

Marc took the remaining chair, and Chubb sat by his feet. "Go ahead."

She ran her hands through her hair and looked at the ceiling. "I'll try to keep this short."

"Take your time. We're not rushing you." I rubbed my hand along Sunny's back.

"Tabby's apprehension worsened the last couple of weeks. Sometimes she wouldn't allow me to go with her to feed the cats. At first I thought she needed some time alone. She was an adult, and I honored her wishes. Some evenings when she returned from caring for the cats, she'd write in the puzzle magazines she loved so much."

Chubb whined and crossed the room to where Kylie sat. She stroked his sides with both hands. "We talked to one of the local cops. He pretended to care but pulled me aside. He confided that he knew about Tabby's brain injury and seizures. It didn't matter that her seizures occurred in Dallas at the hospital. The cop thought she'd imagined trouble on the island."

Marc's arms dropped to his thighs and he leaned forward. "Do you remember the cop's name?"

"Ian Patterson. Why?" She gripped the arms of the chair. "Are you going to tell him what I said?"

He shook his head. "No way, but I plan to keep an eye on him. Let's get back to your story."

Seconds ticked by while Kylie gawked at Marc. "You promise? I don't trust the local cops. If it wasn't for y'all, I wouldn't trust the sheriff's department."

"I promise." Marc kept eye contact with the young lady.

I almost spoke to reassure Kylie, but Marc seemed to have convinced her.

Lacey Jane repositioned herself, and Sunny hopped onto the floor then lay at our feet.

Kylie crossed her arms. "We visited the library a few times. Tabby's daughter thought paying for Wi-Fi was a waste because she didn't believe her mom capable of using a computer anymore. Tabby didn't need my help, but I saw some of the pages she printed out."

She was about to drop a big clue into our laps. "What was she researching?"

"Articles on counterfeit generic drugs." Her whispered words blazed through my brain.

Marc whistled. "No wonder she was upset. What happened to the articles?"

"When Tabby disappeared, I grabbed the pages before I ran. After tonight, I wonder if I should continue to run."

"Absolutely not." I stood and pain shot up my leg, forcing me back on the couch. "Kylie, I still believe you're safer here with us. We haven't known you long, but your best chance of survival is to stick with us. If there is some kind of counterfeit drug ring, we're all safer together. If the individuals involved killed Tabby, it's possible they're after you."

"I know, but the local cops did nothing." She pulled both legs into the chair but stretched her arms enough to continue petting Chubb.

A lump formed in my throat. How many people had lied to Kylie and abused her? It was a wonder she had faith in us. "Kylie, we can trust the sheriff and David. They have frustrated me in the past, but both are honorable men."

Marc rested his forearms on his thighs. "Lacey Jane and I will research this on the down low. I'll avoid the local cops. While I'd like to think Ian Patterson was only having a bad day when Tabby spoke to him, we won't assume anything."

My text ringtone played, and I glanced at my phone, reading the message that flashed on the screen. "It's David. He's on the way over to check on you and Lacey Jane. This is bigger than the four of us. It's bigger than Tabby. It might even be more than the sheriff's department can handle, but they'll know the right contacts to make."

Tense moments ticked by where nobody said a word. I didn't want Kylie to feel like we were ganging up on her, but I wanted to keep her safe. She stared at the floor.

Marc pointed to the window and stood. "He's here. Are you ready, Kylie? Or do you want me to stall him?"

She planted her feet on the floor. "May as well face the music. Stalling only prolongs the torment."

Chapter Eighteen

THE BUZZ OF MY phone woke me the next morning before my alarm went off. I reached for it before opening my eyes. "Hello." My voice croaked.

"Morning, sunshine." The sound of Marc's voice woke me right up.

"Good morning. Where are you?"

"I'm about to go for a run, and I'm missing my best girl." If being Marc's girlfriend meant morning calls from him, I could get used to it.

I fluffed my pillows and sat up, leaning against the headboard. "Aw. Stupid ankle. Do you want to come over for breakfast? I can offer you granola, yogurt, and fruit." Before his efforts to help me eat healthier, I would've only had sugary cereal.

"I've got Chubb with me."

"No problem. I'll see you soon." I hopped out of bed and landed on my injured ankle. Minimum pain, but I'd be smart and follow the doctor's suggestions. I took a cool shower, in order to not damage the burns, then dressed and braided my hair.

I made it to the kitchen with only a slight limp. Lacey Jane and Kylie sat at the table, eating donuts and drinking coffee. Sunny lay on the rug by the back door.

"Where'd those come from?" The delicacies tempted me.

Lacey Jane smiled. "David brought them by last night after you went to bed."

I plopped into a chair. "He came over a second time?"

My sister continued to smile. "He informed us they found the owner of the truck that hit us." Lacey Jane patted the chair beside her.

Kylie smirked. "At least that was the excuse he gave for showing back up."

"Who owns it?" I sat beside my sister and gave her a one-arm hug. It was nice to have her staying with me for a while.

Sunny crossed the kitchen and lay beside me. I leaned down and rubbed her back.

"A retired marine." My sister got up and poured me a mug of

coffee. "He'd been eating dinner with a real estate agent at Tony's Pizzeria. Ivey Gilbert is his agent. When the marine went to get his truck, it was gone, and Ivey drove him to the police station. While he filled out the report, the police got the news about the accident."

"Is it possible he rammed y'all before his dinner with Ivey?"

Lacey Jane placed the flowery mug of coffee in front of me. "No. They were discussing business from the salad course to dessert. He's got an alibi."

My body felt like lead. It would've been too easy to think they'd catch the driver so quickly. "Sounds like he might be moving to the area. What's the man's name?"

My sister picked out a donut hole. "David didn't tell me. Or else I forgot." She shrugged.

I laughed. "It sounds like you're really sweet on David. Like more than a little crush."

She stuffed the donut hole into her mouth and shrugged.

Kylie propped her arms on the table. "They're sweet on each other—it's definitely a mutual thing. He didn't leave until well after midnight. I went to bed after he informed us about the marine but couldn't sleep. Danger has been a constant in my life, but this is different."

Lacey Jane swallowed and licked icing off her thumb. "How's it different?"

"In Texas, I always saw my attacker coming. With Tabby's murderer still free, I could really die if the killer comes after me. Not just suffer. You know what I mean?"

Her matter-of-fact acceptance of the situation chilled me. "I think it's possible we're all in danger. Nate's going to loan you his old truck, Kylie. It might appear to be a clunker, but it's reliable. What about Susan? Did you talk to her last night?"

"We texted each other. She plans to have Tabby cremated when the coroner releases her body. Until then, she'd like me to help her at the house."

"I didn't think you were comfortable with her." I doctored up my cup of coffee with sweetener and vanilla creamer.

"It's probably just my imagination. My clothes and stuff are at Tabby's, so I need to go there at some point." She reached for a chocolate donut with chocolate icing.

Double chocolate meant double yum. I sipped my coffee. "Man, if Marc doesn't get here soon, I'm going to cave in to temptation."

Lacey Jane said, "Kylie, don't go by yourself. When Nate gets here, the three of us can drive over together."

I ran my finger over the rim of the mug. "There's no need for either of you to take unnecessary risks."

Kylie twirled her hair. "Susan didn't arrive in Heyward Beach until after Tabby's death, so she can't be the killer."

"If you feel uneasy, don't go back alone." My sister frowned.

Kylie laughed. "My imagination is getting the best of me. I'll be safe with Susan. She offered to let me live in Tabby's house until it sells, and she gave me the Jetta. The worst thing about living with Susan is she smokes too much. At least she goes outside, but the smell clings to her. Again, it's not my house. I should accept her offer with grace and save the money I make working for you." She pointed at me.

"Speaking of work, let's go over this morning's schedule. It'll be a big help if you take the early shift of dogs needing to walk. After lunch we'll go with you to Tabby's house."

Kylie's shoulders relaxed. "All right. I didn't really want to confront her all by myself."

Lacey Jane stood and pointed to the donuts. "Do you want me to remove temptation?"

"Yes, please." The doorbell rang, and I laughed. "I bet that's Marc. Good thing I behaved."

"I'll let him in." Kylie left me alone in the kitchen with Lacey Jane.

"I'm not used to you eating healthy, and you rarely let a guy tell you what to do." Lacey Jane closed the donut box and shoved it into the pantry.

"I'm not so bullheaded I won't listen to good advice. A decade of bad food choices can't be erased, but I can make better decisions about my diet now."

"I'm proud of you, Sis. Maybe I should follow your lead. Between school and work, I don't have time to prepare healthy meals. Sandwiches, chips, and cookies are my staples."

"I should've set a better example for you."

Marc entered the kitchen wearing sweats and a T-shirt. "Kylie's getting ready for the morning rounds and wants to know where the schedule is."

"I'll show her." Lacey Jane disappeared.

"At least you and Sunny didn't leave because of me. Chubb's in the backyard. I didn't want to bring him inside all sandy."

"The gate should've been secured. Do you have a key?" I opened the back door, and Sunny strolled onto the deck.

"Nope. I closed the hasp, but the lock is missing."

"I didn't remove the lock, so where is it? There were only three keys to it. I'll check with Lacey Jane and Nate to see if they know anything." I hobbled to the refrigerator and pulled out yogurt and strawberries then placed them on the kitchen counter beside two empty bowls and plates. "David brought the girls donuts if you want one."

Marc pulled a box of granola from the cabinet. "We're in this to-gether."

"I like the sound of that." We each created our yogurt bowls then sat at the table. "What's on your agenda today?"

"The usual. What about you? Are you planning to look for clues to Tabby's murder?" His knee touched mine under the kitchen table, and chills raced up my spine. Good chills.

"Maybe, but first I need to work. I'm giving a lesson to Yoyo, Ethan and Violet Seitz's black Lab. Then I hope to work on marketing Stay and Play and check on the progress Griffin and Dylan are making on the old kitchen. It feels like I haven't been to the plantation in forever."

"Do you miss it?"

Did I? "In a perfect world, Stay and Play would be closer to the beach. The plantation is beautiful, but it doesn't fit my personality."

"I understand. It's formal and you're casual."

My body relaxed in a comfortable way. Marc got me. "You're right. Marc, you're a well-respected attorney. You wear suits and ties to work. I mostly wear shorts and T-shirts. You need a girlfriend who is upper class. Well educated. She should dress nice."

He formed a T with his hands. "Time out. I need you." The tendon in his jaw tightened.

"You need me to what?" I wiped my hands on a paper napkin and searched his eyes.

"I just need you to be exactly like you are." He held my hand. "Be yourself. I don't want you to change a thing. Not your hair, career, style, or desire to solve murders. You're perfect for me just the way you are, Andi Grace."

My body grew hot. "Even if I don't eat healthy foods?"

He pressed his lips together and met my gaze before speaking. "The only reason I'd like you to eat healthy foods is so we can be together longer. I'd like for you to live a good and healthy life."

"I could still get sick. Lots of diseases aren't related to diet." Was he the kind of man who'd leave a wife or girlfriend because she was ill?

"True, but why not make good choices when it comes to eating and exercise?"

"Good point, Counselor." I leaned toward him and kissed his cheek.

"Su-weet." He tweaked my nose. "Wade called me last night. He told me the truck that hit the girls belongs to a marine. Upstanding man. Decorated and all that. Then he asked if we'd join him and Hannah for dinner tonight at Tony's Pizzeria."

I clapped my hands. "Yes. Hannah's got a little crush on Wade. What'd you tell him?"

"That I needed to check with you first. It sounds like you're in favor of us going on a double date with Wade and Hannah."

"You bet I am. I'll even order a salad. How's that?"

"You're making me happy, but if you change your mind, I'll still enjoy our date." He took another bite of yogurt.

I bit into a juicy strawberry. Marc's logic made me want to dance for joy, but the pain in my ankle made dancing impossible for now. He was thinking about our relationship both now and down the road, motivating me to board the wellness train. Exercise and a healthy diet might work for longevity of life as long as I didn't get killed solving murders. I'd need to exert an abundance of caution in order to enjoy a full life with Marc.

Chapter Nineteen

AFTER YOYO'S LESSON, I followed Ethan and Violet to their vehicle. "I can tell you've been practicing with him. Keep up the good work."

Violet gave the dog a treat and pushed the car fob which closed the van's back door. "Is Monday too soon for another lesson?"

Ethan's hands were propped on his hips, and he looked toward the construction work.

I checked my schedule on my phone app. "I can make Monday work. Violet, what do you do?"

"I'm the new children's librarian at the main library."

All right. This day kept getting better. I kept my expression neutral. "I guess you know Leslie Nichols. Her son is running for state representative against Hannah Cummings."

She released her thick red hair from the elastic band. "Yes, I know her. All she talks about is how great her son is. Even if I didn't like Hannah, I'd vote for her just to shut Leslie up."

Ethan's swung his head to face his wife. "Honey, you shouldn't say that."

Violet shot a frosty glare at her husband. "Why? It's the truth."

"Still, it's rude."

Violet flushed. "Ethan makes a good point. Sorry."

"No need to apologize to me." I adjusted my crutches to relieve the irritation at my armpits. "Have you met Danny?"

"Yeah. When he comes into the library, you'd think royalty had arrived. His nose is in the air. He only asks us peons where his mother is then walks away without so much as a thank you. He's the most arrogant—"

"Seriously, Violet. Stop gossiping." Ethan glanced at me. "She doesn't have red hair for nothing. You should see her when she really gets riled up."

I laughed. "No, thank you. In all fairness, there's something I should tell you. I'm not gossiping because it'll be in the police report. Danny attacked me. He's the reason I'm on crutches."

Violet shrieked. "I knew he was a horrible person. Why'd he assault you?"

I gave them the short version of the story. "He's very volatile these days. Watch yourself around him. If he comes to the library again looking for his mom, be nice."

Her eyes widened. "You better believe I won't antagonize him. Ethan, does he go to your pharmacy?"

Ethan slung his arm around his wife's shoulders. "I can't answer your question without breaking HIPAA regulations. If you see him in the store, fine, but I can't say anything." He held up his hand when she opened her mouth. "And if you should see him there, you know I won't tell you what medications he takes."

She shot him a pouty face. "That's what I get for marrying a man with integrity."

Yoyo barked.

"Sounds like it's time for y'all to go." I stepped back. "I'll see you Monday. Remember, be consistent with Yoyo."

They told me bye and rumbled away in their fancy van.

I spent the next few hours on more dog training lessons. As the last family left, a familiar truck pulled up the drive and around the plantation house. Soon it stopped near me. Leroy Peck reached toward the passenger seat and picked something up.

I backed away, unsure about the man and the mysterious object. Was he the killer? Did he have a gun? He opened his door and stepped out, holding a cardboard box bigger than a shoe box. "Andi Grace."

"Leroy, what can I do for you?" I planned to ditch the crutches and hightail it to the woods if he revealed a hidden bomb or weapon.

"I found this little fellow along the side of the road. He's so pitiful, and I was afraid a regular shelter wouldn't take him. It'd be a shame for him to be put to sleep." A furry black head with a white muzzle popped up. "I can't keep him on account of my landlord, but I've been calling him Gus. No tags. Nothing. He's dirty and looks malnourished. Will you take pity on him?"

The cat hater had rescued an abandoned dog. My heart melted. "Of course I will."

"He needs a bath in the worst way. I had to hang one of those air fragrance things on my rearview mirror just to survive the drive over here."

I reached out, and my crutches fell to the ground. "Uh, let me think how we're going to do this."

Leroy retrieved my crutches without dropping Gus. "Why don't you just take me to the closest bathtub."

"Thanks." I pointed to the dog barn. "I've got an area in there for bathing dogs. One day I'd like to add an official grooming area."

"You lead, and I'll follow."

Leroy didn't seem scary or hateful like the man Kylie described. "Why don't you like cats?"

He snorted. "You're the first person to ask me. Most folks act like I'm whacked."

I waved to Dylan and Griffin as we passed them at the old kitchen renovation, and we continued our slow pace to the barn. "You didn't answer my question."

"A feral cat caused my accident."

"I thought you fell off a roof."

"I did." He clutched the crumpled box and kept his eyes straight ahead.

Wow. The man was harder to get an answer out of than Marc used to be. "Was there a cat on the roof with you?"

His nostrils flared. "If you must know, while I was replacing the shingles, a cat meowed. I crawled around and found the darn thing in the chimney. After I got him free, he attacked me. Scratched my face and neck all to pieces. Next thing you know, I'm rolling down the roof and falling through the air. Tree branches slowed my fall but none were strong enough to stop me. Last thing I remember was hitting the ground."

I stopped at the barn door and faced him. "Oh, Leroy. I'm so sorry. It makes sense you'd be skittish around cats."

"Didn't say I was scared of 'em, but they're dangerous. Tabby shouldn't have gone around saving all the feral cats. Leastwise not save them while letting them roam free."

"Cats are different than dogs."

"Word around town is, when you find a dog, you connect them to an owner." He pushed open the barn door. "Where's the tub?"

Sunny barked from the play area.

"That's my German shepherd." I tossed her a treat and kept moving toward our destination in the far corner of the shadowy barn.

"Fancy." He looked me up and down then placed Gus into the stainless steel tub I'd splurged on. "I'll do it if you pass me the dog shampoo. It'll take at least two washings, and I doubt you're in any condition to handle the job on a bum leg."

"It's my ankle, but I can't let you bathe Gus."

"Don't see why not. If I'd shown up with a clean dog, you would've taken him in. Don't see no difference."

"Okay, I see your point, but you're not on my payroll."

Leroy deflated before my eyes. "I get it."

I felt like a big jerk. "You know what, I probably should rest my ankle. Are you sure it's not too much trouble?"

His chin lifted and his shoulders straightened. "Ain't no problem."

"Thanks, Leroy." I reached for the shampoo from the shelves of dog supplies, including towels and cleaning products. "This one is all natural and good for smelly dogs."

Leroy leaned close to the dirty mutt. "How about flea shampoo?"

I swapped products. "Here you go."

"Go rest your ankle. I've got this under control."

I left him alone long enough to play toss with Sunny. When she lay on her favorite pillow, I returned to Leroy and sat on a wobbly barstool near the tub. "You're good with him. Why don't you live in a place that allows dogs?"

"I never considered it before." Brown water swirled down the drain as Leroy rinsed the dog. "I think one more washing should do it. You definitely need to treat him for fleas."

"Yes, sir." I observed his gentle manner with Gus.

"Deep down Tabby and I got along fine. I guess Kylie told you differently."

"Yeah. She was very protective of Tabby. It's understandable she'd fear you."

"Enough said. Tabby told me she grew up in a home with abuse. Arguing with Tabby was kind of a release for us. People tiptoe around or shun those they don't understand. When we weren't arguing, we compared stories. Had a lot in common." He shut off the water and lathered up the pitiful dog.

It made sense they'd become friends. "You both were in work-related accidents. What else?"

"We're survivors. At least we were until she was killed." He remained focused on his task. "Both of us had seizures and lost our jobs. When she first grew suspicious about some kind of crime on the island, I believed her."

"Did you see anything concerning?"

He shook his head and ran clear water over Gus, who stood in the tub, gazing at Leroy with adoring eyes. "No, but I'm a man who enjoys working with his hands. Tabby used her smarts. Know what I mean?"

"You seem smart to me."

He shrugged. "Thanks. Tabby thought long and hard before she mentioned her suspicions to Kylie. When they shared her information with the cops, she was devastated the cop sent her away. She kinda lost hope that she could contribute to society." He shut off the water and hung the water sprayer on its hook. "The only thing I've noticed when I'm out fishing is the jet skis. It's a rough ride if you leave the creek and head to the ocean on one of those things. I've seen more lately than ever before."

"What about shrimp boats?"

"Most folks claim shrimping is a dying industry, but you can't prove it by me." His thin curly hair stuck out, almost clownlike. "Most nights I see at least one shrimp boat, even though it's not the right time of year to go shrimping. On the weekends, I may see two or three."

"Marc and I saw a shrimp boat yesterday. Sounds like I should investigate what's going on."

Gus shook, splattering both of us with drops of water.

Leroy chuckled. "He's going to be a keeper."

I smiled but his story saddened me. Poor Tabby and poor Gus. "We all want to feel like we matter, even dogs. You've given Gus a gift today by rescuing the little runt and taking care of him. Your actions probably saved his life."

"It's important to make a difference in the world. Once your identity is ripped away from you without any warning, it's a burden to bear. Tabby and I both took seizure medicine after our accidents. It's part of the reason nobody will hire me for construction work."

"You can still work?" I passed him a soft clean towel.

He dried the dog. "Yeah, but I'm limited on the hours because of my disability. DDS could come down on me if I work too many hours. My back won't allow me to work as much as I'd like, so I'm stuck."

"Gotcha." There was something I was missing. Probing deeper might lead me to the answer. "Limited because of the seizures? Leroy, did you ever take gabapentin for your seizures?" The kaleidoscope was tumbling into focus.

He cradled Gus in one arm while drying him with the opposite hand. "No, but I took it for pain. The docs told me I wouldn't get hooked on gabapentin like narcotics. They gave it to me for my back, and that stuff is wicked powerful. I gave it a month and quit because it made me dizzy and tired. When I stopped, I went through withdrawal. Don't wish that on my worst enemy."

"Did Tabby tell you what medication she took to control her seizures?"

"Phenytoin. My doc tried different meds on me. The best drug without side effects for me personally was topiramate. I haven't had a seizure since, and there are few side effects for me." He shrugged. "Everybody's different."

"Andi Grace, where are you?" Dylan called out.

"We're back here giving a bath to our newest dog."

He joined us and did a double take when he got a clear look at Leroy. "You're the man who doesn't like cats."

"Dylan, there's more to the story. This is Leroy Peck. Leroy, this is Dylan King."

"I'm in the construction business and used to know your old man." Leroy tucked Gus into his arms. "He did good work."

"What are you trying to say?" Dylan tilted his head.

"I won't judge you on your father's actions, and I'd appreciate you returning the favor."

Tense seconds ticked by before Dylan nodded. "Fine."

"Appreciate it." Leroy passed the dog to me. "I'll see you around."

The damp dog settled into my arms.

"Thanks for Gus. I'll find him a good home."

"Don't forget to treat him for fleas."

"I won't."

Leroy walked out of the barn then Dylan met my gaze. "He brought you a dog? How'd you convince him to give the fleabag a bath?"

"He offered because of my ankle. I'm going to take him off my suspect list. Wait until you hear his story."

Dylan snorted. "You may convince me he's okay, but persuading Kylie that Leroy is fine will be a different matter."

Chapter Twenty

I DROVE KYLIE TO our afternoon appointments to observe her skills with the dogs on my schedule. All of the day's families lived on the mainland, but I planned our route to be as efficient as possible. Kylie's gentle touch and kindness with the dogs convinced me she'd be a good employee. When we finished, I drove us toward the island.

Kylie twisted her hair in circles. "Dylan told me Cranky Butt came to the plantation today."

I slowed at a stop sign. "Yeah. About that. Leroy claims he and Tabby didn't argue for real. Were they like little kids at school? One punches the other in the arm or pulls their hair as a sign of affection?"

"You think arguing was the way they exhibited their fondness for each other?" Her arctic expression gave me a chill.

"It crossed my mind." I drove over the bridge to the island.

"I never considered that possibility. When my parents argued, it was time to hide or run." The hair twisting slowed. "I guess it's possible. Tabby was livelier after an argument with Leroy."

"There you go. Leroy didn't treat her like an invalid, which sparked her to life."

"If they liked each other, he wouldn't be on your suspect list. Is that what you're implying?"

"Exactly, but I'm keeping Susan on my list as a long shot that she did it for the money. I promised to go by Tabby's house with you. Are you ready?"

"Okay." Kylie dropped both hands into her lap. "Andi Grace, I've seen you in church. My parents never took me, but a friend used to invite me to youth group. I always went with her because we ate at her house and sometimes I slept over. Which meant I got a couple of good meals and had a safe night." She dropped her head and stared at her lap. "It sounds self-serving when I say it out loud."

"No, it doesn't. God loves you, and I believe the friend who invited you to church was a way for God to reveal his love to you." I lessened my speed, giving her a chance to reply before we reached Tabby's place.

Kylie stared straight ahead. "I loved going to church with my friend, but I always knew I'd have to return to my parents. Attending here with Tabby was different. Tabby gave me my first Bible, and she answered my questions." Kylie sighed. "Believe me, I had a ton of questions."

"It sounds like you've got one now."

She nodded. "Now that Tabby's gone, I'm not sure how to live without fear. As long as she was alive, I felt safe."

I eased into Tabby's driveway behind Susan's blue Mercedes rental. "You're an adult, and you've made friends in Heyward Beach. We'll protect you from your parents if they show up. Can they afford to travel to South Carolina from Dallas?"

"Not unless they make a big score." She stared at her hands.

"Score? Like what?"

"You know. Sell drugs or act as a mule for their dealer." Her tone was matter of fact.

Chills broke out on my arms. "I used to believe money was the root of all evil, but I'm beginning to wonder if it's drugs. From your experience, do you think Danny sounds like a drug abuser?"

"All kinds of people get hooked on drugs. Prescription drugs, heroin, meth, you name it. Abuse doesn't care what your name is or how much money you have. If you're not careful, they'll take control. I know Danny's an attorney from a good family, but that doesn't mean squat. Tell me more about him."

As fast as possible, I shared what I knew. "He's running against Hannah Cummings for state representative. Part of her platform is taking a stand against drugs, but I doubt that's his motivation for running."

"You said he can be charming and turn angry just like that." Kylie snapped her fingers.

"Yes." My eye twitched.

"Dad was the same way." She rolled her head. "I'm tired of talking about him, though. It sounds like Danny might be taking drugs, but he probably can afford his habit without having to resort to selling or smuggling drugs into the country."

"I guess it's good to know what I'm dealing with." I patted her arm. "You ready to go inside and face Susan?"

She released a heavy sigh. "Let's go."

After we made it to the door and rang the bell, I turned to Kylie. "This is a really nice house. I bet it sells fast."

"Yeah, it makes me sad."

"Why?" I glanced at the wide front porch with plank flooring. The white rockers invited people to sit a spell.

"It feels like my home. It's the first place I enjoyed living, and I bet an investor buys it to rent it out. Then it'll just be a vacation house and not a real home."

"I see what you're saying, but it could also be a place where families come together once a year and grow closer."

Kylie's eyes grew wide. "You always see the glass as half-full, don't you?"

"I try to stay positive."

The door opened, and Susan swayed with it. "I didn't expect company this afternoon. This isn't the best time." A mixture of booze and cigarette smoke swirled around me.

The woman was snockered.

Chapter Twenty-One

I DON'T KNOW who was more embarrassed by Susan's behavior, Kylie or me. We told Tabby's daughter we'd get in touch with her the next day then left.

Kylie latched her seat belt. "I've never been around a rich drunk. Can you believe she was still polite?"

"I think some people get mean while others get melancholy." We finished the short drive to my home in silence. "I've got to get ready for my date."

Lacey Jane met us at the front door. "Are you ready for your transformation, Andi Grace?"

"Why aren't you at work?"

"It's still spring vacation." She grabbed my hand and led me to my bedroom. "Take a shower while we plan your wardrobe."

Kylie looked me up and down. "Do you have any appropriate clothes for dating?"

Lacey Jane burst out laughing.

"I wear nice clothes to church." I entered the bathroom and locked the door behind me while their laughter continued. My thoughts flitted between our encounter with Susan, the murder, and my date.

Before long, I was clean and sitting on a barstool in my bathroom. Lacey Jane styled my hair with a curling iron and some kind of product that smelled like fruit.

Kylie knelt at my feet and used colorful tape to make my injury feel better and look pretty at the same time. She lifted my foot so I could see it. "Well?"

"That feels so good I can hardly tell it's been hurt. Where'd you learn to wrap an ankle?"

Kylie stood. "You'd be amazed at what I picked up as a PCT at the hospital. I hope the bright blue is okay, but if you wear pants, it won't show."

Lacey Jane pointed to the bed in the other room. "No problem. I brought over a couple of tops for you to try. Both will look nice with black slacks. You can wear one of my dresses another night."

"I have clothes." I frowned at my sister.

"This is a date, and you need to act like it." Lacey Jane shook her finger at me.

I had no comeback. Marc was my boyfriend. I'd be myself, but it wouldn't hurt to put some effort into our relationship. "I appreciate the help."

Lacey Jane and Kylie finished my hair, did my makeup, and debated the appropriate top.

I allowed them to plan my evening while I thought through the clues. The day we'd found Tabby, Chubb had tried to dig in the dunes. We'd stopped him and never imagined we'd later find a bag full of money. Had the deputies found fingerprints or anything useful from the bag?

There'd also been cigarette butts close to Tabby's body. Did they contain fingerprints or DNA evidence?

Cigarettes. Susan was a smoker, but she claimed to have been in Dallas at the time her mother was killed. How could I learn if that was the truth? "Kylie, when Susan arrived, were there tags on her suitcase? Like the ones they attach when you fly?"

Kylie tilted her head and met my gaze. "No, but she had a small bag on wheels. She probably didn't check it."

"There goes that theory. We need to find out exactly when she flew in. Any thoughts?"

My sister lifted an off-white top off the bed. "This is the one. Please, tell me you have a strapless bra."

"Of course I do." I pulled one out of my drawer. "See? I'm not a complete tomboy."

"Good. You're going to wear this off-the-shoulder sweater with your skinny black slacks and my leopard print flats. They're stretchy and should work with your wrapped ankle."

"What if I stretch them out too much?" My sister's model-like thinness left me doubting.

"It's a risk worth taking. Now, get dressed and try not to mess up your hair."

"Wait a second. Kylie, you said Susan's a neat freak. Maybe she threw away the tickets from her flight."

"I don't know. She's pretty high tech."

"Meaning?"

Lacey Jane piped in. "I bet she used her phone app. They have barcodes you can show for your flight instead of paper tickets."

"Oh. I didn't realize."

Lacey Jane wrapped her arm around my shoulders. "You never travel. It's not surprising you didn't know people store flight tickets on their phones."

"One day I'm going to Paris. You can teach me about the app then."

The doorbell rang, and we all squealed.

Kylie said, "It's bound to be Marc. I'll stall him in the family room."

The memory of Danny's attempt to get inside earlier in the week washed over me. "Look before you open the door."

"These days I always check." She left us alone.

In the other room, Sunny barked. A happy sound. Not threatening.

"Hurry." Lacey Jane urged me. "At work, Marc doesn't like it when clients are late for appointments."

I changed clothes and stood in front of the bathroom mirror with my sister. Strangers might not guess we were related with the differences in our appearances. "I look amazing. Thanks, Sis."

She shrugged off my comment and reached for the still-hot curling iron. "I want to tweak this side."

I stood still. "What are your plans tonight?"

"Kylie and I are meeting David and Dylan for burgers then we may go for a walk on the beach. Can I take Sunny with us?"

"Sure. She always enjoys a beach walk." I smiled. "I like the thought of you and David together, and not because he carries a gun. You two seem to complement each other."

"Close your eyes." She blasted my pretty curls with hairspray. "This should hold for a while against the humidity. You look very pretty."

"Thanks to you." I hugged her then reached for my crutches. "I'm going to try to walk. These are for just in case."

I limped into the family room. Marc was talking to Kylie. He wore khaki jeans, a plaid cotton shirt, and blue pullover sweater. The man took my breath away. He glanced toward me and stopped talking. His mouth dropped open.

Kylie turned toward me and gave me two thumbs-up.

The room grew silent.

"Hey, Marc."

"Wow! You look nice." He walked past Kylie and kissed my cheek. "Let me rephrase that. You're beautiful."

My face grew warm. "You do, too. Uh, I mean, you look very handsome." Gorgeous even, if you could call a man gorgeous.

"Ready to go? We're meeting Wade and Hannah at the pizzeria."

Lacey Jane patted our shoulders. "You two kids have fun. Marc, her curfew is midnight. Have her home on time."

"Curfew?" Marc's eyebrows rose.

"That's the same speech she gave every boy who took me out. Ten o'clock was my first curfew, but I figured you two are adults. Midnight should do it."

Marc laughed.

I pointed at her. "Seems like you have a date, too."

"Yep, and my date packs heat. So don't be late."

I gazed at Marc. "We better leave before she grills you." I limped toward the door, carrying but not using the crutches.

"Why aren't you using your crutches?" He opened the door for me.

"I think my ankle is wrapped tight enough to try walking, but I'll have these just in case."

He grabbed my crutches and offered me his arm. I held on as we descended the porch steps. The girls had pampered me until I felt like a fairy princess. Marc could definitely play the role of handsome prince. Going on a date was just what I needed. No talk of murders or disasters. Yep, it'd be a good night.

Chapter Twenty-Two

MARC AND I WALKED into Tony's hand-in-hand. Hannah stood in the entry area talking to Danny. Her posture was stiff, and he held out his hands with shoulders slumped. The expression on his face told me he wanted something from Hannah.

I let go of Marc and touched Hannah's arm. "Hannah, I'm so sorry we're late. It's my fault. Where's Sheriff Stone?"

Danny's chin shot up, and his eyes narrowed. "You called the sheriff? Hannah and I were having a civil conversation."

Marc stepped in front of Danny. "It looked to me like you were the only one talking. How'd you get out of jail?"

"Bail, baby. The charges won't stick. The judge knows it, and so do you." He poked Marc's chest with his finger.

Marc's jaw tightened. "Hannah, do you have anything to say to Danny?"

"Not unless it's to tell him to leave me alone, but I've done that. He refuses to back off."

Marc nodded. "You heard the lady."

"It's a public restaurant. You can't kick me out." Danny clenched his fists.

"No, but I can." Tony joined us with a large pizza paddle in his hand.

Danny muttered something unbecoming a gentleman and stormed out of the restaurant.

"*Mi dispiace.*" Tony shook his head. "I'm sorry about the riffraff. I keep hoping the boy will wake up and become respectable. You know what I mean?"

Wade stepped through the doorway, wearing dark jeans and a solid button-up. "By the looks on your faces, you ran into Danny. He brushed past me on the sidewalk, mumbling obscenities. No law against cussing, and I didn't want to be any later."

"Shh, shh." Tony lifted his hands. "Come with me to the best table. Tonight's on me to make up for the unpleasantness."

We all tried to argue, but Tony led us to a table for four. "I'll return with drinks and appetizers. Relax and forget about it." He shuffled away with his arthritic gait.

I obeyed Tony and relaxed into my seat. "He's always so nice to me."

Hannah's eyes widened. "I'm impressed he got Danny to leave."

Marc nodded. "Tony has a soft spot for Andi Grace."

I shrugged. "He's special to me, too."

Marc squeezed my hand. "We probably should discuss what just happened so we can enjoy our dinner."

Hannah pulled hand sanitizer from her pretty brown leather purse and squirted some on her hands. "Danny must be worried about his recent arrests. He's still pushing me for a debate, and I feel like it's too soon."

Wade sat beside Hannah and placed his hands on the table. His muscular chest strained the buttons of his shirt. "If you agree to a debate, you better brace yourself for it to be ugly."

"What about his attack on Andi Grace? Can that prevent him for running for office?" Hannah stopped rubbing her hands together.

"The witnesses didn't mind saving her, but so far nobody's willing to make an official statement."

My pulse soared. "Are you kidding?"

"Afraid not." He ran a hand over his light beard. "Try not to worry about it. You've got a good attorney."

"Yes, I do." I squeezed Marc's hand. "What about the murder? Did your deputies pick up the cigarette butts on the beach Monday morning?"

"Yes, but we didn't get any hits with people in the system." Wade's calm expression encouraged me to ask more questions.

"Did you try to match it to the victim?"

"It's not like TV, where they run DNA in minutes. We're doing the best we can."

"What about Susan's flight? Can you find out if she arrived earlier than she claims? Kylie thinks Tabby's daughter has financial problems, and this afternoon she was plastered. It's possible she's trying to drink away her problems."

Wade rubbed his forehead. "Andi Grace, I'm handling the investigation."

"One last question." I didn't give him the opportunity to stop me. "Have you heard anything about counterfeit drugs in Heyward Beach?"

"It's a national problem."

Tony appeared with four Cokes and a platter of bruschetta and meatballs. "Enjoy. I'll be back with your dinner shortly. Manicotti casserole and supreme pizza."

Marc placed his arm along the back of my chair. "Let's enjoy our dinner and forget about Danny and the murder. Plenty of time to discuss all of that later."

I rested my head on his shoulder for a moment. "You're right. What should we discuss?"

Wade stuck a paper straw into his drink. "Basketball season is wrapping up. I suggest we discuss March Madness and what teams we're cheering for."

"I used to think you were a Blue Devils fan because your dog is named Duke." I reached for the little white plates in the center of the table and passed them around.

With his fork, Wade speared a meatball. "John Wayne was my hero growing up. It may be silly, but I used to watch his movies with my dad and grandfather. One of my favorite quotes is, 'The reason there are so many stupid people is because it's illegal to kill them.'" Wade chuckled. "It always makes me smile."

Hannah nudged his arm. "I remember him saying that in a movie. *Iwo Jima?*"

Wade wiped his mouth with the paper napkin. "Yeah. Most people don't know much about John Wayne."

"My favorite quote is, 'Courage is being scared to death and saddling up anyway.' His magnetism appealed to men and women." Hannah tossed her dark hair behind her shoulder.

"Yeah, but not many women our age have watched his movies." Wade ignored the food and studied Hannah.

"Daddy and I used to watch them when Mom went to her volunteer meetings." Her eyes sparkled.

"Cool." He nodded and turned back to eating another meatball.

Juliet deserved credit for matching Wade and Hannah together. She had a way with people like I did dogs. "Oh, Hannah. I may have a dog for you."

Marc laughed. "I hope you wanted a pet, because Andi Grace is known for finding homes for dogs in need. It's pointless trying to resist because she'll wear you down."

She lifted her hands palms up. "I don't need a dog right now because of the election."

Wade lifted his hand. "Listen to Marc. I've seen Andi Grace in action. Whatever dog she has in mind is going to become your new best friend."

Chapter Twenty-Three

STUFFED, THE FOUR of us walked, or limped, in my case, to the parking lot. I carried a little box with my leftover tiramisu. It was too delicious to waste, but I'd been too full to eat another bite.

A firetruck's siren broke the peacefulness of the evening. The red fire engine with its honking horn, sirens, and lights flashing flew past us and up Main Street toward the beach.

I shivered. "Do you think a rental home is on fire?"

"It's possible." Wade pulled out his phone. "Let me check."

Another siren blasted, and we turned to watch. A firetruck full of men dressed in their protective gear barreled by.

"This isn't good. There aren't a lot of homes in that direction." A plume of black smoke rose in the evening sky, blocking our view of the moon and stars. The island was small and the smoke came from the direction of my home. I gripped Marc's arm. "This is a nightmare."

Wade slid his phone into his jeans. "Andi Grace, they're heading to your street."

"Whose house is it?" All other sounds faded as I waited for Wade to respond. "Wade! Tell me it's not my house."

His gaze shot to Marc then back to me. "I'm sorry."

My legs weakened, and I slumped against Marc. "My home. Marc, give me your keys. I've got to see it."

Wade said, "The firemen won't let you get close."

A deputy's SUV and another firetruck sped by.

"It's my home, and I'm going. Even if I have to walk."

"Let's go then." Marc nodded, and we left Wade and Hannah standing on the sidewalk.

Wade caught up with us. "I'll be right behind you."

I hopped in Marc's truck and dialed Lacey Jane's number. *Please God, don't let her be in the house. Please keep my sister and Sunny safe. And Kylie too.* My prayer almost became a refrain. I repeated it over and over.

"She's not answering."

"Call Wade. See if he can track her down instead of coming to the house. Call Nate, too. Lacey Jane said they were going out."

"Right. And they were supposed to take Sunny with them." I dialed Wade's number.

"Andi Grace, we're right behind you."

"Wade, I can't get ahold of Lacey Jane. Can y'all find her? She may be with David. I hope she is. Oh, and Kylie should be with her. Make sure they're both safe. Please?"

"I'll find them. Hold on." After a muffled pause he came back on. "Hannah will call Nate and Juliet. We're on this. Once we track down the girls, we'll let you know."

"Thanks." I disconnected. My cold skin tingled.

Marc stopped at the barricade at the corner of my street. Sand Piper Way. It was a short street with older traditional beach homes. Nothing fancy, but this was where I lived.

A policewoman motioned for us to turn around.

Marc rolled down his window and explained the situation. It was my house and we wanted to make sure no people or pets were there. The woman spoke, then Marc turned to me. "She wants to see your driver's license."

I opened my purse, found it, and handed it to him without uttering a word. Motions. Meaningless motions.

Up ahead flames engulfed my beach cottage. Firefighters fought the out-of-control blaze.

I'd raised my siblings in the little beach cottage. I'd grieved the loss of my parents. Juliet had even lived with us there for a while. Sad memories. Happy memories. The place was my home.

Marc returned my license and parked on the side of the street. "She said we have to stay on this side of the safety zone."

I opened the door. The side mirror caught my reflection. Pretty clothes and a fancy hairdo. Had we turned off the curling iron? "How could I have been so careless?"

Marc came around his truck and stood in the grass beside me. "What?"

"I bet we forgot to turn off the curling iron. It's all my fault." I coughed. "My vanity destroyed my home." My eyes fixated on the destruction as the fire devoured the house. The image blurred, and I whimpered.

Marc held me to his side but didn't say a word.

"I'm so mad at myself. This didn't have to happen." I bolted away from him and headed to the house.

Firefighters sprayed water at the flames on both ends of my little home. How could one little curling iron cause so much utter damage so fast?

Marc caught up with me. "Andi Grace, you can't get any closer. Let the firemen do their job."

"What if Lacey Jane and Sunny are inside?" I didn't slow.

He rounded on me and placed his hands on my shoulders. "Listen. They were going out. They took Sunny. Maybe they're on the beach where you can't get good reception."

"Is that why Lacey Jane hasn't called me back?"

"I don't know, honey. Let's go search for her."

"What if she went out but decided not to take Sunny?" Another fire truck arrived.

Policemen moved the barricades, allowing the new group of fire-fighters to run past us and help extinguish the fire.

"Andi Grace, I don't know where they are." He bent his knees enough so we looked at each other eye-to-eye. "There are two things I know for sure. You won't survive if you try to enter that inferno." He pointed at my cottage.

"And?" My heart pounded hard against my ribs.

"We've not been gone long enough for a simple curling iron to have caused this blaze. I'm not a fire investigator, but this wasn't an accident."

My nose stung, and I coughed, strangling against the black smoke. "Why?"

"I'd say because you're on the right track to catching Tabby's killer."

In the past, I'd been scared or mad. Never had I experienced such fury as I did when Marc hypothesized Tabby's killer might have set my home on fire.

"I need my Suburban."

Marc shook his head. "It's too close to the fire. Where do you want to go? I'll drive you."

"If they won't let me in the house to search for the others, I need to drive around the island and go into town if need be. Standing here isn't accomplishing anything."

Flames shot out of my office window. People in the crowd screamed.

I pointed to it and moaned. "My dog walking calendar's in there and my notes on Tabby's murder. As well as the puzzle pages."

"I doubt this is a typical arson, but do you recognize anybody in the crowd?"

Neighbors stood watching the fire as if in a trance. A few friends from church gathered in a circle, held hands, and bowed their heads. Next to them was a familiar figure. "There's Susan. She smokes. Could she have started this fire with cigarettes and a lighter?"

He sighed. "Doubtful. Seems like the arsonist used something more flammable like kerosene or gas."

"Why is she here?" My legs shook.

"Tabby's house is on Dolphin Drive. It's only a few blocks away. Maybe she saw the fire and walked over to see what was going on. Do you still want to leave? The police are pushing people farther away from your house."

"I guess because of the intensity. It makes sense."

Marc slid his arm around my shoulders. "I'll take you to look for Lacey Jane."

We squeezed through the growing crowd. Thanks to the darkness of the night, nobody spotted me. Everybody's attention was on the structure that used to be my home.

An explosion shook the ground. The blast threw us to the sandy street. Glass pelted the ground around us. Metallic shrapnel flew through the air.

Marc covered my body with his and protected my head with his arms.

Screaming people ran past and over us.

Another blast rocked the air, and a huge rectangular sheet of steel landed a few feet away then skidded toward us.

"Move!" Still covering me, Marc rolled us away from the flying piece of metal. It skidded to a stop with a puff of sand dust.

I blinked and tried to make sense of what I saw. Big. Steel. The puzzle pieces fell into place. "It's the door to my Suburban."

Marc lifted me and raced to his truck.

I held on tight. Sand Piper Way had become a war zone. We were in real danger. Others bumped against us in their haste to escape the terror. Marc tightened his grip on me.

Soon we were cocooned in the safety of Marc's truck while others hurried past us. I sat in Marc's lap in the passenger seat. My entire body trembled. I struggled to get a full breath. "Why is this happening?" Tears streamed down my face. "Where's my sister?"

"Shh." Marc held me against his chest and stroked my back. "Keep the faith."

"Faith? How? This is a disaster of biblical proportions." I sobbed and struggled for air at the same time.

"Hold up. You're phone's vibrating."

I pulled away from his strength and reached into the pocket of my dirty black slacks. "It's Wade."

Marc pointed to the phone. "Aren't you going to answer?"

"What if he has bad news?" Could I handle any more disasters? My hands trembled, and I hesitated to answer.

"He might have something good to report."

Fear immobilized me. Good or bad, I couldn't seem to control my fingers enough to answer the call.

Chapter Twenty-Four

THE SUSPENSE prompted me to ignore the fear and answer Wade's call. "Hello."

"Andi Grace, I found them. We'll meet you at the pier." The sheriff's words came out low and matter-of-fact.

I licked my dry lips. "What about Sunny? Is she with you?"

"Yes. They're all safe." The big stern sheriff's voice wobbled a bit. "Hannah is comforting the girls, and Sunny's standing beside me."

Sweet relief poured through me, and I collapsed against Marc. "Thanks, Wade. We're coming." I disconnected the call. *Thank you, God.*

Marc's arms went around me. "Well?"

"Wade found all three of them. We have to go to the pier."

Marc kissed my temple before releasing me and jogging around the truck and sliding behind the wheel. He turned the truck around without hitting any of the remaining spectators, while I texted Nate and Juliet. I breathed in and out with slow, deliberate breaths. I wanted to appear calm and strong. It didn't take us long to reach the pier. The others stood by Wade's truck, silent and looking toward the smoke in the sky from my burning house. I swallowed back a lump. Nobody had been killed. We were all safe. That would become my mantra when I started to feel sorry for myself over the loss of my home. I would ignore the temptation to throw a pity party, and be thankful.

Lacey Jane and Sunny ran to me. Sunny leapt forward and placed her big paws on my shoulders and licked my face. I rubbed her back and buried my face into her neck. My sweet dog had seen me cry often after my parents died. She'd listened to my fears and joys. She was truly my best friend.

Lacey Jane shoved between me and my dog, crushing me against her. "I'm so glad you're safe." Her tears dampened my shirt.

I hugged her—I needed to put on a brave face. "Same here." I swallowed hard. "Thanks for taking Sunny with you."

My sister stepped back and gasped. "What if I hadn't brought her?" She covered her mouth with one hand.

"I can't think about it." Sunny had been with me almost thirteen years. She wouldn't live forever, but if she'd died in the fire...A wave of nausea hit me.

Sunny rubbed against my leg, and I dropped to the ground and hugged my faithful companion. "I wonder if I left the curling iron on."

Lacey Jane knelt beside me. "No. I packed it in my toiletry bag. We didn't use the oven or stove. You'd barely left with Marc before David arrived."

"Oh, baby girl. I'm not trying to blame you, and I'm relieved to hear the curling iron didn't cause the fire. I'd hate to think we lost our home because of a careless accident." My voice wobbled.

She touched my knee with trembling fingers. "What are you saying?"

"I think somebody set the fire." I stood and turned toward the ocean and breathed in fresh tangy air.

Wade joined us. "Glad to see you two together. What do you think started the fire?"

"What or who?" I glanced at him but kept trying to breathe in the fresh air. What I really wanted to do was stick my head in the ocean and wash out the fire's stench.

The sheriff stepped closer. "It doesn't surprise me you believe somebody intentionally set the fire. Why?"

"Oh, Wade, the puzzles. I was trying to solve Tabby's crossword puzzles at Daily Java on Tuesday morning. Danny, Erin, and Hannah all knew I had them with me. What if the killer was there and also saw me studying the books? They might have broken into my house tonight to get them. It's a good thing I made copies and gave you the originals."

"No, it isn't. If you'd turned the books over to us and let us solve the puzzles, nobody would've come after you or broken into your house."

My hands shook and the nausea returned. "You're right. I'm sorry, Wade."

Lacey Jane stood between the sheriff and me. "Don't you think she's suffering enough?"

Wade sighed and ran a hand over his face. "It's my turn to apologize."

I looked at him. "We're friends. Don't worry about it." Wade's comment was the least of my concerns. My house was burning to the ground. The Suburban was gone. It'd been like my second home and integral to my business. I'd loved that thing probably more than normal people would understand.

He held out his hand, and we shook. "Friends."

"Wade, we'll be over there if you need us." Lacey Jane linked arms with me, and we ambled over to the others.

Wade followed us to Marc's truck. "If you don't mind, I'll join you. Something might register in your memory, and I'd like to listen."

I nodded. "Sure."

Lacey Jane said, "What was the explosion?"

"The Suburban caught fire and blew up." I shared the details as I remembered. "Wade, Tabby's daughter was on my street watching the fire. There were also friends and neighbors."

"Noted." He leaned against the truck beside Hannah.

Marc pointed in the direction of my burning house. "The flames are going down. Wade, how long does it take to put out a fire?"

"They're all different. Let's wait here. One of my men will contact me when it's safe to check on it."

Safe? Would I ever feel safe again? In one evening, I'd lost my home and SUV. Most of my worldly belongings had been in the house. But my family was okay. Maybe it truly was time for me to walk away from solving Tabby's murder. "Hey, Marc?"

"Yeah?" He ran a hand along my arm.

"Can I sit in your truck? I need to think."

"Sure." He walked beside me and opened the door. "I know you need a place to stay. Griffin is living with me or else I'd offer to let you have the guest room. What about the plantation house?"

"It's a possibility. Lacey Jane's roommates are still away for spring break, so Kylie could move into the apartment with her for a few days. If the other girls don't mind, she might be allowed to stay longer."

"Does Nate have extra space?"

"His condo is small, and it's a mess." I tried to smile but couldn't hold it. "I know what you're thinking. I'm messy, but Nate takes it to a different level."

He raised his hands in surrender. "You don't have to explain it to me."

"Finding a place to sleep may be the least of my worries. I don't have a vehicle, clothes, food, books, or family pictures. I've lost it all, but I've got my family and Sunny." My voice cracked, and I swiped at tears leaking out of my eyes. "I need to be thankful, and I am. I only lost my stuff. It doesn't matter. It can be replaced. We're all safe." My new mantra had already been called upon to remind me of my blessings.

"True, but show yourself some mercy. Losing your home and belongings is a big deal. It's okay to grieve the loss. You're human."

Marc's words comforted me, and I sank back in the seat. "Kylie doesn't have a car either. She's borrowing Nate's old truck. How will I get to the dog walking appointments?" I sneezed then coughed.

"Rent a car for a few days. You can't solve all of your problems tonight. It'll take time." He rubbed my shoulder. "Take one step at a time. Maybe a shower and wearing clean clothes will help your outlook."

I pinched the bridge of my nose with shaky fingers. "I'm wearing the only clothes I own."

"Right. Sorry." Marc took a deep breath. "It's going to get better."

"You're right. You don't deserve my anger." I stared into the distance. No more shooting flames. "The smoke isn't as thick. Do you think we can go back?"

"It's doubtful. The fire investigator will wait until it's safe to go through the rubble before he searches for signs of criminal activity. After his investigation, and if it's safe, you can sift through the debris to see what survived."

I glanced at the dirty and torn top my sister had loaned me before my date. "All of my worldly possessions and the memories attached to them no longer exist. Poof."

"Wait a minute. You can control your memories. Maybe you have photos in a cloud. Maybe you don't. Either way, don't give the arsonist a bigger victory." He cradled my face in his hands. "You're a fighter, Andi Grace. Maybe the bravest person I know. Grieve then get back in the ring." He kissed the top of my head.

"Grieve first. That much I can do." Tears fell from my eyes, and Marc wiped them away one by one. Tomorrow would be soon enough to get back in the fight.

Chapter Twenty-Five

AFTER THE FIRE and explosion, Kylie, Lacey Jane, and I decided to stick together and spend the night at my sister's apartment. Safety in numbers might not be working for us, but at least we survived the fire. Lacey Jane's roommates planned to return Sunday which gave us two more days to figure out living arrangements.

I sent a text blast to all the contacts on my cell phone, asking my customers to meet me at Daily Java with spare keys. Every single person agreed without grumbling. To show my appreciation, I'd worked out a system with Erin to give each of my clients a cup of coffee for the inconvenience. Kylie and I scrambled to keep the new keys organized, and when we completed our task went our separate ways.

Dressed in my sister's jeans, sea turtle T-shirt, underthings, and shoes and socks, I stood in front of my demolished house late Friday morning, listening to my insurance man. George Long had been a friend of my dad's, and he treated me like a daughter. Mr. Long had rented a Highlander for me to drive until the insurance cut me a check to replace the Suburban.

My mind zoomed in and out of the conversation. Practical versus emotional. I needed to listen to what he said, but threatening tears told me the grieving process wasn't over.

When our meeting ended, I headed to meet Kylie at Tabby's house.

I pulled onto Dolphin Drive and parked the Highlander along the curb in front of Tabby's beach cottage. The blue Mercedes and Nate's old truck filled the driveway. I took deep breaths and swiped at tears pooling.

Kylie and Sunny walked toward me. I checked my appearance in the mirror. Red nose and bloodshot eyes wouldn't fool anybody.

Kylie opened my door. "Are you sure this is a good idea?"

"No." My feet touched the street with only a tinge of pain, and I bent over to love on Sunny. "We can drive away now if you're scared. I wouldn't blame you."

She laced her fingers and placed them over her stomach. "If Susan killed her mother, I want to help prove it. If she's innocent, we'll be safe."

"Sounds like you're in."

"All in." She straightened her shoulders. "Where are your crutches?"

"I don't need them anymore." I shut the door.

"Where'd you get the new wheels?"

"My insurance man rented this for me. The thing has so much technology it'll take getting used to. My Suburban was old and dependable. This Highlander is so nice, I'm afraid to get it dirty."

Kylie laughed. "You can't live at the beach without sand, dust, and salt water. It's going to get dirty."

"True." We put my German shepherd in the back of Nate's truck. I slipped her a dog bone from Kylie's stash in the cab. Sunny curled up on an old blanket in a shady corner of the truck and chewed on the bone.

Kylie and I walked to the front door of the white house, and I reached for her arm. "It's not too late to back out."

She shrugged away from me and pressed the doorbell. "I'm doing this for Tabby."

Susan opened the door barefoot but wearing black slacks, a white blouse, and a red scarf. "Hi. How are you two? Come in and I'll get you something to drink. I'm sorry about the fire. Are you okay?"

I'd never seen the woman flustered. "We're fine."

We entered the house and followed Susan to the open kitchen. A white palette with features and appliances to make a professional cook jealous. The pinewood floors added warmth. While I liked more color, the room had a pleasant atmosphere.

"Would you like water or coffee?"

"There's no need to fix coffee." There wasn't a crumb to be seen on the counters.

Susan pulled expensive bottles of water from the large refrigerator and passed one to each of us. "I was at the fire until the explosion. Did the fire department save anything?"

"I'm afraid not. It's completely gone." I twisted off the lid and took a gulp of water. I'd been thirsty since the fire. "Wow, this is the most delicious water I've ever tasted."

"It's my favorite brand, but I'm not one to beat around the bush. Have a seat at the table and tell me why you're here."

I took the closest chair, Susan sat at the head of the table, and Kylie chose the seat across from me. "Why were you at the fire?"

She blinked once. "I heard the sirens and decided to follow them. Call it curiosity or boredom. Either way, I was there."

"Did you see anything suspicious?"

"Such as?" Her perfect eyebrows rose, placing more emphasis on her blue eyes. Mascara, eye shadow, and liner magnified the beauty.

"A spectator acting unusual? Maybe you heard a weird comment? I'd like it if the cops arrested the culprit and put him, or her, away for a long time."

"I didn't observe anything suspicious." Susan tapped a manicured finger on the table. "The cops haven't released Mother's body yet, and I've got meetings in Dallas on Monday. I need to get home."

Kylie said, "If your offer to house-sit is still open, I'd like to accept. I can also handle the cremation with the funeral home and save Tabby's ashes for when you return to Heyward Beach."

"Great. You're hired. Is there anything else?" Susan smiled and looked from Kylie to me.

"Yes." My palms grew damp, and I took another sip of the refreshing drink. "Feel free to say no. Honestly, you have no reason to agree." I shook my head and started to push from the table. "You know what, never mind."

"Andi Grace, I find it best to state what you need. Often the answer is yes. I'm not sure what I can do for you, but ask."

"Straightforward. Nice. Since I'm currently without a house—"

She sat taller and her eyes sparkled. "You want to buy my mother's house? Yes. We can avoid using a real estate agent and save money. Let me show you around. I'll include the furnishings. You lost yours, and I don't need Mother's. It's perfect."

I threw up my hands. "No, wait. I can't afford anything until the insurance pays me." Even then I doubted I could afford Tabby's house.

"Then what did you want to ask me?"

"I wondered if I could stay here with Kylie until the house sells."

"Of course. Spend a few weeks here and get a feel for the place. I won't list it yet. If you decide you like it here, make me an offer. Lowball me even. It'll be worth it not to have the hassle of trying to sell this place." She brushed back a strand of hair. "You two can move in tonight. I'll book a flight back to Texas for Sunday. That'll give me today and tomorrow to finish going through Mother's belongings and convince you to buy this place." She winked.

"The location is perfect. Close to the creek and a very short walk to the beach. As much as I'd like to make you an offer, it's too expensive."

I stopped myself before dreaming about living here.

"You won't know unless you try." Susan stood. "I need to make a few calls. Kylie, I haven't disturbed your room. Andi Grace, take the other guest room for now. The master will be ready for you when I leave. I'll schedule a cleaning lady."

Susan didn't give the impression money was a problem for her. If she planned to fly out on Sunday, I didn't have much time to investigate her. Guilty or innocent.

"Thanks, Susan. Like you said, I lost everything in the fire, which means I need to buy some clothes."

Susan opened a kitchen drawer and retrieved a key ring. "Here's a key for you. I'm not sure why Mother had so many spares. There's an alarm system, and the codes are attached." She held up a small plastic attachment hanging on the needlepoint keychain.

"Thanks. We're meeting my sister for lunch. Can I bring you anything?"

"No, thank you. If I'm not here when you return, make yourself at home. Kylie, what are your plans today?"

Her eyes widened. "I'm working for Andi Grace. Is there something you need me to do when I get off work?"

"Do you have time to take these bags of clothes to a charity?" She pointed to six white bags stuffed full.

"Sure."

Kudos to Susan for donating to charity. "Kylie, I can help you carry them to the truck."

"Truck?" Susan's voice rose. "Did you buy a truck?"

Kylie twirled her hair around a finger. "No. It belongs to Andi Grace's brother. He's loaning it to me for now."

"I put a rush on the men at the dealership. You shouldn't need the truck after tomorrow."

Kylie stilled. "Why are you helping me?"

"You were special to my mother. Goodness gracious, you agreed to move to South Carolina and live with her. Your actions took a huge burden off me, and you should be rewarded." Susan tilted her head. "I never worried about her welfare knowing you were with her."

Kylie's face turned red. "Susan, I can't thank you enough."

"You earned it, but you're welcome. I'll see you two later. I need to visit the funeral home director about the cremation." Susan left us gawking in her wake.

I smiled. "Let's take the bags and grab some lunch. Daily Java?"

"That'll be a treat for sure." Kylie picked up four bags, leaving two for me. "You know these will stay cleaner in your Highlander. What if we put them in the back?"

Susan popped back into the house. "Do either of you wear size nine shoes?"

Kylie shook her head. "I'm a seven."

"I do."

"Fine. I'll let your sort through Mother's shoes in the closet. Take what you like and give the rest to charity. You can also go through her clothes. She might have a few respectable tops for you to wear. Your dogs probably don't require you to dress up."

Wham. Despite the kind offer, her words and the tone slammed my career. I couldn't figure Susan out, and her neutral expression didn't help. I needed clothes, and Susan was offering some. Simple as that.

"Thanks, Susan. It's nice of you to offer. I'll look through them before donating them to the women's shelter."

Kylie and I lugged the bags to the guest room where I'd stay.

Kylie whispered, "Tabby has nice blouses and some cute T-shirts. I bet you'll find something you like. Can you believe how nice Susan is being? She plans to repair the Jetta for me."

"It's very generous. Let's get out of here, and I'll go through the shoes and clothes later." We told Susan bye and didn't say another word until we reached the driveway. "Kylie, do you have a problem with Susan?"

She shrugged. "I saw a lot of arguments between Susan and Tabby. Susan didn't make it easy for Tabby at first. Once I agreed to come here, Susan chilled out. Still, I've seen Susan's mean streak. If you know what I mean."

"I know she's a successful business woman, and I see how she can be intimidating."

"She's used to getting her own way." Kylie glanced at her phone. "Hey, why don't you have lunch with Marc? Lacey Jane needs my help with a project."

"Really? What kind of project?" I walked to the truck and lowered the gate. Sunny leapt to the ground and walked to my side.

"Just a little something. I'll catch up with you later." She drove off in Nate's truck before I could question her more.

I'd already removed Kylie from my suspect list, but she was being secretive for a reason. I just needed to figure out what she was up to. First, I'd ask Marc to have lunch with Sunny and me.

Chapter Twenty-Six

"WELL, KYLIE'S keeping a secret. What do you think it is?"

Sunny and I got into the nice SUV with the new-car smell, and I texted Marc and asked about his lunch plans. He was tied up in court, so I took Sunny to the pier and bought each of us a hot dog at the little restaurant frequented by the fishermen. I finished my lunch and enjoyed my Coke. Sunny snoozed at my feet. The sun shone bright and warmed me down to my bones. An illogical sense of peace flowed over me.

Leroy walked up to the bench where I sat watching seagulls fly overhead. "Andi Grace, I've been looking for you. I was real sorry to hear about your house fire." He swayed back and forth.

"Thanks, Leroy. How are you?"

"I've got something to tell you, but not here. Are you up to a walk?"

"Sure." I attached Sunny's leash, and we followed Leroy to the beach. High tide didn't give us a lot of room to spread out, but the water was flat and quiet, making conversation easy. "What's up?"

"I believe Tabby may have been on to something." He rubbed his freckled hands against each other with a scratchy dry-skin sound.

I reached for his arm. "What?"

"Keep walking, real casual like. We don't want to look suspicious." He kept his focus straight ahead.

One foot in front of the other, I ignored the flicker of pain in my ankle and allowed Leroy to lead the conversation when he was comfortable.

We passed the first beach groin before he spoke again. "Last night I saw a shrimp boat in the water, just like Tabby mentioned. I was fishing from the pier and didn't put much thought to it. When your fire started, the others left me all alone. I don't believe they were being nosy, mind you. They left to see if somebody needed help. I'm an old man, not much good if you're in a crisis."

"That's not true. You rescued Gus. You're a hero to him." I paused a moment for Sunny to relieve herself.

"Thanks, but we're getting off track. I didn't leave with the others.

Instead, I stayed at the pier, watching the shrimp boat. A jet ski appeared out of nowhere and stopped right next to the vessel. If I'd had my binoculars, I'd know more. Something happened, though. I'm sure of it. The interaction took no more than five minutes, and the jet ski sped off, heading south. It came from the north end of the island. Not sure if it came from the creek or all the way down from one of the other islands. The water wasn't too rough, so either direction was possible."

"Leroy, this is huge." I resisted the urge to do a backflip.

"Keep walking. We don't need to get ourselves killed, like Tabby."

My heart picked up its tempo. "Do you think the fire was a distraction? If law enforcement officers were at the fire, there wouldn't be anyone around to see the crime on the water. Whatever the crime is. Smuggling?"

Leroy shrugged. "It's possible, but I thought most drug smuggling happened in California and Texas."

"I think all coastal states are affected."

Sunny looked behind us and barked.

Two runners approached.

I tightened my grip on the leash. "I need to go back. My ankle's throbbing." I raised my voice loud enough for the runners to hear as they came up then passed by us on the narrow stretch of beach. Both men wore athletic shorts and masculine tank tops.

"Sure, sure." Leroy reached for my elbow as we turned. "Do you need to lean on me?"

"I just don't want to overdo it." I continued speaking in a loud voice.

"How's Gus?" Leroy held on to my elbow.

"He's eating and gets along well with the other dogs. Sometimes strays don't have social skills, but Gus does fine in that area. It makes me think he lived in a home at one time. We've put out feelers to find his owners."

The men passed us again. One turned and smirked at me but didn't slow his pace.

Danny Nichols.

What was he doing? Was he even sober enough to run? Of course, I didn't know where he'd started from. Maybe it was all for show. But why? And who was the other guy?

"Do you know that fellow?"

"I'm afraid so." Eating the hot dog might not have been a good decision the way my stomach rumbled.

Leroy scowled. "He's up to no good."

"How do you know?" I believed Leroy but was curious to hear his logic.

A wave washed up and splashed my borrowed jeans. The cool salt water hit my tender skin, and I shivered.

Sunny leapt away and barked.

"This isn't the first time I've seen him around." He removed his fishing hat and scratched his bald, freckled head. "I'll keep a watch on him."

"No, Leroy. Danny is dangerous. He attacked me the other day. That's how I hurt my ankle."

"I'm aware."

We crossed the thicker, dryer sand and reached the parking lot.

"Be careful, Leroy."

"You too, Andi Grace."

I held my hand out. "Can I add myself to your list of contacts?"

Leroy stood taller and gave me his cell phone. "Absolutely."

It didn't take long to add my information and return the phone. "See you later."

"Yes, ma'am." He turned away and entered the building connected to the pier, and I headed to the Highlander.

Danny stood between me and the vehicle. He still wore the shorts but had added a sweatshirt. "I thought you might come this way. We need to talk."

Sunny growled, and I backed away. The last thing I needed was another confrontation with Danny.

Chapter Twenty-Seven

I BACKED TOWARD the building's entrance while pulling my phone out of my pocket.

Danny smiled like he hadn't attacked me or come to my home trying to break down the door. "I'm sorry about what happened the other day."

Sunny's growl deepened.

"You attacked me, Danny."

He held his hands out toward my dog. "Easy there, girl."

While Danny's attention zeroed in on my German shepherd, I tapped the circle on my phone with my free hand and glanced down to find Marc's number. One quick swipe, and the phone dialed him.

Sunny stood between Danny and me and barked.

"Call her off, Andi Grace."

"She's protecting me from you." My hands shook.

"You make it sound so ugly." Danny took a giant step forward. "In reality, it's a simple misunderstanding. I need you to drop the charges, sweetheart."

Sweetheart? Gag! "Stay away from us."

Sunny's tail snapped up. She spread her legs wide apart. With her chest puffed out and ears pointed to the sky, she emitted a low growl. Her front teeth bared.

"Danny, if you take another step toward me, Sunny will attack you. She's protective of me and doesn't know you." If Marc could hear me, or if I was recorded on his voicemail, I wanted it to be clear who did it. I'd repeat Danny's name as often as I could.

"Drop the charges, Andi Grace. Tell the sheriff it's a misunderstanding." He glared at me but kept his distance from my protective dog.

"Danny, there were witnesses."

"Yeah, but nobody is willing to testify." His smug grin shook me.

"Did you threaten them? Bribe them? How'd you get them to back off?"

"You could say they saw the light. Being a witness for you wasn't beneficial for any of them. Hence, you don't have a single person who'll testify."

He was going to get away with attacking me. I needed to stall him. Keep him talking. "Danny, did you set my house on fire?"

"You're losing your mind if you're going to accuse me of attacking you *and* setting fire to your house. You can't prove either one." His eyes dipped down to Sunny, as if gauging the danger.

Chills sprinted up my spine. "You did set the fire."

"Prove it." He pointed at me.

"Danny, you can't get away with hurting people and destroying their property. The cops will figure it out."

His eyes narrowed. "Are you wearing a wire? Why do you keep saying my name?"

"No wire, and thanks to you, I'm not even wearing my own clothes."

He lunged for me and grabbed the neck of the sea turtle T-shirt, ripping the seams.

Sunny leapt at Danny with a ferocious bark and sank her teeth into his arm.

I swung at his head with my fist and dropped the cell phone. I screamed. "Help!" People on the pier wouldn't be able to see me, but they might hear me yell. Or maybe a person at the snack bar inside the building would spot us. "Help!"

"Get your dog off me!" Danny released my shirt and focused his attack on Sunny. He tried to pull his arm out of Sunny's mouth, but she didn't loosen her grip.

"Leave my dog alone." I slapped Danny's back.

Three men ran toward us from the pier, hollering. Leroy and two others. The tallest and possibly youngest man grabbed Danny by the hood of his sweatshirt.

I wasn't alone. "Sunny, release."

Sunny growled but let go of Danny.

Sirens assured me we'd all be safe from Danny. I knelt and hugged my German shepherd. "Good girl. I'm so proud of you."

Leroy's shadow covered us. "Did he hurt you, Andi Grace?"

Each of the other men held tight to Danny's arms. One wore a marine ball cap and the other wore a Vietnam Veteran cap. They didn't appear to be afraid of him, and I doubted he could pay them off. At least I hoped they wouldn't cave in to the despicable man.

"Leroy, I couldn't be any better. Thank you for coming to my rescue."

Danny struggled to break free from his captors, but they held firm.

Leroy reached for my phone and passed it to me. "Those guys are the real heroes."

"All three of you are my heroes." Tears welled in my eyes, and my nose burned.

In no time, the police arrived and hauled Danny away. Again. It was too bad we hadn't found proof he set the fire. I called Wade and begged him to come question me because Kylie kept insisting we couldn't trust at least one of the local cops. Today's attack hadn't been as bad as the first time, but I wanted to be taken seriously. I also wanted the names of the men who'd left their fishing gear on the pier to help me.

The Navy man walked over to me. "Andi Grace, it's me. Frank Hoffman."

I hugged the man who enjoyed working on his yard and had assisted me when I'd helped the cops solve Heyward Beach's last murder. "Of course I remember you. Thanks so much for your help today. I didn't know you fished."

He shrugged. "You made me realize I need more friends. It's not going to happen working alone in my yard, so I took up fishing. Looks like I made two friends today."

"Why haven't you come help me at Stay and Play?"

He shrugged. "I didn't want to be a burden."

"Never. You're always welcome to visit." His response told me I needed to be intentional about inviting him to help. "Frank, I know Leroy, but who's the marine?"

"He's new to the area. Come on over, and I'll introduce you." He signaled for me to follow him.

I led Sunny to a bench where the marine sat with perfect posture. He stood when we reached him.

Frank said, "Andi Grace, I'd like you to meet Isaac Gage."

I gripped his hand tight. "Thank you so much, Mr. Gage." My gaze shifted to the insignia on his ball cap. The man was a marine. The truck who hit Lacey Jane and Kylie had a Semper Fi bumper sticker. "Did you by any chance have your truck stolen earlier this week?"

His head jerked back. "How'd you know?"

"The thief T-boned my sister. Seems like we're destined to meet through a crime."

The color drained from his tanned face. "Lacey Jane Scott is your sister? Or are you related to the other girl?"

"I'm Lacey Jane's older sister. Did you meet her through the accident?" She hadn't mentioned the truck owner to me, but it'd been a crazy week. Anything was possible.

"No. The sheriff told me her name. How is she?"

A bit shorter than six feet tall, trim and fit like you'd expect a marine to be, but I kept staring at his eyes. They looked vaguely familiar. "She's fine."

"Good. I felt terrible about the incident." His posture relaxed and the intensity of his brown eyes lessened.

"Mr. Gage, you were also a victim. We don't hold you responsible." Interesting he blamed himself. "That man who attacked me also assaulted me earlier this week and was arrested. The witnesses declined to testify in a trial against him. Your hat makes me think you're a marine. Honor and courage are basic concepts to the Marine Corps. Will you testify for me? Against Danny Nichols?"

"You can count on me." His complexion returned to a normal color.

Wade pulled into the parking lot followed by Lacey Jane, who screeched to a stop, taking up three spaces, and ran to where we stood.

My sister threw her arms around me. "Andi Grace, what am I going to do with you? David called and said you'd been attacked again."

Mr. Gage remained close without hovering.

I held tight to my sister for a moment but Sunny tugged on the leash, forcing me to release Lacey Jane from our hug.

Frank held out his hand. "I'll take Sunny for a calm walk. Give you time to catch your breath."

"Thank you." I smiled at my friend. I refused to let us drift apart again. I'd do better.

Sunny trotted off with Frank, showing me she not only trusted the older gentleman but didn't fear Mr. Gage.

"Lacey Jane, this is Isaac Gage. He's one of my rescuers." I waved my hand toward the man. He was a stranger, but he'd come to my rescue. "Mr. Gage, this is my sister."

The marine closed the gap between us and shook hands with my sister. The man's eyes looked so much like Lacey Jane's it took my breath away. The shape of their noses was similar. I dropped my eyes to their hands. I had my dad's hands. My sister's hands and toes weren't like any of ours, but her hands favored this stranger's.

I stumbled to the bench.

Lacey Jane and the marine gazed into each other's eyes, and I knew. They were connected. But how?

Did they recognize the similarities? How did they feel? Were they oblivious, or could I be imagining things? Stress affected people in different ways. Maybe I was losing my mind like Danny had suggested. How could Lacey Jane and the marine be related to each other if I wasn't in the mix?

I was the oldest child. Nobody alive in our family had memories of my birth. Had I been adopted? There were lots of stories of couples thinking they were infertile, but after they adopted a child, they were able to conceive. That must be what had happened. No. Wait. I wasn't the person who looked different.

Lacey Jane was the most different, but I remembered my mom being pregnant with both of my siblings. What was going on?

I counted to ten in French to calm myself then tried to rein my thoughts into some semblance of order.

When Nate and I were young, a few times my mother had taken off at night after bedtime. I was old enough to remember, but I'd never been sure where she went.

Other times she'd gone away to artist retreats. Mom and Dad had argued often during those days.

Pieces of the puzzle that were my mother fell into place. Arguments, late nights, Dad's smile not reaching his eyes, sadness, her weekends away, then marriage counseling.

Mom seemed to be the problem. Dad had always taken care of us nights and weekends. He'd often been the one to give us breakfast and get us ready for school while Mom slept. My mouth grew dry. I didn't want to believe it was possible, but there was only one logical conclusion.

My mother had an affair.

Chills covered my arms. If it'd been a local man, the entire town would've talked about it. Somehow, she'd met Isaac Gage. They had an affair, and Mom must've gotten pregnant. Two questions plagued me. Had my dad known? The bigger question was, did Lacey Jane and Isaac Gage realize there was something bigger happening than two strangers randomly meeting?

Chapter Twenty-Eight

WADE AND OFFICER Ian Patterson questioned each of us. Before it was my turn, Marc arrived with a squeal of his truck tires. Across the parking lot his gaze connected with mine, and he stopped the truck in the first available space. He leapt out, leaving the door wide open and the keys in the ignition, if the dinging alert was any indication.

His presence soothed my nerves, and I hobbled over to him. "You came."

"Girl, you're going to give me a heart attack one of these days."

"Sorry." I hugged him hard. "I guess it's a good thing we're eating healthy foods and exercising."

"Very funny." He kissed the top of my head.

I loosened my hold on him. "I think you left your truck running."

"Well, I'll be." He jogged to the truck and removed his keys.

We ended up sitting on the beach where I'd eaten the hot dog earlier. It seemed like a lifetime ago instead of probably an hour. "Marc, thanks for coming. I called you, but you didn't answer."

"I'm so sorry. I about died when I listened to your message, but you did a great job letting me know what was happening. We'll let Wade listen to it." Marc leaned close and kissed me full on the mouth, in front of anybody who wanted to watch.

Oh, baby. My heart raced, and I squeezed closer to him.

"Andi Grace. Marc. Break it up." Lacey Jane tapped both of us on the shoulders, bringing the glorious kiss to an end. "Officer Patterson called your name."

Marc held my face. "Are you okay?"

"Much better now. Will you go with me?"

"You bet." We walked to Wade's official truck, and Marc shook hands with the sheriff and the local cop.

Officer Patterson took the lead. "Ms. Scott, tell us what happened between you and Dan Nichols."

"Danny was waiting for me in the parking lot here. He claimed he only wanted to talk to me, but if it hadn't been for Sunny, I probably wouldn't be standing here with y'all right now."

"Dan said your dog attacked him. Unprovoked."

I crossed my arms. "Sunny would never do such a thing. Danny grabbed me by the neck of my shirt so hard it ripped." I pointed to the tear in the T-shirt. "In fact, it's not even my shirt. It's borrowed. My dog protected me."

Wade held up his hands. "Start from the beginning. We won't interrupt you."

I explained in detail what had happened. "You can ask the men who left the pier to help me. There was Leroy Peck, Frank Hoffman, and Isaac Gage. They'll tell you the truth."

Officer Patterson frowned. "We'll question them, but I can't promise they'll testify in court."

I set my hands on my hips. "Why wouldn't they?" I'd been tricked once by this kind of behavior. It wouldn't happen twice. I was prepared if the cop or Danny tried to talk a witness out of testifying.

"You never know what'll happen." His lips flattened, and I couldn't read the expression in his eyes behind the dark sunglasses.

I believed all three men were full of integrity, and I wouldn't doubt them. "Have you discovered who set my house on fire?"

"The fire department is leading the investigation. I expect we'll get word from them today." Officer Patterson's tone didn't instill much hope.

I stared at the police officer. Had he been at the fire? I'd seen him around town, but I didn't really know him. Kinda standoffish, if you asked me. I angled toward Wade. "I asked Danny if he set the fire, and he didn't deny it. You can also check Marc's voice mail. I called him for help and left a message of our entire conversation."

"It's true. Here, have a listen." Marc mashed the appropriate buttons and held his phone out. The conversation between Danny and me played.

The four of us gathered around and leaned close to listen. When it ended, Officer Patterson didn't look as cocky as before.

"That should convince you that Sunny's attack was provoked. You also heard me ask about the fire. I'd appreciate it if you'd consider the possibility that Danny is the arsonist."

The officer stuffed his little notepad into his shirt pocket. "He didn't admit anything."

Frustration set in, but I didn't want to say something I'd regret. "Am I free to leave? I've got a busy day."

Wade smiled. "You're free to go. I may have a few more questions later."

Officer Patterson swung toward the sheriff. "Like what kind of questions?"

"You never know." Wade imitated the cop without cracking a smile. "Who's next on your list, Ian?"

I walked away with Marc at my side. "What do you think? Is Patterson a good guy or corrupt cop?"

"Time will tell. Have you decided where you're going to live?"

I stopped at the Highlander and patted the hood. "These are my new wheels for now. My insurance man rented this sweet ride until I get their check, and I'm going to live in Tabby's house with Kylie until Susan sells it."

"That may not be long enough to rebuild." Marc pinched his lower lip between his thumb and finger.

"You're not going to believe this, but Susan wants me to buy the place." Buying Tabby's house would simplify my life, and it was awesome. Still, I couldn't let myself get excited just yet.

"Can you afford it? It's closer to the water than your place, which makes me think it's more expensive."

"I guess we'll find out. It's been a whirlwind day."

"Sounds like it." He wrapped me in his arms.

"Thanks again for coming." His embrace warmed me. "Oh, I almost forgot. I've got somebody for you to meet. Isaac Gage. The marine."

"The guy who had his truck stolen?" Marc pulled back just enough to look at me but also keep me in his arms.

"Exactly. I can't wait to get your impression of the man." I bit my lower lip. "He's one of the men who came to my rescue."

"Do you think he killed Tabby?" Marc ran a hand over his face. "Or was he driving the truck when it hit Lacey Jane?"

I shook my head. "It might be bigger than a murder. Judge for yourself." I clasped Marc's hand and led him to Mr. Gage then tapped the older man on the shoulder. "Mr. Gage, I'd like you to meet Marc Williams."

His hand shot out to shake with Marc. "Isaac Gage. My friends call me Ike."

A slow easy grin spread across Marc's face. "Nice to meet ya, Ike. Seems like you picked a bad week to visit Heyward Beach. We're usually a quiet coastal community."

"I've heard a rumor to that effect, but my experience has been different." Ike clasped his hands behind his back. "First my truck was stolen, then Ms. Scott was attacked. But I consider it a blessing to have been here. Do you two know Officer Patterson very well?"

I shook my head. "He's not a local. He's only lived here the last couple of years. Why?"

Mr. Gage inched closer and crossed his arms. "The young man gave me numerous reasons not to give him my statement. Financial issues for me, waste of time, and my safety were the main three. He basically did everything but refuse to take my statement."

Marc pulled out his cell phone. "If you don't mind, I'm taking notes."

Ike grinned and pulled out his phone. "I didn't want to chance anything to memory, so I took my own notes. I can text them to you."

"Have you seen my sister?"

He pointed. "She's over there speaking to one of the deputies."

"Okay." The feeling he and Lacey Jane were related grew stronger. "Mr. Gage, did you ever live in Heyward Beach? You seem familiar to me, but I can't figure it out."

"Please, call me Ike. I've been to Myrtle Beach a few times but never stopped here. It's been over twenty years since I've been in the area."

"Why now?"

He laughed. "You ask a lot of questions. Are you a reporter?"

"I'm a dog walker with curiosity issues." My face grew warm.

Marc elbowed me. "She's also helped solve a couple of murders. Trust me, it's easier to just answer her questions. She'll find out anyway."

His eyes twinkled. "I'm retired, and my wife died in January after a lengthy battle with lung cancer. I decided it was time for a change, and here I am." He gazed across the parking lot toward Lacey Jane.

His story touched my heart. "I'm sorry about that. Do you have children?"

"My wife was an actress, and we never got around to starting a family. I've got a brother in Kentucky."

Lacey Jane and David strolled across the parking lot and joined us. My sister introduced David to Ike.

I nudged Marc and widened my eyes. Did he see what I saw? Was I so desperate for a parent I was imagining a connection between Ike and Lacey Jane? Of course, it wouldn't make him my parent, but Lacey Jane would be in luck if my suspicions were true.

Marc tilted his head. "Excuse me, I need to speak to David for a minute."

The two stepped far enough away I was prevented from hearing what they said, so I watched Ike and Lacey Jane interact. He asked for a recommendation on coffee shops.

Her expression grew somber. "Daily Java is my favorite. I used to work there."

"Oh, I've been there. In Beaufort I'm used to lots of options, but this is a small town. I can get used to going to the same coffee shop. Where do you work now?" His face remained neutral, probably a trick he learned in the military. Did he suspect Lacey Jane was his daughter? Had he come to Heyward Beach intentionally to find her, or was this some big coincidence?

"I work as a law clerk for Marc. I'm also in school taking paralegal classes."

"Why not become a lawyer? You seem intelligent." He jingled change in his pockets.

"I might one day, but it's expensive. Becoming a paralegal gives me the opportunity to make more money and save up for college."

I wanted to help pay for her education and had secretly been trying to find a way. Nate was happy with his landscaping business. I'd settled into the dog walking business in order to have a flexible schedule while raising Nate and Lacey Jane after our parents died. Nate had never shown much interest in attending college, but he'd taken online business classes. Lacey Jane and I had dreamed of going to college. I was getting closer to making the plantation profitable and hoped to help send my sister to college.

Ike said, "I guess you've applied for scholarships."

Lacey Jane cleared her throat. "Don't you think I'm too old for them?"

He shook his head. "No, I don't. You should meet with a college planner. They can help you pick the best school for your major and assist you in finding scholarships you qualify for. My niece is a college planner." He pulled a business card from his wallet and passed it to my sister. "If you're interested, give me a call. I can have her contact you."

In ordinary circumstances, I'd be suspicious of Ike's intentions. Instead, I became more and more convinced Ike and Lacey Jane were related.

Chapter Twenty-Nine

LACEY JANE FOLLOWED me to Tabby's house, and Kylie handled the afternoon dog walking appointments. My ankle throbbed, so I plopped down on the light blue couch. Sunny got comfortable at my side, and I didn't have the energy to make her stay on the floor. Hadn't Susan told me to make myself at home?

I heard the click of her shoes on the wood steps, then Susan appeared, dressed like she was at her executive job in Dallas. "How was your day?"

I ran my hand over Sunny's back. "It was fine. Do you mind my dog?"

"No. This will soon be your home. Act like it." She smiled.

Too tired to object, I nodded. "My sister will be here soon. I hope we don't disturb you."

Susan shook her finger at me. "Your house."

Lacey Jane entered with numerous shopping bags. "I bought you some new clothes. To be honest, some are from the new consignment store, but they'll be new to you."

"Appropriate for dog walking? I don't need anything fancy."

Sunny shifted and dropped her head into my lap.

"You've got a boyfriend. It's time to up your wardrobe." Lacey Jane glanced at Susan. "Don't you agree?"

Well-balanced eyebrows rose over Susan's expertly made-up eyes. "Definitely. What you wear is a language. The right clothes will show how much you care. If you're dating a handsome man, dress like it."

"I don't really do fashion." At the sight of my sister's crest-fallen face, I relented. "Show me what you bought. Maybe it's time to find my style since I have nothing to wear. Literally."

"That's the truth." Lacey Jane proceeded to pull out shorts, pants, skirts, T-shirts, and nicer tops. She showed me ways to mix and match to make my wardrobe seem bigger. "I stuck with blues because they emphasize your eyes and complement your complexion."

Susan had watched the entire demonstration. "Lacey Jane, you have a talent for fashion and possibly marketing. Nice presentation."

"Thank you, Susan." My sister beamed.

Susan glanced at her watch. "I'll be in the office. I've got a conference call in five minutes." She pulled a water bottle from the refrigerator on her way to Tabby's office connected to the back of the kitchen.

I liked the open floor plan of Tabby's house This area was big, yet somehow cozy. I patted the cushion next to me. "Have a seat. We need to talk."

"Let me guess. Ike Gage?" She settled in next to me, and Sunny hopped off the couch and wandered to the kitchen.

"Yes. What do you think of him?" I twisted around to face her easier.

"He's charming. I like him." Her smile dimmed. "But not in a creepy way. You know I'm interested in David."

"Yuck and yes. Ike's old enough to be your father." I watched for a reaction.

She blinked rapidly. "What are you trying to say? I've got a dad, and Peter treated me like an uncle. Both are gone, and I don't want to care about anybody else in the same way. It's not meant for me to have a father figure in my life, and I made my peace with the issue when Peter died."

"I understand, but how does Ike make you feel?"

Her brown eyes grew wide. Eyes like Ike's, not my dad. "Uh, you're kinda freaking me out right now."

"Humor me for a minute. I'm trying to get a feel for everybody we've crossed paths with the last few days." I definitely needed to figure out Ike Gage, maybe more than I needed to solve Tabby's murder.

Lacey Jane sank into the couch cushions and closed her eyes. "He makes me feel safe. Protected. And it's so weird, but I feel cherished. Maybe because he was a marine and it's his job to protect Americans."

Goose bumps covered my body. "This might not be the best time to deal with Ike, but I can't drop the issue." I licked my lips. "If I can give you the opportunity for stronger family ties, I need to. I'm your sister, but what if you have more family in the world we don't know about?"

She reached for a throw pillow and held it against her stomach. "Are you suggesting we go to one of those genealogy sites that connects you with people on your family tree? We'd need to research and find one that's legit."

I swallowed hard. "That's not what I meant, but learning more about our roots could be fun. Wait, this is coming out all wrong."

"Probably because you don't want to say whatever's on your mind. I'm a big girl and can handle whatever you want to say." Her words sounded confident, but her lower lip trembled.

I inhaled deeply and tried to collect my thoughts. "You two have a connection. You and Ike Gage. I see it between the two of you, but I don't feel it for myself."

"Andi Grace, please get to the point." Irritation laced her words.

"Don't be upset, but I think you're related to Ike. You favor him."

She gasped. "Then you're related to him also."

I shrugged. "Maybe not."

Lacey Jane's complexion paled. "Impossible. I can't be related to Ike if you're not." Her voice was a mere whisper.

I reached for my sister's hand. "It's not impossible."

"You're scaring me." She leaned forward and grabbed my arm with her cold hand. "What do you think is happening?"

I touched her hand with mine. "I think it's possible Mom had an affair."

Lacey Jane pulled away and leapt off the couch. "That's crazy talk. I've got to go."

"No, stay. We need to consider the possibility."

"Forget it, Andi Grace. I know who my parents are." She stormed down the wide hall.

I followed her to the front door. "Lacey Jane, wait. Let's discuss the possibility."

"I can't talk about your crazy theory anymore." She raced to her car and sped away.

Susan joined me at the front door. "Family tiff?"

I couldn't tell her our fight wasn't any of her business. After all, the woman had allowed me to stay in her home, and she'd no doubt heard the entire discussion. "You could say we had a disagreement."

Susan patted my shoulder. "Your family seems tight. I imagine the issue will work itself out."

I wasn't convinced, but I closed the door. The arsonist hadn't taken away my siblings or my dog. Pushing Lacey Jane away had been all my fault.

I followed Susan to the family room with Sunny at my side. Thanks to Susan's graciousness, I had a temporary residence. I studied Tabby's daughter. The woman was on my suspect list, which meant I was living with a potential killer. At times she seemed hardnosed, and other times her kindness appeared. I needed to come to a conclusion about Tabby's daughter. I hoped she was innocent, but the woman was a mystery to me.

Chapter Thirty

I ORGANIZED MY meager belongings in the guest room at Tabby's house then headed to buy toiletries and underwear at the nearest general store. Sunny rode shotgun.

I ran my hand over her head. "You have dog supplies at the plantation, but we'll buy more for our temporary home. How do you like our new digs? Would you be more comfortable at the plantation house?"

Sunny's ears pointed up, and her tongue hung out.

I parked at the little store and lowered the windows enough for Sunny to have fresh air while I shopped. When I returned to the Highlander, I passed a safe chew bone to my sweet German shepherd.

Sunny gave me a happy bark then hopped into the back seat and gnawed on her treat.

"Let's go check on Gus." I headed south and hummed along to country tunes on the radio until we reached the turn from River Road to my plantation. I meandered along the driveway to the dog barn, where I parked the Highlander under a shady tree. I rubbed Sunny's back. "I could get used to this car . . . er . . . SUV. If I can fit dog supplies in here, it beats shopping for a new vehicle." My hand stilled. If I kept this vehicle, was I taking the easy way out?

I rolled my head back. There was so much to deal with. New home, vehicle, dog walking supplies, clothes, furniture, food, dishes, and all the items we needed in life. I fought back a wave of panic. All of these were replaceable.

What about the irreplaceable parts of my life? I'd lost all of my family pictures, my mother's jewelry, and my journals. There'd been many notes in them I'd written when going through other catastrophes.

Sunny nudged the back of my arm with her nose, and my tears plopped onto the console.

I swiped them away and checked the mirror. "Oh, look at me. What a mess."

In my peripheral vision, I noticed Dylan approaching us. It was well known he didn't like to deal with crying women. Time to pull myself together. Crying wouldn't solve my problems. I hopped out of the Highlander and Sunny followed.

"Nice wheels."

I slid on my sunglasses and pasted a smile on my face. "My insurance agent leased it for me until we settle my claim."

"I was really sorry to hear you lost everything." For him to address the issue was a sure sign of his growing maturity.

"Thanks. At least I had my phone and purse with me when my home caught on fire." Keeping the conversation neutral would help Dylan not stress, so I changed the topic. "Whatcha working on today?"

"The Stay and Play sign arrived. Wait 'til you see it." He waved for me to follow. We entered the barn, and Dylan pulled a white hand-painted sign from where it leaned against the fence of the dog area. "Ta-da."

Hand lettering on an oval wood sign. *Stay and Play.* "It's gorgeous."

Dylan turned it, allowing me to see the words on both sides. "This one is to hang on a post near the sign for the bed and breakfast. It'll make it easier for owners to find us, and I ordered a bigger sign to hang on the barn."

"Do you think we need another sign pointing visitors back here instead of wasting their time searching for us?"

"I'm one step ahead of you." He set down the two-sided hanging sign and lifted a small stake. "We'll position this so the arrows point toward the main house and the barn."

"Dylan, you've taken on so much responsibility. You deserve a raise." I took a deep breath. "Give me time to get a better handle on our financial outlook. I won't forget you."

He coughed and dipped his chin. "I've got a home here, and Juliet feeds me lots of meals. I'm good for now."

"Thanks, but I plan to do right by you."

"No worries." He backed toward the door, as if trying to leave before I did something mushy. "I need to help Griffin, but I'll have these up by the end of the day."

After his escape, Sunny and I headed to the kennel area to find Gus. The black and white bundle of fur lay on a dog bed with his head on his paws looking at me. "Hi, Gus."

He blinked, and when I held out a treat to him, he came to me in slow motion. One cautious step at a time.

"It's okay. We're going to take good care of you and find you a forever home."

Sunny wandered over to a water bowl and ignored us.

I sat on the ground and played gently with Gus, hoping to earn his trust. "What a good boy. You're special and deserve to be taken care of. If I can't find you a new home, you'll live with Sunny and me." Gus was as much homeless as I was.

His gaze met mine, and I reached for my phone in order to text Hannah. She wanted a dog, and Gus needed a good home. It was worth a shot to introduce them. **I've got a dog for you to meet. Are you available?**

My phone rang, and I expected to see Hannah's name on the screen, but I didn't recognize the number. "Hello."

"Andi Grace, this is Leroy. Can you meet me at the pier? Now?" His voice had a panicked tone.

"I'm on the way." I settled Gus back into his crate. When he whimpered, Sunny joined him. "Alrighty, then. Sunny, you're in charge. I'll be back."

If I pushed it, I could make it to Leroy in twenty minutes. Not wanting to waste time, I didn't alert Dylan or Juliet to my whereabouts. I jumped into the Highlander and high-tailed it to the pier.

I pulled into the parking lot in time to see Danny head to his blue convertible, carrying a large backpack. He wore jeans and a black hoodie and shot a quick glance my way. He wasn't used to my temporary vehicle and showed no sign of recognition before he slithered into his fancy car. Sandy gravel sprayed out as he made his exit.

How'd he get released from jail so fast? Did the cops book him, or had his friend Ian Patterson let him off? I'd find out what happened as soon as I met Leroy.

I parked and grabbed my key fob, phone, and wallet and ran as fast as my ankle allowed to pay my fee, then stepped onto the wood walkway.

At the end of the pier, Leroy leaned on the railing. He faced the Atlantic, and his back was toward me.

"Leroy, I'm here." I'd hurried enough to be out of breath. The sun peeked through gathering clouds, and a cool breeze ruffled my ponytail.

"You missed it. I get why people doubted Tabby. It happened so fast." He adjusted the bill of his cap.

"Tell me what happened. I'll believe you." I patted his shoulder.

He pointed out to the sea. "It's like she said. See that shrimp boat in the distance?"

The faded red and white vessel bobbed in the waves while puttering away from the beach. "Yes."

"It stopped with the nets out. Most people would assume nothing unusual. A jet ski came from the north and disappeared behind the boat. I'm a durn fool for not bringing my binoculars. I couldn't see what happened for like five minutes or so."

"It's doubtful you would've seen what happened with them on the other side of the boat. Do you always bring your binoculars when you fish?"

"Naw, I learned it from Tabby. Once she got suspicious, she carried them almost every time she left the house. She even put a sticker on them with her name in case she had a seizure."

"Sounds like a good idea. What else happened?" I converted my ponytail to a messy bun so it'd quit slapping my cheeks.

"The jet ski appeared and came toward the beach. By then I could see two people were riding the watercraft. The guy in back got off and swam to shore with a bag. When he reached the beach, another guy met him. They swapped bags. Land man ran to the parking lot, and water man swam out until the guy on the jet ski picked him up." Leroy snapped his fingers. "Simple and quick as that."

"Were you the only person who saw the switch?"

He pointed to a couple wrapped in a quilt who were simultaneously drinking and fishing. "They're too sloshed to have noticed. Been drinking for hours."

"So it was only you."

He sagged against the railing. "That's right. I doubt the cops will accept my story any more than they believed Tabby."

I watched the shrimp boat disappear, making its slow journey over the incoming waves. "How about Deputy Wayne? He's in charge of Tabby's murder." Random raindrops pelted my head while I awaited Leroy's answer.

At last he nodded and pushed away from the rail. "It's worth a shot. If the situation was reversed, I'd want somebody to stand up to the men who killed me. Seems like it's the least I can do for Tabby."

Chapter Thirty-One

LEROY FOLLOWED me to the sheriff's office, and he told David what he'd seen from the pier. David treated the older man with respect and took notes. Afterward, we went our separate ways.

My growling stomach alerted me it was time for supper. I swung by Tony's and picked up enough pizza and salad to feed a small army then sent out a text inviting my closest people to join me. It turned out only Susan, Kylie, and Marc ate with me. Lacey Jane texted claiming she had other plans and asked me to give her some space. Meanwhile, Nate was helping Juliet at the bed and breakfast.

Susan only ate salad, but the rest of us put a dent in the supreme pizza.

Kylie wrapped the leftovers and placed them in the refrigerator. "I'm heading to the plantation to hang out with Dylan. Do you want me to bring Sunny home?"

Relief rippled over my shoulders. Home. She nailed the truth. Tabby's house was my temporary home.

"Yes, please. I want her here with us, but I dread the thought of driving out to the plantation tonight. I'm whipped."

Susan said, "Hold up, Kylie. I'm flying out Sunday, and I'd like for us to spend a little time together tomorrow. I'm going to have a surprise for you."

Kylie's eyes sparkled. "I like good surprises."

"I guarantee it'll be a good one." Susan removed one of her expensive water bottles from the refrigerator.

"I can't wait." Kylie waved and took off in Nate's old truck, leaving me alone with Marc and Susan.

Marc and I sat on the couch, and Susan chose a black wooden chair with white and blue cushions. The pattern complemented the blue couch. Throw pillows of the same material as the chairs had been tossed on the couch and tied the pieces together. Nice and sophisticated. Unlike my cozy home, which had gone up in flames.

I leaned into the comfy cushions. "Susan, are you taking the night off?"

"I've got boxes of photographs to go through before morning. By the time I leave, this place will be ready for you to settle in."

"Your mom had good taste in furniture. It coordinates so well."

Susan lifted a hand to her chest. "Thank you. I worked with an interior decorator. We wanted a tranquil place for my mother to live. Her life as an ER nurse was busy and chaotic, and it seemed appropriate for this home to be the opposite. I hope it helped her healing process."

Marc slipped his arm around my shoulders. "Your mother was a gem."

"I appreciate you saying so, Marc. I worried she'd have trouble thinking clearly and making decisions."

"Tabby was smart and observant enough to suspect there was something going on at the beach. She also made friends and took care of the feral island cats." Marc ran his fingers along my shoulder.

"Mother always had a big heart." Susan nodded. "More than once she mentioned her concerns to me about a shrimp boat and smuggling. Unfortunately, I chalked it up to an overactive imagination or boredom."

I said, "I think she was on to something, but I haven't figured out what yet."

Susan twisted the top of her water bottle back and forth. "It won't bring Mother back."

My lower lip trembled. Was Susan too brokenhearted to deal with the crime? "Don't you at least want her killer caught?"

"Of course I do." She took a delicate drink from her water bottle, leaving a smear of lipstick on the plastic. "I'm not equipped to catch the person who did this, but it doesn't mean I want them to get away with it."

"Did you two get along?"

"She's my mother, and I loved her, even though we didn't agree on everything. For instance, her move to Heyward Beach didn't make sense to me. In the end, I went along with her plan but insisted on hiring Kylie to come here with her." She picked up magazine from the side table and fanned herself. "Mother cared about Kylie, but she wasn't happy I forced them together. We were two strong-willed women used to being in charge, which led to a certain amount of tension between us. At the end of the day, we loved each other. I hope you understand."

Mothers and daughters. I missed my mother every day, even though

I didn't always understand her artistic nature. "Susan, can I be blunt?"

Marc groaned.

Susan's gaze bounced from Marc to me. "Yes. I much prefer it when a person gets to the point instead of hem-hawing around."

"Are you having financial problems?"

One brow arched. "Do I need money from my mother's estate? No. There have been rumors my company is having some financial issues, but we're solid. I can't reveal more than that at this time. What else?"

"If I could see your plane ticket, I'd completely move you off my list of suspects."

"I think you missed your calling, Andi Grace. You should've been a cop." Susan moved to the kitchen counter and picked up her cell phone. She made a few swipes before handing it to me. "Here's my travel itinerary. Plane tickets and the information about the car rental."

Marc moved his head close to mine and gazed at the app. "This shows Susan flew out after her mom died."

My shoulders slumped, and I passed the phone to Susan. "Thanks."

"You're welcome. I find it's better to face conflict and move on. Is there anything else you want to know before I fly out on Sunday?" Her tone was calm, and her eyebrows perked up.

"No, ma'am. You're officially off my suspect list. I appreciate your graciousness."

"Good to know. It's comforting to know you're looking into my mother's death." She smiled. "If you're considering suspects, what about the man who hates cats?"

I shook my head. "Leroy said when they were alone, he and Tabby got along. Arguing about the cats made them feel alive."

"I can see my mother needing the conflict. She always enjoyed the craziness of the ER. Maybe it was a mistake to offer her a carefree life." For the first time, I saw doubt in Susan's eyes.

Marc's foot shook. "Susan, Tabby mentioned you often, and she was very proud of you."

"I appreciate you telling me that." Susan white-knuckled her phone. "Andi Grace, resolve the conflict between you and your sister. Don't wait until it's too late."

My throat grew so tight I couldn't speak.

Susan met my blurry gaze. "I'm going to turn in now. Night." Tabby's daughter disappeared without another word.

"Good night." Marc waved then turned to me when we were alone.

"Is there a problem with you and Lacey Jane?"

"Oh, Marc." I dropped my head to his arm and slapped my hand over my warm face. "I plowed straight into an issue with the grace of a clumsy oaf. I completely bungled the conversation, and now Lacey Jane says she needs space."

His brow puckered. "What's the issue?"

I stood and paced, ignoring the slight pain in my ankle. "Didn't you see it today? I tried to signal you. Ike Gage? Lacey Jane?"

Marc rose and placed his hands on my shoulders. "They're connected because it was his truck that hit Lacey Jane and Kylie."

"I know that, but it's more than a wreck concerning them." My legs shook.

He frowned. "What are you talking about?"

"Ike and Lacey Jane are very similar. I feel like they're related."

Marc met my gaze. "How so?"

"I think Ike might be Lacey Jane's biological father."

His eyes widened. "She's adopted?"

"No." My chest tightened, making it hard to breath. "I remember my mother being pregnant. I sang to my siblings before they were born by leaning close to Mom's belly."

"Andi Grace, you're entering choppy waters. What are you suggesting?"

"I think my mother had an affair." I gulped.

Marc shook his head. "Please tell me you didn't say as much to Lacey Jane."

I nodded. "Yeah, I'm afraid I did."

Marc huffed and moved toward the kitchen. "She adores you, Andi Grace. If it's true, she'll be crushed."

"Don't you see? If it's true, she'll have a father." I followed him to the kitchen, reached for his hand, and led him to the back porch where Susan wouldn't hear us. Hurricane wall lanterns cast a warm glow over the area.

He ran his hands through his hair. "Did you consider Lacey Jane may feel like you're pawning her off on Ike Gage?"

"That wasn't my intention." I shivered and blamed it on the night breeze.

"Think about it. Lacey Jane's the youngest and struggles to feel equal to you and Nate, even though she's a grown woman. Presenting her with a different father destroys the family she believes in. The worst thing is, you don't even know if it's true or not. With one random hunch, you rocked Lacey Jane's world."

I dropped into a wicker chair still shivering. Pure intentions could still hurt. If I hadn't decided to find Tabby's killer, Lacey Jane might not have been in the car accident. No accident meant no Ike Gage in our lives. When would I learn to mind my own business?

Marc sighed. "You don't always have to try so hard to fix things."

Could I help it if I enjoyed helping others? It couldn't hurt for me to step back and consider the consequences to my actions before I jumped into a situation. Marc had made a good point. If I'd waited, my sister wouldn't be mad at me. Who knew what she'd do with my suspicions? "Marc, we've got to find Lacey Jane. She might be in danger from Danny and too upset to realize her life is at risk. I've got to save her before it's too late. If he attacks her, it'll be my fault."

"No, it won't." Marc reached for my hand. "But it can't hurt to make sure she's safe." We rushed into the house.

"If I hadn't distracted her with my dumb theory, she'd be focused on the trouble on the island."

"This isn't the time to debate the issue. If you're concerned about Lacey Jane's safety, let's find her."

I snatched my purse and keys and dashed out of the house, breathing a prayer along the way. We needed to find Lacey Jane before Danny or one of his drug thugs did.

Chapter Thirty-Two

"I'LL DRIVE THE Highlander." I gripped the key fob. "Please keep trying to get in touch with Lacey Jane. Maybe she'll take your call."

Marc opened my door then jogged to the passenger side.

Clouds and cool fog blocked our view of the moon and stars, making the night darker than normal. Scattered raindrops splattered the windshield. I found the right control knob and adjusted the wipers before calling Nate.

"Hello." His voice almost brought me to tears. *Almost.*

"Nate, have you seen Lacey Jane?"

"I'm at the plantation with Juliet, and she's not here. What's up?" His happy tone broke my heart because I'd have to tell him what I'd done.

"We had an argument, and I can't find her." I drove toward the pier.

"She'll show up. It's not the first time you've made her mad."

"True, but this was the worst." I glanced at Marc, who shook his head, indicating he hadn't gotten a response. "Can you help me look for her?"

"I'll try to find her, but it seems like the theme of our family for the past week is to search for each other. An adult version of hide and seek, if you know what I mean. Do you want to warn me what I'm getting myself into?" He'd gone from sounding happy to worried.

"It's bad and all my fault. For now, let's focus on finding Lacey Jane." I took a deep breath. "I'll tell you about it later."

"I think she blocked me from our tracker app." He sighed. "If I can't reach her by phone or text, I'll drive to Conway and stop at the apartment."

"You might check the local bars too. Thanks for your help, Nate."

"Hey, she's my sister, too. I'm absolutely gonna help." He chuckled. "We may have to gang up on you when I get to the truth."

"Huh, I have no doubt you'll be on her side. Shoot, I'm on her side.

163

I meant well but ended up hurting her." We hung up, and I pulled into the pier parking lot.

"No sign of her car, but I'll run inside to double check." Marc was out before I could object.

I sat in the idling SUV. Where would she have gone? She was upset and her college friends were in Florida.

"She wasn't inside." Marc slid into the passenger seat and looked straight ahead.

I drove past my burned house, Tony's Pizzeria, and Marc's office without seeing a sign of my sister. "Nate's going to check at her apartment, so I guess stopping at the bars is my next move."

Marc fiddled with his phone.

"Are you mad at me?"

"No."

I turned onto Highway 17. "It sounds like you might be."

"I hate for Lacey Jane to deal with her potential birth issues all by herself."

"I'm not any happier about this than you are."

"Then why'd you bring it up today?" He didn't once glance at me.

The light ahead of us turned yellow, but I stepped on the gas and shot through the intersection before red glowed. "I don't believe Ike's here by accident. What if he was looking for my mother? If they had a relationship but went back to their spouses, it's possible Ike didn't know my mom died. Ike's wife passed away recently. It could be he wants to find my mother. Don't you think it's better for me to connect the dots and tell Lacey Jane than for her to hear about it from a stranger?"

"A stranger you suspect of being Lacey Jane's biological father." He pointed to the next light. "You might want to stop this time. The cops like to hang out at the gas station on the corner. Best coffee around if you're in a hurry."

I stepped on the brakes and eased to a stop. "I'm sorry, Marc."

His posture relaxed. "I'm not the one you need to apologize to."

"I did." At least I thought I had, but I'd do it again. "I'll make it right."

"Andi Grace, your sister is a grown woman, and if it turns out Ike is her dad, she'll deal with the situation. As an adult. Green."

"Green?"

"The light. It turned green."

"Oh." I moved forward into the dark rainy night. "Do you really think I baby my sister?"

Marc burst out laughing. "I know you do. I guess it's natural, but I see her differently."

"How?"

"Working with Lacey Jane, I've learned how smart and capable she is. When she looks for an answer, she doesn't stop until she finds it. Her dogged determination reminds me of you. She's also kind when she interacts with clients. Sympathetic while paying close attention to details. Given the opportunity, she'd make a great attorney."

My ringtone played an old Neil Diamond love song, and I snatched it up while driving. "Nate, did you find her?"

"Our little sister answered my call and told me to leave her alone. She's at Daily Java with some man. Isaac Gage. Do you know him?"

"We just met, but he's nice enough. Thanks for your help. I gotta go." I slowed to pull a U-turn. "She's at Daily Java."

In less than ten minutes, I parked at the coffee shop and stepped out of the Highlander. The rain had stopped, but it was humid.

Marc met me at the front door but leaned against it, preventing me from entering. "Hold up. Do you know what you're going to say? Or will you race inside and make a bad situation worse?"

I paused. He'd nailed me. "You're right. I don't have a plan other than to hug my sister and possibly cry hysterically."

Marc took my hand and led me to the deserted coffee shop patio. We sat on a bench. "She's not a four-year-old runaway. Your sister is a grown woman. Do you hear me? Grown. Woman."

"Yeah, I hear you." I swallowed hard. "You might even say she's an angry grown woman. Look, there she is sitting with Ike."

"Sounds mature. I bet she contacted him to get some answers." Marc reached for a loose strand of my hair and wrapped it around his finger. "How do you want to proceed?"

I peeked around his shoulder. My sister's arms were on the table, and she leaned toward the older man. They appeared to be deep in conversation. No smiles. Serious expressions. "What if I leave a note on her windshield? It'll show I trust her and can allow her to handle the situation instead of barging in like I'm prone to do."

He smiled so big his dimple appeared. "Su-weet. I'm proud of you."

Unsure whether to punch his arm or kiss him, I made the more pleasant decision. I pressed my lips against his cheek, and when he turned his face, we transitioned into a full-blown kiss.

Chapter Thirty-Three

AFTER A RESTLESS night of tossing and turning, I readied myself for the day and headed to Tabby's kitchen to prepare a pot of coffee.

Kylie and Lacey Jane sat at the kitchen table eating muffins. Both studied the screens on their phones.

"Good morning." My voice croaked, causing both of them to glimpse up from their phones.

"Hey, Sis. Have a muffin. Erin gave them to me last night when she locked up." Lacey Jane pointed to a plate of delicious-looking muffins with brown sugar topping.

I counted to ten in French to stop myself from saying something I'd regret. As much as I wanted details of Lacey Jane's conversation with Ike, I wouldn't quiz her relentlessly. Had she found my note? Was this a test? Did she want to see if I really could butt out? I lifted my chin. "They look like blueberry. Thanks."

Kylie said, "Sunny's in the backyard, and Susan disappeared with an Uber driver on a mysterious errand."

"Wow, it's kinda early to run errands." I searched the cabinets until I located a solid white mug. Tabby's mugs lacked the personality of mine. On the other hand, a boring mug was better than nothing. "I wonder why Susan didn't take the fancy rental car."

"Rich people are different than us." Kylie squeezed her eyes shut. "Sorry. I forgot you're rich, too. You seem normal."

Lacey Jane snickered. "My sister ain't normal."

I laughed. "I've got a sick feeling when I meet with my accountant, he's going to reveal something that didn't get paid, like a lien for the renovation on the main house or a tax bill that slipped through the cracks."

Lacey Jane patted the empty chair next to her. "Have a seat. I got your note last night."

I sat beside her and gave her a one-armed hug. "Marc drilled it into me that you're an adult, and I don't always have to jump into your business. He deserves the credit for me honoring your privacy."

"You're wrong about giving Marc all the glory. I'm sure it took a lot of discipline on your part to leave us alone. So thank you." She smiled. "I bet you're curious."

"Dying, actually."

Kylie buttered a blueberry muffin. "Would you two like some privacy?"

"It's fine. After all we've been through the last few days, you're practically family. Feel free to listen." Lacey Jane passed the glass coffee carafe to me.

Kylie dropped the butter knife on the table then picked it up and set it on her plate. "That's the nicest thing you coulda said. Thanks."

I filled my mug and doctored my coffee, but I didn't rush Lacey Jane to share her story.

My sister added more coffee to her mug before she looked at us. "My conversation with Ike started with little things like our families and jobs. Finally, I asked Ike if he knew our parents. By the second cup of coffee, he admitted he knew Mom."

Kylie stood so fast her slat-backed chair wobbled. She grabbed the dog leash. "As much as I appreciate being included, you two don't need me for this conversation. I'll be with Sunny. If you don't find us in the yard, we've gone for a walk."

Lacey Jane sipped her coffee while Kylie beat a hasty retreat out the back doorway. At last we were alone.

My pulse pounded in my neck, but I held my tongue.

She focused on the table. "Ike met Mom in Myrtle Beach twenty-five years ago. He came here with some of his marine buddies for a week of golfing. His marriage was in trouble, and he needed time to think. Meanwhile, Mom was unhappy with life in general. All of her time was spent taking care of you, Nate, and Dad. She missed painting. There was an artists' convention or showing or some sort of event, and Mom came to see what other artists were doing. Ike said she was depressed after meeting the professionals. They were people who seemed to find time to paint, and Mom was too busy to fulfill her passion."

Her words proved my theory Mom had been unhappy. "How'd they meet?"

Lacey Jane shrugged. "They were staying at the same hotel. It had a pool and bar on the beach, which is where they met. Get the picture?"

"Both were depressed and drinking?"

"You got it. Ike said Mom was beautiful. She laughed at his jokes and so on and so forth." Lacey Jane shuddered.

Deep down I'd known things weren't great between my parents, but a small part of me didn't want to believe my own instincts. "How'd you feel hearing his story?"

"Torn." Her gaze met mine. "It was a love story with no hope for a happy ending. Sweet at times, yet bitter too. It wasn't fair to Dad, and you know how much I loved him. As Ike shared his version of what happened, I felt like collateral damage, but I couldn't stop listening. Your hunch was correct."

"I'm so sorry. I wish I'd been wrong." I clasped her hand.

"Me, too. Kinda." She sipped her coffee. "They danced to beach music played by a local band. One thing led to another. Ike avoided sharing the gross, intimate details, but he fell in love with Mom."

"Did he say why he returned to his wife?"

"Their last morning together, Mom and Ike agreed not to see each other again. When he returned home, he confessed to his wife about the affair. He said it was a struggle, but she forgave him. He'd made a commitment to her and wanted to honor his marriage vows."

"Whoa." Not what I'd expected.

"A few months later Mom sent a message to him through one of his friends on the golf trip." She paused for a few moments, pressing her lips together. "I don't know why this is so hard to say. It's obvious what happened. Mom was pregnant. Her note said she didn't want to lose her family. He called Mom, but she begged him not to rock the boat. She didn't want Dad to find out about the affair. She asked him to stay away."

"Do you believe Ike?"

Lacey Jane nodded. "Mom sent him pictures of me on my birthdays and holidays."

I grabbed my sister's arm. "I remember she often wanted to take pictures of us as a group and individually. I always thought she took more of you because you were the baby."

"I was also the most adorable child." Lacey Jane gave me a saucy smile then sobered. "Mom mailed pictures of me to Ike's work address."

"So his wife wouldn't see them?"

Lacey Jane nodded. "He showed me the photographs she sent to him every year until she died."

The hair on my neck stood up. "Does that mean he came to Heyward Beach with the intention of finding you? Why else would he have the pictures with him?"

"Yeah, his goal was to find me, no matter how long it took." She looked out the window. "If you hadn't introduced us, Ike still would've tracked me down."

"Are you mad he never contacted you before now? And Mom lied to you—to us—your entire life."

"Ike said the plan was to tell me when I turned eighteen. They were going to let me decide if I wanted to meet him or not."

I rubbed her back. "I wonder what you would've decided."

Lacey Jane laughed. "After my reaction to your hypothesis, I doubt meeting Ike was an option. It would've been too cruel to Dad. I could never hurt the only man I knew as a father."

"Why did you get together with Ike last night?"

"I was furious and wanted to prove you wrong. I contacted him, and he agreed to meet me." She threw up her hand like a traffic cop. "Before you lecture me on stranger danger, I told him it needed to be a public place. The coffee shop seemed to be the perfect place. We were at Daily Java over three hours. Erin locked the doors at closing time but insisted we stay. She baked muffins and cookies in back and was very gracious to give us privacy."

I needed to do something special for Erin. "You were a good employee to Erin when you worked at Daily Java. I'm sure she was happy to do something nice for you."

"I guess."

"So what's next for you and Ike? Blood testing?"

Lacey Jane shook her head. "I know he's my biological father. I may have known it deep in my heart the moment I met him. It's probably the reason I was so mad when you suggested it."

"Getting to know Ike doesn't make you disloyal to Dad. He treated you like the baby, sure, but he never showed favoritism toward any of us. Dad didn't treat you differently than he treated Nate and me. I was the oldest, Nate was the boy, and you were Dad's princess. He loved you the same as he loved us. Different but the same."

Her posture relaxed and a smile touched her lips. "He always called me *his little princess*. Were you ever jealous of me since we're both his daughters?"

My heart swelled. "I can honestly say I was never jealous. We all fell in love with you the day you were born."

Her smile disappeared. "Do you think Dad knew the truth?"

I pulled my hair into a ponytail and fanned myself with a napkin. Tough question. "I have no idea. He didn't keep a journal, so we'll never know for sure what Dad knew."

Lacey Jane stared at her hands but didn't say anything else.

I took a deep breath. "You brought joy to our household, and our family was stronger because of you. Mom and Dad fought less. I can't tell you if Dad knew the truth, but he adored you."

"I adored him, too. If Dad was still alive, it'd be harder to get to know Ike."

"I know, but Dad's not here. Why not start a relationship with Ike? Your biological dad is alive, and you have nothing to feel guilty about. I'm happy for you, and Nate will be, too, when he learns about Ike."

"You and Nate have always been my family. I don't want Ike to hurt our relationship."

"I like him, and Nate will, too." I touched her sternum with my finger. "Your heart is big enough for all of us."

She hugged me then sniffed. "Let's talk about something lighter."

"For instance?"

"Have you figured out who killed Tabby?"

Chapter Thirty-Four

LACEY JANE'S QUESTION had spurred me on to find Tabby's killer. Maybe focusing on a problem that I could handle would lift the veil of despair covering me. Feeling sorry for myself wouldn't solve the murder or any of my problems.

I dressed in my new jeans and light blue long-sleeve T-shirt. My phone vibrated on the bedside table and Marc's name appeared, so I swiped the screen. "Good morning."

"Morning."

My heart twisted. "Are you still mad at me?"

"I wasn't mad last night."

"Okay." I hoped he was telling the truth. His tone didn't sound angry. "What's up?"

"It's Saturday, and I was wondering if Chubb and I can hang out with you today. We can take it easy or look for clues."

Nice. I relaxed. "I was planning to visit Phyllis and ask about her gabapentin prescription. Do you want to meet me at her place?"

"I'm already in town. How about if I swing by and pick you up?"

"Sounds good. See you soon." Thank goodness I'd bought toiletries at the dollar store. While I wasn't a fashionista, it made me happy to apply mascara and a light touch of lipstick. After applying antibiotic cream to the healing scratches on my face, I was ready to face whatever the day held.

The doorbell rang, and I headed to the front hall. Kylie was watching a home decorating channel. "I've got it, Kylie. Have you heard anything from Susan about your surprise?"

"No. Do you think it's safe for me to be here alone with her? Lacey Jane left to find Nate. I think she plans to tell him about Mr. Gage."

I nodded. "It'll be good to get that conversation behind her. As far as you and Susan, I've marked her off my suspect list."

"Um, you evaded my question." She frowned.

If I was going to quit being a bossy pants, I needed to allow Kylie to make decisions on her own. "I feel like you'll be safe, but if you're uncomfortable, then don't stay here. Do you want to hang out with Marc and me?"

"I had a late night. May as well stay here." Kylie stretched out on the couch and continued watching the show about flipping houses. "Have fun."

I grabbed the dog leash off the chair in case we needed it later. "Come on, Sunny. Let's go."

Marc was waiting for me on the front porch, wearing a nice pullover sweatshirt, jeans, and aviator sunglasses. "It's a beautiful day. Are you sure you want to fight crime? We can kayak on the river or marsh."

"We'll feel better once the killer has been arrested and secured behind bars."

His lips touched mine briefly. "I expected as much. You look pretty."

I almost tripped at his compliment. Marc was a man of few words, and I squelched the desire to shed tears at his kindness. The emotions of this week were about to push me over the edge. "Oh, thanks."

Sunny barked and ran to the red truck, where Chubb hung his head out and replied with his own yap.

Once the dogs were situated in the backseat, Marc pulled away from Tabby's house. "Have you heard any news on the fire?"

"No. The chief is still processing the evidence. Yesterday, I had friends call and text me. People could see the flames and smoke on the other side of Highway 17."

Marc ran a hand over his face. "I'm not surprised. The fire was huge, and the fire department did a stupendous job of containing it. If it'd been a windy night, the flames could've spread quickly and destroyed more property."

I reflected on his words until we reached our destination. We left the dogs in the truck with windows lowered. When we reached the porch, I rang the bell and waited.

Phyllis opened the door. "Andi Grace, I didn't schedule you for today."

Leave it to Phyllis to be blunt. "You're right, but I wanted to ask you a couple of questions. If you don't mind." I'd suspected her in the past of wrongdoing but only had questions this time.

"I have a church luncheon today, but I can spare a few minutes." She waved us in and led us to the kitchen. "Pumpkin and Captain are in the backyard. I'm afraid you might be right about those obedience lessons. I found a chewed-up shoe under the couch this morning."

"I'll call you Monday and arrange a time to meet. First lesson will be free."

"Thanks. So what do you need to ask?" She cut into a pan of brownies and began arranging them on a pretty blue-and-white serving dish.

Medicine vials were in a ceramic bowl on the counter.

"I didn't mean to snoop the last time I was here, but there were capsules spilled on your counter. Gabapentin."

"It's legal for me to take them." Her hands stopped moving. "How'd you know they were gabapentin?"

"I looked at the bottles."

"I should've known. Don't expect me to give you a recommendation." She frowned. "I have every right to take medicine a doctor prescribes."

"I'm not accusing you of anything wrong, but I couldn't help notice they were different colors."

Marc sat on a bar stool close to Phyllis. "We've discovered drug abusers like gabapentin. Have you ever had a dealer try to sell you some?"

Phyllis waved her hand as if fanning herself. "No, but a man in the drug store's parking lot asked if I was interested in selling my supply. He offered me a lot of money, but I refused. It wasn't easy, though. You know pastors don't make much."

I knew the pastor's wife had an addiction to gambling. "Phyllis, selling your prescription medicine would've been worse than gambling."

"Not really. Once I'd sold my stash, it'd be over. Unlike the ability to gamble every day."

Marc crossed his arms. "It's illegal to sell your prescription medication. If the insurance company discovered what you were doing, you could be accused of insurance fraud."

"Yeah, Larry said the same thing."

Marc said, "Also, once you sold some of your gabapentin, those people might pressure you to get more and sell it to them. Please, don't let them tempt you into selling what you have."

Phyllis lay the spatula in the sink. "I never considered the implycations. I didn't sell any, if that's what you want to know."

I noticed her hands shook. "Who knows you take gabapentin?"

"Larry and my doctors know what I take." Phyllis tapped her cheek. "The ladies in my prayer group also know. Otherwise, I can't think of anybody else."

"Does your group meet in a public place?" Who could've heard her confess to taking the pain medication?

"Last month we met at Leslie's house. We move around, though. Sometimes we get together at the coffee shop or the library, and we've even met for lunch at Tony's. It's hard to say if anybody overheard me ask for prayer to not feel pain and to get off gabapentin."

"Leslie Nichols?" Danny's mother was in the same prayer group as Phyllis? Warning bells clanged in my skull. "Is there any chance Danny was around when you met at her house?"

Phyllis lifted her chin. "I don't recall seeing him, but he's running for state representative. He's a valued member of our community. A lawyer, no less. If he overheard my request, there's no way he'd reveal my problem."

"Why did you fill your prescription at different pharmacies?" I itched to take notes but refrained, not wanting to interrupt the flow of conversation.

"My insurance company insists I get my refills through a mail-order place."

"I understand, but you seemed to have quite a few capsules spilled on the counter, and if you want to cut back, why do you have so much medication?"

"I was afraid to stop the refills in case I need to take some. What if I'm in pain and don't have the medicine? Do you want me to suffer?" Her eyes fluttered.

"No, I don't. I'm just trying to put all the pieces together."

Phyllis reached for the aluminum foil and covered the plate of brownies. "I've got to go, but you're barking up the wrong tree if you think Danny's involved."

"If not Danny, who do you think?"

"It's too bad my husband isn't a priest."

"You wouldn't be married to Larry if he was a priest." In addition to the fact he couldn't blab what people confessed.

"Yeah, but people confess things to priests all the time."

It'd be pointless to argue with Phyllis. "I know you're in a hurry. Thanks for talking to us."

Phyllis walked us to the door and ushered us out.

Once we were in Marc's truck, I pulled out my notes. "If Leslie is a member of the same prayer group as Phyllis, I bet Danny knew about the pain medicine."

"Danny's done some despicable things to you, but I'm struggling to picture him selling drugs."

The dogs panted in the backseat, and I filled a new plastic bowl with spring water and gave them treats. "You all are so good."

Marc pulled away from the curb, humming a country tune.

"Let's go back to the duffel bag full of cash. How's it linked to Tabby's death?"

Marc ran a hand over his face. "Cash is involved in smuggling."

"True. Suppose Tabby came across the bag and wanted to turn it in to the cops. Maybe she was afraid the smugglers would catch her, so she buried it. The bad guys find her, but she won't tell them where the bag is, and they kill her. Danny or one of his friends could be the killer."

"I know he has anger issues, but it's hard to picture him killing Tabby."

I leaned against the headrest and closed my eyes. "If you'd seen him attacking me, you'd believe him capable of anything."

Marc's warm hand closed over mine. "I'm sorry he hurt you, but there's a difference between attacking a person in the heat of the moment and getting involved in selling drugs."

"Don't you see? Tabby could've made Danny mad. If people hadn't helped me, I could be as dead as Tabby. I really believe it's possible he's involved." The image of her body and Monday morning's events replayed in my mind. Chubb had tried to dig in the dune, but we'd stopped him. His dog senses told him there was something there. "Marc, yesterday I saw Danny carrying a backpack at the pier parking lot when I went to see Leroy."

He slammed on the brakes. "Did you tell anybody?"

"No. I guess I was so relieved he didn't see me, and Leroy was waiting, so it just kinda slipped my mind."

A horn honked, and Marc started driving again. "We can't jump to conclusions, but I'm glad you saw him with a bag."

"It's more than just seeing him carry a bag at the pier. I saw him right after Leroy witnessed the exchange of bags on the beach."

Chapter Thirty-Five

MARC PARKED HIS truck in front of Tabby's house.

Susan and Kylie stood in the driveway next to a Jetta. White, like Tabby's car that had been T-boned, but different. Bolder and bigger.

"Marc, look." I smiled. "Do you think Susan bought Kylie a new car?"

Marc scratched his jaw. "It's got a temporary tag, so maybe she did."

"I don't understand why, but I intend to find out. What if it's a bribe? Maybe Susan is guilty and trying to buy Kylie's silence." I reached for the door handle and stopped. "Wait a minute, I don't want to always be wary. Maybe Susan bought the car out of the kindness of her heart."

"Look at you not being suspicious. Good job." He leaned over and kissed me. "Although your natural curiosity has helped put a couple of killers in prison."

"Aw, thanks." I slipped out of the truck, mindful of my ankle.

Marc let the dogs out, and they followed him to the driveway. "Ladies, did somebody get a new car?"

Shock described Kylie's expression best. "It's mine. Susan decided it'd take too long to repair Tabby's car, and she wanted to make sure I had a dependable set of wheels."

Susan's smile surprised me—and this explained why she'd taken an Uber.

"It seemed the least I could do. After all, Kylie uprooted her life and moved to South Carolina to take care of my mother. And she agreed to house-sit until Andi Grace decides to buy the house."

I held out my hands. "As much as I love this place, it's not in my budget."

"You haven't even asked the price." Susan reached into her Kate Spade purse and retrieved an envelope. "I decided to make you a proposition. Think about it and get back to me. This offer expires in one month, at which point I'll list it with a real estate agent."

I accepted the envelope she passed my way, knowing it'd be so easy to start over in this home that was already built and furnished. The house was even closer to the ocean and marsh than my current homesite. "I'll need time to think and pray about the decision."

"I knew you would, which is why I'm paying Kylie to stay here with you for now." Susan lifted her chin. "I changed my flight and plan to leave later this afternoon, but my contact information is in the envelope. Let me know when you decide."

Kylie's eyes grew wide. "You're leaving today?"

"Yes. I've gone through Mother's belongings and paperwork. Did you realize Mother kept a secret stash of Moon Pies?"

"I wondered about that. Every time we went to the grocery store, we bought Moon Pies, but I never saw them again. Where were they?"

"In the drawer under her nightgowns. It's amazing she didn't gain weight, but I guess walking every day helped. They're in the pantry now." Susan adjusted her sunglasses. "I can sell the house long distance, so nothing's holding me here."

Kylie clasped her hands together. "What about Tabby's ashes? Aren't we going to spread them over the water together?"

Susan shook her head. "At first, I thought it'd be like a final farewell from me to my mother. It turns out sorting through her belongings provided enough closure."

"Okay." Kylie drew the word out. "How can I help you prepare to leave?"

"Come inside and let's go over a couple of things, then I'll be on my way." She led Kylie into the house.

I turned to Marc. "Should we alert Wade or David about Susan's imminent departure?"

"Can't hurt to text them." While he tapped a text, I turned the envelope over in my hands.

"Should I review her proposition before she leaves?" I waved the sealed offer in front of Marc.

"Yeah. Why don't we sit on the deck where you can have some privacy?"

We led Sunny and Chubb to the backyard and filled a water bowl for them. They noisily lapped it up, and I refilled the bowl.

Once we were comfortable on the white slip-covered outdoor couch, I opened the white envelope and read over the offer. My heart beat slow, steady, and hard. My pulse thundered in my ears. How was this offer even possible? "It's affordable. Look, Marc." With a shaky hand, I passed the paperwork to him.

He took his time reading the offer. His brow puckered until he finished and returned the pages to their proper order. A smile stole over his face, and he whistled. "I don't know how you can pass up this opportunity."

"Me either."

His phone vibrated, and he checked the incoming message. "Wade said they don't consider Susan to be a suspect at this time. She's free to go."

"Alrighty then. How about if we go to my old homesite? Maybe we can get some answers about my fire. Seeing the remains may give me clarity and the ability to say yes before Susan changes her offer."

Marc stood and held out his hand.

I hugged him instead of holding his hand. "When my house burned to the ground, I thought my world was spiraling out of control. My home was destroyed. You know how I struggled to consider selling it when I inherited Peter's plantation."

"I know." Marc ran his hand up and down my back, and chills followed the path of his touch.

"My house was old and needed work. If I decide to rebuild in the same spot, I'll change the floor plan."

"But?"

"Tabby's house is amazing. There are so many modern gadgets, and it's all clean and new. The place still has that new-home smell. You know what I mean?"

"Yep. Do you think you can be comfortable here? The place is immaculate almost to the point of being sterile."

I laughed. "I can easily put my touch on this place. With a few tweaks here and there, I can add my personality."

"I believe you, so why do you want to go to the other place?"

"It's time the fire chief, or arson investigator, gives us some answers." I stepped back. "This is your day off. I understand if you'd rather spend your Saturday kayaking or something more fun."

"Nothing compares to spending time with you, Andi Grace. Come on. Let's go to your old place."

My heart melted at his words. I'd never understand how I'd gotten so lucky with Marc. I was so full of emotion, I could only nod and walk by his side.

The dogs followed us to Marc's truck. Without vacationers on the island, we reached my burned-down house in less than two minutes.

The sight of my home punched me in the gut. The wound to my

soul was fresh and painful, despite the knowledge I could buy Tabby's place.

Marc reached over and held my icy hand in his warm one. Time lost meaning as I looked at the desolation in front of me. "What kind of accelerant would be used to burn something completely to the ground?"

"Gasoline is the first thing that comes to mind. Kerosene, maybe?" He rubbed his thumb along my knuckles. "I'm sure the fire chief has answers for you."

My gut churned and anger swirled deep in my belly. Answers wouldn't turn back time or restore my home, but maybe justice would be served. I took a deep breath and counted to ten in French. "There's no crime scene tape. No smoking embers. I'm going to walk around and see if anything survived."

Without arguing, Marc released my hand and hopped out.

I didn't want the dogs to get hurt, so I gave them treats before joining Marc in the middle of the street. "Thanks for not trying to dissuade me."

"By now, I know it'd be a waste of energy, but we need to be careful." He pointed to pieces of metal and wood randomly spread around. "You don't need any more injuries."

"True." I approached the cinderblock foundation. "It's unbelievable how small it appears. Three bedrooms, a family room, a kitchen, an office, and bathrooms full of laughter, tears, and love. All gone."

Marc slipped his arm around my shoulders. "I know this must be ripping you apart."

Tremors shook my body. Tears coursed down my face. "Thanks for not reminding me how lucky I am." Emotion stopped me from saying more.

He wrapped me in his strong embrace, and we stood beside the home I'd chosen to live in and raise Nate and Lacey Jane. I didn't know how long I cried, but Marc never got restless. If he was uncomfortable with my meltdown, he hid it well.

At last I edged away and swiped at the last tears. "This is ridiculous. I'm sorry for my behavior. No one and no animals were harmed in the fire. I should be grateful. No, I *am* grateful. Let's get to work."

"Whoa, hold up there. Don't be so hard on yourself." Marc placed his finger under my chin and applied enough pressure for me to look up and meet his gaze. "You haven't given yourself time to mourn. Basically, all of your earthly belongings are gone. No more books, clothes, dishes, laptop, and all the other things that are part of your daily life. They're familiar and comfortable."

"Marc Williams, you are something else." Tension eased from my body. "Thanks for not judging me harshly."

An SUV from the fire department turned onto the street, ending our conversation.

"Maybe we're about to get some answers." Marc reached for my hand, and we stood in front of the rubble of my home.

The fire official stepped from the vehicle with a clipboard in his hand. He wore a blue shirt tucked into rugged dark pants and walked with an air of authority. Quick determined steps. He stopped a few feet in front of us.

I took a deep breath. Please, Lord, give me strength.

Chapter Thirty-Six

THE MAN STUCK OUT his hand as if wanting to shake with me. "I'm Bernard Holden, the investigator in charge of your fire."

"Andi Grace Scott and this is Marc Williams." I met his firm grip with strength I'd mustered from deep inside. "What can you tell me about the fire? Was it intentional?"

"The cause is undetermined."

I crossed my arms. "Are you saying it was an accident?"

"It means there are causes we can't rule out yet. We're offering a reward for any information, and the local police have interviewed your neighbors. If there are witnesses, we'll find them."

"Can I look through the remains?"

"Sure, but I don't think you'll find much." He checked the pages on the black clipboard. "Have you ever buried a pet on your property?"

"No, sir. Why?" My knees shook.

"We found a bag of dog bones, but we can't be sure they had been buried. How long did you live here?"

"Almost thirteen years. What kind of bag?"

"Plastic. Dark green like for lawn waste."

A wave of dizziness hit me.

Marc squeezed my hand but focused on the firefighter. "Why are you suspicious about the bag?"

"Pets should be buried at least three feet deep. The bag of bones we found wasn't buried and it was covered with a layer of soot and ashes. Not dirt. The bag was located near your property line, not close to the house. There was also a note in the bag." He pulled a photograph from between his pages. "Back off or you're next."

I held out a hand. It trembled. "May I see it?"

He passed the photo to me. "Block letters on an index card. No fingerprints."

"Drat." My right eye twitched. "I don't recognize the handwriting."

Marc said, "Do you believe the threat is directed at Andi Grace?"

Firefighter Holden rubbed his forehead. "It's the theory we're going with for now."

"We all know the warning was meant for me." My heart raced. "It's not random. The arsonist knows me. He knows how much I love dogs, which is why there's a bag of bones. The note is freaking me out. Is the threat meant to hurt me directly or hurt me by attacking Sunny? Don't forget she attacked Danny."

Marc rubbed my shoulder. "You're safe now."

"But for how long?" *Back off or you're next.* "What if the note had been destroyed in the fire? I wouldn't know to quit searching for Tabby's killer."

The investigator tilted his head. "You knew the cat lady? She sure had a big heart. Ms. Malkin insisted we call her Tabby."

I nodded. "Sounds about right. How'd you meet her?"

Marc stepped away and lifted the phone to his ear.

A smile appeared on the investigator's face. "Our first encounter was at a fire on the island. My unit came here when an intoxicated young man knocked over his grill and caught his yard on fire. Tabby happened to be feeding cats at the time. She stood to the side, waiting patiently until we got the situation under control. Then she asked if we needed one of the strays at the fire station."

"What'd you do?"

"At first, I told her we didn't need a pet, but she proceeded to explain how there was a ginger cat who was malnourished and in bad shape. She thought the cat might revive under the watchful eye of the men and women at the firehouse. Before I knew what had happened, I agreed. The very next day she brought the cat to us."

"I love matching dogs to people. How's the cat doing?"

He gave me a thumbs-up. "We named her Blaze, and she's thriving."

Marc rejoined us. "Firefighter Holden, would it be okay for us to walk around the remains?"

"Call me Bernard." He held up a finger and typed into his phone. "A couple of firefighters are nearby and will go through the place for you. Is there anything specific you hope to find?"

I turned toward the ocean side of the island and caught a slight breeze. I gulped in the fresh air. "If any pictures survived, I'd like them. There was a fireproof lock box in my office. Our birth certificates and my mother's rings are in it."

Bernard made a list on a fresh sheet of paper on his clipboard. "What else?"

"I'm not sure. Can I just poke around myself?"

Marc pulled blue latex gloves and surgical face masks from his pockets. "I brought supplies."

The firefighter looked at Marc then me. "The site has been cleared of carbon monoxide and toxic gases, but it'd be safer if you let us perform our duties."

Defeat rolled over my shoulders. I took a deep breath and counted to ten in French. "I understand. Thank you."

I moved to the driveway like an obedient child. Or a mature adult.

Marc joined me. "I'm impressed you didn't charge over the man and tackle it on your own."

"Hey, I can be reasonable."

A white pickup truck arrived and parked behind Bernard's official SUV.

I waved to the men, and they nodded toward us before joining their comrade.

Marc said, "You're reasonable but also headstrong and determined to handle things on your own. I was trying to pay you a compliment."

"Oh, then thanks." I grew warm.

Muted sounds of the ocean hitting the beach and rolling back out to sea brought me a measure of comfort. I couldn't go back in time and stop the arsonist, but I could move forward with renewed determination to find the killer.

Chapter Thirty-Seven

TOWEL-DRYING MY hair after a long, hot shower in Tabby's guest bathroom, I made my way to the dining table. The firefighters had scoured through the rubble of my home while I stood watching, and they'd found a few cherished items. My fireproof lockbox with our birth certificates and my mother's jewelry had survived. They also found a few tools, a metal cooking pot I'd bought at a consignment store, and my gold cross necklace.

I poured myself an ice-cold Coke and sat at the table with the few items spread out on the table. I drank and heard myself swallow in the quiet house.

Marc had dropped me off but promised to return with pizza from Tony's. Kylie was walking Sunny, and Susan was on her way back to Texas.

Rarely was I alone. No dogs were scheduled for the rest of the day.

The peace and quiet made me uneasy. After another sip of Coke, I hopped up and found the remote controllers in a sweetgrass basket on the table beside the couch. With the press of a power button, music swelled into the room. "I Love Paris" by Harry Connick Jr.

Had Tabby liked the song? I relaxed into the music, closed my eyes, and swayed to the tune. Why did I dream of going to Paris? I lived on the island of Heyward Beach, and I wouldn't trade my life. Still, I longed to visit France one day.

The front door opened, and I turned down the volume before peeking to see who'd entered.

Kylie knelt beside Sunny and unfastened her leash.

"How was your walk?"

"Uneventful, just the way I like it." She headed to the refrigerator. "Is it okay if I drink one of Susan's bottles of water?"

"Help yourself." I loved on Sunny.

Kylie took a small sip. "It seems like water this nice should be savored. I think these things are over three dollars a bottle."

"They're all yours."

She took another sip. "I stripped the sheets off the master bed and washed them. They're in the dryer now. What can I help you do?"

"Would you like to stay in the master bedroom?"

"No, I'm settled in my room." She shrugged. "You should have the master, especially if you're considering buying this place. Susan said if I can convince you to make this your home, she'll give me a bonus."

"Are you kidding?" I stood, and Sunny walked over to her water bowl.

"No, she said it'd be like paying a Realtor." Kylie twisted the blue top onto the plastic bottle. "I'm not hiding it from you."

"Thanks for that." At least Susan hadn't resorted to hypnotizing me or trying to brainwash me. "Let's check out the bedroom."

"I'll grab the linens from the dryer and meet you up there."

I climbed the stairs. The entire second floor consisted of a landing with a small sitting area and a door to the master suite. I entered with bated breath. Neutral and unimaginative. Eggshell white walls without a single picture hanging. One slick chrome chair with a floor lamp and small side table filled the corner between the large front window and the smaller side window. A beige loveseat without colorful throw pillows. There wasn't a dresser for my clothes.

I laughed at myself. I barely had any clothes to put into a dresser. Still, the room depressed me.

Kylie clomped up the stairs and dropped the sheets onto the bed. "What do you think?"

"There's no personality. Was Tabby a minimalist, or did Susan remove it all?"

"A little of both. Did you check out the closet? It's bigger than the bedroom I grew up in." She opened the door with a flourish and the lights automatically popped on.

"Wowsers!" A fancy teardrop chandelier hung over a modern white dresser. "I've never seen anything so sparkly."

She laughed. "I know. I've never seen such a fancy light."

"Extravagant and probably too fancy for me."

Kylie laughed. "There's more to this closet. Check out this wall of shelves for your shoes."

"I've never had that many shoes."

"You can use it for whatever you want if you buy the place. Look at the sectionals where you can hang clothes. Honestly, Tabby used one area for jackets and one for blouses and slacks, and she even hung up her shorts."

I sat on the little white bench at the end of the white dresser. So much white.

Kylie walked from one side to the other with slow methodical steps. "Roughly ten feet." She repeated the process in the opposite direction. "Seventeen feet. Ten by seventeen. Can you believe it? I always wanted to explore the entire house, but I didn't want to intrude on Tabby's privacy."

"It's too much for a simple girl like me." I exited the closet and entered the master bathroom. No surprise to find another white room, but what a room. The floor had been made of brown, black, and gray pebbles with a soft white grout. Double vanity sink, freestanding tub, and a shower with eight knobs. How would I ever figure them all out?

Kylie elbowed me. "Just breathe. There's no shame in owning something nice."

I turned in a circle, absorbing the fantastic mind-blowing bathroom. "This is beyond nice. Let's do something normal. Do you want to help me rotate the mattress?"

"Why?"

"You're supposed to rotate them every three months."

"If you say so. Let's do it."

We each took a corner of the mattress and shuffled around.

The doorbell rang, and Kylie dropped her section. "I'll get it."

Sunny's footsteps raced to the door, and she barked.

"It's probably Marc with supper, so I can go." I released my precarious hold on the mattress, leaving it catty-cornered on the box springs. I headed toward the stairs. "Do you want to join us?"

"I've got a date with Dylan. We're going to see a movie then go out to dinner." She passed by me. "I should probably get ready."

"Absolutely." I went downstairs to let Marc inside. "Hey, there."

Chubb barked and squeezed past us to Sunny. The two dogs scampered away.

"Hi. You hungry?" Marc entered the large foyer and headed to the kitchen.

I followed him and two boxes of pizza to the kitchen counter. The spicy aroma stirred my appetite. "I'm starved."

He let the dogs out.

I turned to pull out plates and paused. What would've been an automatic response at my home was now something I needed to think about. In three tries, I found white plates and napkins. "Do you want a Coke?"

"Sure. Did you make a salad?" Marc's dimple appeared, giving me the impression he knew the answer.

"Sorry. I got busy with other things. Do you want one?"

"Not tonight." He lifted the lid of the first box. "Your choices are supreme or veggie."

"I'll take a slice of each." I let the dogs out the back door. "We can eat on the deck, if you'd like."

He glanced at me. "Your hair's wet, and it's getting cool. I think we'll be more comfortable in here."

I moved my few belongings that had survived the fire to the kitchen counter then fixed our drinks. We sat at the maple table, and Harry Connick Jr. continued to croon. Marc reached for my hand. "It's nice to have you all to myself for a change."

His words filled me with a quiet joy. "I agree."

I ate my first slice without saying a word. "Deep down, what do you think I should do about this house? It's furnished and the location is better than my house. Although every home on the actual island is in a good location."

He wiped his mouth with the napkin. "Do you like the place?"

My gaze drifted over the large room. Fresh and clean. New. Nice TV and sound system. Good furniture. "What's not to like? I really think it'd be easy to put my personality into this place. It's kinda exciting to think about it."

Kylie appeared, wearing a trendy dress and boots. "Dylan's out front, and we're running behind. Marc, please help Andi Grace finish turning the mattress. Otherwise, I'm going to get stuck trying to lift it again."

My face grew warm. "You could've said no when I asked."

"I know, but I thought we could turn the thing by ourselves. Who knew a king-size bed was so heavy? Gotta go." She turned on her toe and disappeared down the hall. A few seconds later the door clicked shut.

I avoided making eye contact with Marc and bit into the slice of vegetarian.

"How about a grand tour after we finish turning the mattress? And why are we turning it?"

"I read a magazine article at the dentist's office. It said you should rotate your mattress every three months." I avoided meeting his gaze.

Scratching on the back door brought Marc to his feet. While he opened the door and gave the dogs water, I envisioned changing up the neat and orderly environment. My gaze stopped on the lockbox and jewelry.

Time to get back to solving Tabby's murder. If my hunch was correct, we'd catch the arsonist at the same time.

Chapter Thirty-Eight

AFTER DINNER, WE entered Tabby's bedroom and slid the mattress onto the floor.

Thump.

I looked to see what had fallen.

A brown leather journal with a leather strap lay on the floor. I froze. "Marc, do you see what I see? Tabby's initials are on the cover."

"Su-weet." He reached for the book and studied the cover. "Feel how soft this is."

I moved closer and ran my hands over the surface. "Swanky."

He laughed. "True, and I'm sure you believe there's a clue inside."

"There's got to be a clue. At least I hope so, because I struggled to make sense of Tabby's puzzle books." I held my hand out for the journal.

Marc placed Tabby's diary on the bedside table. "Let's finish your bed first then search for clues."

"You're always logical." I gripped one side of the mattress. "Do you remember which side used to be up?"

His eyes grew wide. "Yeah." He patted the top.

It only took a few minutes to finish the process, but I was winded. "Thanks."

Marc shook his head. "May as well make it up. You'll be glad when it's time to go to bed tonight."

Again, the man made a good point. "You're right, but I can't wait to get into the diary."

"I believe you, but this won't take long." He snatched the white fitted sheet from the pile of fresh linens and we began the process of making the bed.

"These may be the softest sheets I've ever had." I tucked the corners around the mattress.

"I agree. It appears Tabby didn't have trouble spending money for quality products."

"Yeah, but Susan was in charge of decorating. I wonder why she didn't choose bright colors?"

Marc rubbed his chin. "Maybe the neutral atmosphere soothed her or she could've been depressed after her injury. White is fresh and peaceful. It's also the color of innocence. My theory is peace and tranquility."

"I wonder if Tabby added any of her own touches after moving here?"

"It's possible she focused her energy on getting healthy and taking care of the cats on the island."

I reached for one of the four pillow cases and worked on the pillows. "That makes sense. She was smart though, otherwise she wouldn't be the only person to suspect a crime at the beach."

Marc reached for a faded pink and white quilt. It was so old and worn you could barely tell it used to have any pink sections in it. "Is this what you're using for a bedspread?"

"What other option do I have?" I laughed and rubbed the edge between my fingers. "It's the most colorful thing in this room, and it's soft."

"Don't forget smells fresh." He waggled his eyebrows.

"Yeah, Kylie washed all of this today. She's very thoughtful."

We finished making the bed, Marc grabbed the journal, and we hurried downstairs.

Sunny and Chubb each raised their heads when we entered the open family room but must've decided nothing exciting was about to happen because they returned to snoozing on the rug in front of the couch.

I breezed over to the table and patted the spot beside me. "Do you want to look at it together?"

Marc sat beside me, unwound the leather strap, and opened the journal. "It feels like we're invading her privacy."

"I know, but if there's a clue in here to catch her killer, it's the right thing to do. Tabby would want us to catch her killer."

"You're right." Marc opened the book and flipped through the pages. "This goes back to the first of October. Why don't we read it separately? You go first."

"Okay, thanks." I started with the first entry.

Marc left me alone at the table but soon returned with a yellow legal pad and pen. "I had these in my truck and thought you might like to take notes. We're not too far from Daily Java. I think the dogs and I'll walk over there. Would you like coffee?"

"Yes, mocha latte, but I didn't think you drank coffee at night."

"We've got to turn the journal over to Wade, which tells me it's going to be a long night."

"Thanks but sit down a minute." I clicked the pen. "Who do you think is guilty?"

"We've ruled out Susan and Kylie."

"Yeah, and I scratched Leroy from my list."

"Who does that leave?"

"Danny Nichols."

Marc's eyebrows lowered. "What's his motive?"

I wrote down Danny's name and drew a thick line under it. "That's just it. He's running for state representative, and it doesn't make sense he'd be involved in something shady."

"He attacked you in broad daylight in a public place, and he came to your house after he was released from jail. I believe he tampered with the witnesses from your first attack, and he was free within hours of the second confrontation."

"You're right." I wrote each of Marc's statements under Danny's name. "I also saw him with a backpack at the pier after Leroy witnessed the men and the shrimp boat."

"I'd love to know what was in the backpack." Chubb roused and walked over to us, and

Marc rubbed his golden retriever's head.

"Let's dissect your idea of witness tampering. How'd Danny accomplish that?"

Marc appeared to be focused on his dog, but I'd learned when he dug deep for an answer he zoned out.

I started a new list of notes. Tabby's body. Cigarette butts. Possible footprint in deep sand. Duffel bag of money. Shrimp boat. Jet Ski. Gabapentin. Drug or alcohol addiction.

At last Marc met my gaze. "What about Ian Patterson? Kylie claims he didn't take their report seriously. Did he grow up here?"

"No. He's from Myrtle Beach, but he knew some of the guys from sports. They attended camps and competed against each other. I'm pretty sure Ian dated Rachel Farris."

"Name sounds familiar."

"She's Erin Lane's sister and a hospital administrator."

Marc stood and Chubb whined. "I'm definitely going on a coffee run. With a little luck, Erin will be working."

"She's probably baking. Lacey Jane said that's what Erin was doing the other night when she met with Ike." As much as I wanted to pump Erin for information on the local cop, I understood we'd accomplish more if we divided and conquered. "Take my key, and I'll read the journal while you're out."

Marc took the keys, leashed both dogs, and left me alone.

Quiet descended and I dove into the Tabby's entries, determined to find a clue to Tabby's killer.

Chapter Thirty-Nine

I YAWNED AND stretched my arms over my head at the kitchen table. I couldn't wait for the much-needed coffee from Daily Java, but I turned my attention to the journal. If Tabby had suspicions of illegal activity on the beach, she didn't record it in October or November. Her handwriting was neat and so small it strained my eyes. Turning the page to December, I squinted and picked up where I'd left off.

More of the same. Tabby loved the beach and the island cats. She didn't question God about the accident, but she questioned her purpose without a job. It only took one sick stray cat, and she found her purpose. Caring for the wild creatures on the island became her mission.

She began a daily process of bringing them food and milk. She named the cats, and her rough sketches of each one made me smile.

December tenth was the first entry with a mention of the shrimp boat. *I keep seeing shrimp boats out at night but mostly on the weekends.* In this entry she elaborated about the red and white vessel bobbing in the waves and a jet ski stopping next to it. She joked about wondering if this was the way to get the freshest shrimp possible. I laughed.

A few days later, Tabby wrote in her journal about the shrimp boat and another personal water motorcycle. Her term for the jet ski made me smile and I believed she and I could've been good friends, given the chance. The details of the event matched what she'd written on the tenth, except Tabby sketched the water motorcycle below her words. The vessel had been shaded in, and the craft Leroy had described had been dark. I took a leap of faith and believed they were the same boat.

After snapping a photo of Tabby's drawing with my phone, I continued to read and take notes.

A key rattled in the front door, and I headed to investigate. Sunny's excited bark on the porch told me who'd returned, and I opened the door.

"One mocha latte for you." Marc passed the cup to me before entering with the dogs. "The temperature's dropping, but I hope your drink is still warm. I swaddled it in extra napkins."

Not wanting to wait another second, I sniffed the chocolatey aroma then sipped the sweetened cocoa espresso drink. Yum. "It's perfect. What'd you find out about Rachel and Ian?"

Marc unleashed Sunny and Chubb, who beelined it to the water bowls. "They dated for almost a year."

I motioned for him to follow me to the table. "I'll take notes. Keep going."

"Ian was content being a cop. No ambition to try out for detective or anything else. Rachel is a determined woman with clear goals of rising to the top, which explains how she's climbed to the position of hospital administrator. When Rachel decided the two of them didn't have enough in common, she broke up with Ian. He didn't take it well."

"How do you know?" I took another sip of my latte.

"According to Erin, he called and texted her sister at all hours and even showed up at her door a few times. Rachel told him if he didn't back off, she'd file a restraining order."

"Did that work?" My pulse throbbed in my neck. It'd be horrific to have a stalker in a position of authority.

"Erin said it did the trick. He probably didn't want to get canned and decided to leave Rachel alone."

"Thank goodness for Rachel's sake." I shared with him what little Tabby had written about her suspicions. "I've only made it into her December entries though, and this is March. I hope we're getting to the good stuff now."

"Keep reading. Do you mind if I explore the house?"

"Knock yourself out." I turned the page and sipped my coffee. More dates where Tabby saw something she considered suspicious. I wrote down what concerned the woman.

Marc appeared and handed me a small yellow sticky pad. "There's a copier in the office. Why don't you mark pages with clues?"

"Great idea. That'll be quicker." I held out the legal pad. "Do you want to read over my notes?"

"Sounds like a plan." He dropped into the seat across the table from me and took the notes. His fingers curled around mine. "This is nice. Of course, it'd be even nicer if we weren't trying to solve a murder."

"Still, we're spending time together." As far as I was concerned, any time spent with Marc was good.

Sunny lay by my feet, and Chubb settled in beside Marc.

I let go of his hand and lost myself in reading the journal and marking the pages I thought we should copy. The last entry was the day before Tabby died. The handwriting was messier than any of her previous entries. *The man came out of the ocean in a wet suit. His face was covered with a mask. Bare feet. Blue bag. Car near pier. I hid in shadows. He might have seen me. I need to be more careful next time.*

Chills popped out on my neck and crawled up my scalp. "Tabby was afraid the man on the beach saw her." I pointed to the journal entry.

Marc read it then ran a hand over his face. "I agree, but it doesn't mean he killed her."

I shook my head. "In my heart, I believe her death is connected to what she saw. You're a boat guy. Do you know any of the shrimpers?"

He tugged his fingers one at a time, popping them. "Afraid not. Most of the people I used to work with enjoyed boats for pleasure. Sailboats, kayaks, canoes, small yachts, and vessels like that."

"I should've known that as often as I've visited your boat shed. I'll go make copies while you contact Wade." I headed into the home office and turned on a lamp. Shelves full of books lined the interior wall, windows to the back deck took up space on two walls, and an antique secretary hutch desk had been placed in the far corner. More books filled the hutch and could be seen through the glass doors. A cream couch and two chairs with cream upholstery faced the shelves with a coffee table centering them.

Marc followed me and leaned against the doorframe. He glanced at his athletic watch. "It's after eleven."

"Really? Where'd this day go?" I paused. "But it's Saturday night. I'm sure Wade's still awake."

Marc's gray-eyed gaze met mine, and one side of his mouth tipped up. "The things you talk me into."

I shook my finger at him and laughed. "You're the one who said we need to give the journal to the authorities."

"True, but I'll text Wade first and see if he's awake. If he doesn't answer, I'll call him in the morning."

The copier was on a credenza and I studied the buttons before I went to work.

Marc left me alone and disappeared into the kitchen. The sound of his voice assured me he'd reached the sheriff. He soon entered the office. "Wade's on his way over, but he's bringing Hannah. They were on a date when I texted him."

"Nice." Copying only select pages was slower than molasses.

"It looks like Tabby enjoyed reading." Marc turned in a circle.

"She only lived here a little over a year. I wonder if the books belonged to the previous owner." I continued making copies.

Marc walked to the shelves on the left and ran his finger over the spines. "History of South Carolina and Charleston, Bible studies, suspense books, and romances. Interesting selection. Some are fairly current, and there are a few antiques."

I finished the last page. "Wade's job will be easier if I leave the sticky notes in here."

"That'll earn you a lecture." Marc glanced at me.

"My powers of evasion don't work too well, so I may as well be upfront."

Marc chuckled. "Even though he warned you not to get involved?"

I shrugged. "He's got to realize I'm investigating. Tabby was killed, Danny attacked me, Lacey Jane and Kylie were T-boned, and my house burned to the ground."

The doorbell rang.

I grabbed the journal and shoved the copied pages at Marc. "Hide these, will ya? I'll answer the door."

Marc's eyes widened, but he took the paper. "Like where?"

"Somewhere sneaky." I left him and hurried through the kitchen-slash-family room to the large entry hall and opened the front door with a quick swish. "Hi, y'all. Come in."

Chubb sniffed Wade and Hannah's pants, but Sunny stood at my side.

Marc appeared and clapped his hands once. The loud sound echoed in the sparsely furnished entry hall. "Hey, Wade. Hannah. Sorry to interrupt your date. Let me get the dogs out of the way so we can talk. Chubb, come on, boy."

Both dogs followed Marc to the back door, where he let them out.

"Are y'all thirsty?" I breezed past the family room and into the kitchen.

Hannah said, "I'm fine."

"Me, too. Marc said you found Tabby's journal."

"Sure did. Under the mattress." I leaned against the counter and passed the diary to him. "Here you go."

"Why were you snooping under the mattress?" He pulled a clear plastic zipper bag from his jacket pocket and inserted the journal.

"I may buy Tabby's house since mine burned to the ground." A lump formed in my throat.

Wade's eyebrows rose. "Interesting. Can you afford this place?"

My heart missed a beat. "I don't think it's any of your business what I can afford."

He lifted a shoulder. "Some might say you burned your house down for the insurance money."

Hannah sniffed and distanced herself from Wade. "Andi Grace isn't that kind of person."

"No, I'm not. I loved my little beach cottage." I inhaled deeply. "For your information, Tabby's daughter really doesn't want to be bothered with selling this place. She offered me a sweet deal, and I may buy it."

"Okay." His eye must've twitched, because there was no way he winked at me. "For the record, I would never accuse you of setting fire to your house for the insurance money." Wade focused on the journal in the clear plastic bag. "Did you find this with the sticky notes in it?"

"No." I pressed my lips together. The less I said, the better.

Wade appeared to struggle not to smile. "On the other hand, I have no problem accusing you of looking at evidence before you turn it over."

I pointed at the book. "Lucky for all of us I found Tabby's journal." I didn't mention deputies had searched Tabby's house and missed it. "As I read the diary, it seemed like a good idea to mark where the most important information is located. You know, to save time."

Marc crossed the kitchen and stood at my side.

Wade ran a hand through his dark hair. "Andi Grace, have you ever considered applying to the police academy? If you're going to keep butting into our murder investigations, you should get yourself trained."

Hannah's gaze darted from Wade to me. "Oh, dear, I'm sure he didn't mean to be rude, Andi Grace. It's late, and we should go."

With my hands on the counter to brace myself, I leaned forward. "My skin is thick enough not to let Wade hurt my feelings. His desire for me to mind my own business is to protect me. I understand your motive, Wade, but Tabby's killer has taken this too far."

"No disrespect intended. I really think you should consider my suggestion." The sheriff stepped to the white kitchen counter and examined what had been rescued from the fire. "I heard the arson investigator met you at the site."

"You mean my home."

Wade's eyes widened. "Exactly. I'm sorry for being insensitive. Is this all you found?"

"I'm afraid so." The pitiful collection of belongings zapped the frustration right out of me. The lump returned to my throat. "It's been a long and emotional day. Let's call it a night."

Wade clutched the protected journal in his hands and didn't budge. "Investigator Holden also informed me you saw a picture of the threatening note."

"Yes. He said there were no fingerprints. Is that right?"

"Yeah, but the note and bag of bones prove the fire was arson." Wade rolled his shoulders.

I'd suspected the verdict, but my knees wobbled. "Somebody is really out to get me, and if it's the same person who killed Tabby, I could be next." My voice shook as much as my legs.

"We've got a forensic scientist studying the bones. She believes they're old."

Oddly, the information gave me some relief. "At least a dog wasn't killed in order to scare me more."

Marc drew close to me and slid his arm around my shoulders. "Wade, can we have police surveillance? Or should Andi Grace stay at the plantation? Where will she be the safest?"

Wade shook his head. "One of the local cops might swing by every so often, but it's a small police force."

My pulse skittered. "I'm not sure Officer Patterson can be trusted. He didn't take Tabby's complaint seriously. If he's assigned to keep an eye on this place, I don't have much confidence I'll be safe. It might be better not to alert him."

Wade crossed his arms. "I have no control over the local cops."

"Who's in charge of my fire?"

"We're working with the fire department and Heyward Beach Police Department. The combined effort should enable us to get answers faster."

Drat. The more Ian Patterson was involved, the more I might be in danger.

Marc rubbed his hands together. "Okay then, it sounds like the plantation is the best place for you to stay."

A headache blossomed. "Peter was killed at the plantation, which makes me suspicious it's the best place. Don't forget I almost lost my life there, too. I feel safer in Tabby's house with Sunny."

"I don't agree." Marc shook his head. "There are plenty of people at the bed and breakfast these days. Just don't wander off alone. If you stay here, it'll only be you and Kylie."

I lifted my chin. "Don't forget Sunny."

Wade raised his hands. "We're going to leave. You two can come to a decision by yourselves. Just let me know. I'll research Ian Patterson's past and see what I can dig up. I'll also read the journal tonight."

I nudged Marc. "Tell Wade what you found out about Ian, and I'll talk to Hannah."

The men hung back, and Hannah and I walked outside to the front porch. I inhaled the briny ocean fragrance, and my soul sang. "Even with a killer on the loose, the island is my favorite place in the world."

Hannah nodded. "I'd offer to spend the night with y'all, but I need to take care of Gus."

"What?"

"Yeah, I picked him up from Dylan earlier today and fell in love with the little guy."

Her words thrilled me, and I hugged my friend. "You won't regret adopting him."

"Don't forget you offered to help me train him."

"No problem." I leaned against the porch rail. "Don't be too hard on Wade about tonight. I think he worries I'll get myself killed."

"He was kinda hard on you."

I laughed. "I knew he wouldn't be happy I read Tabby's journal but did it anyway. Have you mentioned to Wade your concern about Danny?"

"No. Wade is law enforcement, and I'd hate to risk Danny finding out and getting angrier at me. Even worse he might say I'm trying to influence the election. I don't want Wade to lose his next election because of me." She sat in a rocker. "I'm brave enough to adopt a dog, but I draw the line at crossing Danny. It's not worth stirring the pot."

Wade stepped out the doorway. "Stir what pot?"

Hannah's eyes grew wide.

I stood straight. "You two are invited to have chili with us. How does next weekend sound?"

Marc closed the door behind him. "Can you cook chili?"

I laughed. "You really don't trust my skills in the kitchen."

"And you didn't answer the question." He grinned.

Hannah got out of the rocking chair and stood close to Wade. "I've got a great recipe. I use three kinds of beans and plenty of vegetables. I'll bring it."

Wade reached for Hannah's hand with his free one. "We can work out the details later. Y'all have a good night."

I leaned my back against Marc, and we watched them drive away. With his arms wrapped around me, he kissed my neck then turned me to face him. "What were you two really discussing? I know you didn't invite them over to eat something you've probably never prepared before."

"Busted. What if I'd said grilled cheese and tomato soup from a can?"

"Much more believable." He smiled. "What gives?"

I placed my hands on his shoulders. "We were discussing Danny. Hannah hasn't mentioned her suspicions to Wade yet. She wants to run a clean election. Focus on the issues. You know what I mean?"

"The sheriff's a smart guy, and I believe he can handle the truth. She needs to tell him."

"Yes, but the Nichols family has lots of money and power. Look at how easy it was for Danny to get out of jail after he attacked me."

"You're right. I've seen dirty dealings, but it did shock me." Marc frowned. "If you refuse to stay at the plantation, it might be a good idea if I sleep on your couch tonight."

"I don't want to put you out."

Woof. Woof.

I jumped away from Marc. "That's Sunny."

Ruff. Ruff.

"And that's Chubb." Marc ran into the house.

I only slowed to slam the door and lock it. I wouldn't be stupid enough to leave it wide open for Tabby's killer to walk right in while I was busy with the dogs.

Chapter Forty

WHAT TABBY LACKED in flamboyance, she made up for with lights. The entire backyard was visible from the powerful illumination of the floodlights. The small yard was neat and didn't contain a lot of large bushes where an intruder could hide. Palm trees, a crepe myrtle, and small azaleas. Minimalism might be the theme of this house and the landscaping, but it was pretty. "I don't see anybody."

Sunny and Chubb stood with us on the back porch, panting.

"I'll walk the perimeter. Your fence is probably five feet tall, making it difficult to jump over. Maybe somebody tried and failed."

I prayed for Marc's safety while he inspected the area. He was thorough and took his time checking out the white vinyl fence.

He returned and climbed the stairs to the porch. "I don't see any signs of an intruder, but it doesn't mean somebody didn't try."

"Thanks." I stared out into the yard. "Can you picture me living here?"

Marc met my gaze. "Yeah, I can. It's got good bones, and you can't beat the location. Once you put your designing touch on the interior, I can totally see you living here."

An owl hooted, and Sunny barked.

"Hey, maybe that's what upset the dogs."

"Just in case it's not, let's go inside." Marc held the door open, and we entered the kitchen. "What's holding you back from buying Tabby's house?"

I filled two water bowls for the dogs. Was it because I didn't feel worthy of nice things? I'd spent over one third of my life scrimping. Did I deserve something this nice? Did my old home fit my personality? "I'm not exactly sure. Maybe it's the memories. I already own the land where my home stood."

"You've had a lot of shocks this past year. Why not make it easy on yourself and buy this?"

Exhaustion swept through me. "You make a good point, Counselor. Then again, you usually do."

The front door rattled, and I froze.

"Stay here." Marc headed to the front of the house with Chubb on his heels. Sunny stood at attention beside me.

I held my breath. My ears rang with the pressure to hear who was entering.

Kylie's laughter eased the tension from my body.

Soon Marc, Kylie, and Dylan appeared in the family room.

Kylie said, "You won't believe what we saw. A whale."

Dylan nodded. "We were on the pier, looking at the water, and I think we saw a momma whale and her baby swim past us."

Marc patted Dylan's shoulder. "That doesn't happen often."

"I know. We stood there watching for the longest time, hoping to get another glimpse."

Kylie removed her jacket. "No such luck though. We waited until the fog grew too thick to see anything. Then we went out for ice cream before coming home."

I ran my hand over Sunny's back. "Did you see anybody on the street?"

Dylan shook his head. "Sorry. The way this fog is rolling in, it's hard to make out much. We passed a car, but I didn't pay much attention."

"It was dark and sporty, but I really don't know makes of cars." Kylie's eyebrows lifted. "Except I know what a Jetta is now."

Marc crossed his arms. "What about a cop vehicle?"

"What's going on?" Dylan's eyes grew wide. "Are your questions related to Tabby's murder?"

Marc and I made eye contact. I couldn't read his expression though.

"Guys, you're scaring me." Kylie's voice warbled.

"For your own safety, you should know. Let's sit down." I was too anxious to relax on the couch and chose a cushioned chair instead. Marc took the seat next to me, while the other two sat close to each other on the couch. "Kylie, you were the first person to share your concerns about Officer Patterson. I think we all need to watch out for him. Right now, we could be in danger from Tabby's killer, the arsonist, and Danny Nichols." I lifted a finger, counting off each threat.

The girl grew pale. "I still don't get why Danny's threatening you."

"The only reason I can think of is because I inherited his uncle's estate."

Marc rubbed his chin. "Kylie's right. Why now? The will was read months ago."

I looked at Marc. "Could it be the drugs? He needs to pay for them?"

Kylie shifted closer to Dylan. "You think he's a drug abuser?"

Dylan reached for her hand. "You sound surprised."

"Well, yeah. He's rich. Most drug addicts I know are poor. Even if a person starts out wealthy, buying drugs can make you poor real fast." She twirled her hair. "Then again, I lived in the poor section of town."

Marc crossed the room, reached for my notebook and passed it to me. "Danny is also running for state representative. If he's hooked on drugs, how else could he pay for them?"

Kylie said, "My parents sometimes acted as mules, and other times they sold drugs on the street. It's a dangerous life. Once my dad tried to keep a little something for himself, and his boss in the organization beat the tar out of him."

I wrote as she talked. Poor Kylie. What a life she'd lived. "I'm impressed you escaped."

"You have no idea."

I studied Dylan and Kylie sitting close together. Neither had come from a good home. Dylan's mother had kidnapped him at a young age from his father and fed him lies. He grew up hating his dad until the cops arrested his mother. His dad loved him but bad choices had landed him in prison. Kylie's parents worked together to make her life miserable. How had these two survived and found their way to each other?

Marc paced. "We're assuming Danny's abusing drugs. Oxycodone, hydrocodone, meth, gabapentin, or who knows what. If that's true, he needs money to support his habit." He stopped and looked at each one of us. "What do we know for a fact?"

I gripped the pen so hard my fingers hurt. "He attacked me and came to my home when he was released. I don't believe for one second he only wanted to talk. I also had a run-in with him at the pier."

Kylie leaned forward, arms on her thighs, and fingers laced together. "Shouldn't we be discussing Tabby's killer instead of Danny?"

I turned through my notes. "I've ruled out you, Susan, Dylan, and Leroy Peck. Who's left?"

"The cop?" Her knuckles whitened.

"Hopefully not." I didn't want a cop to be guilty, but I wrote his name down.

"I can't remember Tabby ever meeting Danny. What would be his motive?"

I rubbed my forehead. "Tabby died on the beach. We've seen Danny in the same vicinity as well as a buried bag of money. I also saw Danny with a backpack at the pier parking lot. You asked for a motive though. Cash. Greed. Drugs."

"There could be other suspects we're not considering." Marc stuffed his hands into his pockets. "The more immediate issue we need to decide is where y'all are going to spend the night."

"I'm not going to the plantation. We have a security system here. Kylie, do you know how to use it?"

"Yes."

Dylan said, "I can spend the night and protect you two."

Not having my work calendar was crippling. "Do we have any dogs spending the night at the plantation?"

"The schedule is clear until Monday. Tomorrow morning Griffin will go to church with Juliet and Nate. So I won't be needed to help with the renovation."

I met Kylie's gaze. "I feel safe with you, Sunny, and the security system. What about you?"

She nodded. "I've survived worse situations."

"It's settled then. Everybody sleep in your own bed tonight."

Dylan left, and Kylie turned in.

I faced Marc. "Thanks for your offer to stay."

"I don't like leaving you."

"That's one of the things I, uh, appreciate about you. We'll be fine."

"I feel like a good boyfriend would stay." He ran a finger down my arm and chills popped out.

I didn't want to grow too dependent on Marc. "I've been taking care of myself for years. We'll be fine." I squeezed his hand. "Thanks for offering."

"Call me if you're even a tiny bit scared." Marc ran a hand through his hair. "No, call 911 first. Then call Wade. His place is closer, and he can get here quicker. Then call me."

It was a rare thing to see Marc rattled, and I was touched.

"If you keep trying to solve mysteries, I may have to move to the island. I don't like living so far away. It makes me feel helpless."

"No matter where you live, you're my hero, Marc Williams." I slid my arms around his neck and kissed him.

He kissed me back with an intensity that removed all thoughts of murder, arson, and unidentified dog bones.

Chapter Forty-One

I SAT AT THE KITCHEN table in Tabby's house with a cup of coffee at my side and notes and pictures spread around me. It'd been impossible for me to concentrate on Pastor Mays's sermon while a murderer roamed freely around Heyward Beach. After the service, I declined Juliet's invitation to join her for lunch at the plantation, and Marc was meeting with a client at the jail.

Nate had gone with Juliet, and Lacey Jane had agreed to spend the afternoon with Ike. In fact, my sister had been spending most of her free time with the marine.

Kylie had gone with Dylan to the plantation, leaving me home alone. The house was so quiet, my growling stomach caught Sunny's attention. I found organic granola bars in a cabinet and grabbed one along with a Coke and settled back at the table.

While I didn't have my original notes, I found the new list I'd begun. On one sheet of paper I'd written the word "why." With a felt tip pen, I circled the word.

Why would somebody kill Tabby?

Money? Love? The woman wasn't in a romantic relationship, and Susan didn't seem to need her mom's inheritance. While researching the Dallas news, it'd been easy to discover Tabby's husband had married a much-younger woman. So it didn't make sense he'd kill her for money or love. He'd moved on with his life.

Could Tabby's murder be chalked up to simply being in the wrong place at the wrong time? I tapped the smooth maple table with my finger. What were the most common excuses people used to explain why they killed another person?

I opened my laptop and asked the question in a search engine. In less than a second, there were multiple articles on this very question. I clicked the most official-looking site. It ended with *gov* making me think it was legit.

Before the list began, the author insisted most of the time a murder victim knew their killer. That statement proved true for the previous murders in Heyward Beach.

I continued reading the post and scanned the top reasons. Then I returned to the top of the list and concentrated on each excuse.

I ruled out sex and lust. Robbery, burglary, car theft, and larceny didn't seem to apply. Arson and gambling were also included as reasons on the website. Tabby wasn't a gambler, and my house had been burned to the ground. Not Tabby's.

Arguments. Interesting. Besides Leroy Peck, had Tabby argued with anybody? I made notes on a clean sheet of paper and would question Kylie later.

Next category was drugs and gangs.

My heart leapt. Drugs. Gabapentin. Somebody had wanted to buy the prescription medicine from Phyllis. Tabby and Leroy had each experienced seizures, and he'd tried gabapentin for a short time. Tabby took phenytoin. The news usually mentioned cocaine, heroin, and oxycodone. Had I ever heard gabapentin mentioned on the news? I couldn't remember.

What else?

I read more of the article until it ended with graphs. Math wasn't my thing, and the sight of a graph made me want to walk away. Except the tallest bar belonged to the category of arguments. Lime green. It was twice as tall as the yellow bar representing drugs as the motive for murder.

On a clean page, I added the possible motives from my internet search. Under money, I listed Susan and Kylie. Leroy obviously went under arguments, even though he'd explained the situation. Still, maybe connecting people to motives would open my eyes to the true killer.

Nothing else on the internet list seemed appropriate to Tabby's situation. I turned to my page where I'd written clues and red herrings. The cigarette butts around Tabby's dead body had never been explained. Were they a clue or a bunny trail?

I'd never know for sure about the footprint I'd spotted in the sand near Tabby's body, but the duffel bag stuffed with money was a definite clue. Money had made my list of reasons to murder a victim.

I turned the page and entered random thoughts. Tabby's body. Cigarette butts. Possible footprint in deep sand. Duffel bag of money. Shrimp boat. Jet Ski. Gabapentin. Drug or alcohol addiction.

How many times was I going to come across the name of a drug I'd never thought about before Tabby's murder? I glanced back at the laptop. Gabapentin led some individuals to a euphoric high. Calmness, becoming more social, and a zombie-like feeling had also been reported.

Danny sure hadn't been calm during my interactions with him, but maybe he took gabapentin to keep his cool for campaign events. It seemed like there were better options if you were anxious, but maybe Danny still dealt with pain issues from his neck injury. That made more sense. The post continued and claimed signs of excessive doses of gabapentin included change in mood, tremors, anxiety, and the inability to feel happy.

The doorbell rang, followed by knocking.

Danny had pounded on the front door at my real home. He'd been moody, angry, and maybe anxious. Could the incident where he dropped his coffee at Daily Java have been due to tremors? Was he taking too much gabapentin?

My biggest problem with considering Danny as a suspect was his lack of connection with Tabby. He didn't own a cat, and he spent most of his free time on the golf course. I walked to the door with Sunny and peeked out.

Marc stood on the front porch, and I opened the door. "Come in."

He still wore his nice slacks, button-up shirt, and red tie. "Clouds are rolling in from the west."

I waved for him to follow me to the family room. "The radio station said to expect rain for the next few days. I always carry extra towels with me to dry the dogs before we reenter their homes." I pictured my Suburban and supply of yellow towels for rainy days.

"What's wrong?"

"Nothing. Or everything. Remind me nobody got hurt in the fire."

Marc pulled me close, and I inhaled his familiar scent. "You're safe and so is Sunny. Everybody survived the fire."

"You're right. The Highlander is really nice. High tech and a smooth ride. Buying new towels is no big deal." *Un, deux, trois, quatre...*

"Let me guess. You're counting to ten in French."

"Guilty." My face grew warm. "I'm not going to be a baby. I'm grateful, and I need to act like it."

"Whoa, don't be so hard on yourself. Losing your home and SUV is a lot to deal with." He ran his hands over my back.

I closed my eyes, not wanting to move.

After a few moments, Marc kissed my temple. "Whatcha working on?"

I moved into the kitchen and caught him up on my progress while fixing a fresh pot of coffee.

Marc leaned against the counter, stretched his long legs out, and crossed them at the ankles. "I'm not sure about Danny preferring the golf course. Didn't you see him running on the beach the day you were with Leroy?"

"You're right. He threatened me that day, too." I prepared a mug of coffee for Marc and refilled my empty cup. "I've been trying to find a connection between Tabby and Danny. It's possible they didn't really know each other. Leroy told me about the shrimp boat and the person on the jet ski. He said it happened fast. He understands why the cops didn't really have confidence in Tabby's report. Leroy believes if you weren't looking for something unusual, you wouldn't see it."

"Tabby was patient with the cats in order to earn their trust. It makes sense she'd have the fortitude to keep watching the shrimp boat if she suspected illegal activity."

"You're right." I placed our mugs on stone coasters on the nice kitchen table and grabbed napkins before sitting. "It explains how Tabby caught on to whatever was happening. She took notes in her diary and the puzzle books."

Marc sat in the chair beside me. "Why both?"

"Good question." I sipped my coffee. "Tabby's bedroom is upstairs. What if she was tired after her walks? She used the puzzle books to record dates and minor details. In the journal, she wrote in depth about what she saw."

"That's a good theory." He loosened his tie.

Sunny whined and gazed at me. I let her out the back door and returned. "Suppose Hannah's suspicions are correct. Danny's hooked on drugs. He needs to be extra cautious because he's running for state representative."

Marc reached for his mug. "He wouldn't be the first politician with a substance abuse issue, and he doesn't want the press to get wind of it. Hannah's making a stand to crack down on drug trafficking, and if Danny's hooked, it'll make it harder to get elected."

I slid my notes to him. "This list is symptoms a person experiences if they take too much gabapentin."

"Why focus on gabapentin?" He rolled his sleeves up.

"It's not a controlled substance, making it harder to track. Although Danny could be drinking too much or taking oxycodone or hydrocodone."

"Don't forget benzodiazepines."

"Valium and those kinds of drugs are also tracked."

"Right." Marc ran a hand over his face. "Okay, suppose he's taking gabapentin. Do you think he's buying it off the street? It'd make more sense to doctor shop and go to different pharmacies."

"Good point." I wanted to pound the table. "What are we missing?"

Marc turned to the next page and wrote Danny's name at the top. "What do we know about your old boyfriend?"

I avoided eye contact. "Please don't judge me for poor taste in men when I was in high school."

"Your taste in men is improving." He winked at me.

I met his gaze. "Definitely."

"People change, and it's not always for the better." Marc began writing. "Running for political office takes money. I'm struggling to believe he can keep up with his law career and run for a political office while he's hooked on drugs."

"We ruled out drinking because we've never smelled alcohol on his breath." I sighed. "We need to find out who's contributing to his campaign."

Marc added to his list. "Has Danny had an accident recently? Say in the last five years?"

"He had a neck injury while he lived in Georgia. Let me ask some of the guys if they know of anything else." I texted Nate, Griffin, Wade, and David.

Nate replied to the group text almost instantly. Danny injured his neck water skiing in Georgia. Hospitalized. Physical therapy. Good now.

Thunder clapped, and Sunny howled.

I pushed my phone toward Marc and raced to let my German shepherd inside. "Looks like the storm is here."

He lifted my phone. "In more ways than one."

I stopped in my tracks. "If he's involved with whatever's happening on the beach, is it related to pain meds? Have we finally found a link between Danny and Tabby?"

"I don't believe it's a coincidence. So is he a dealer or buyer?" Marc leaned back and crossed his arms. "It's possible he's running his campaign with money by trafficking drugs."

"That'd be something else." My heart tempo sped up. "Or maybe he's a drug runner. How did the smugglers lose the bag of money? It seems like you'd swap the counterfeit gabapentin for the cash, but maybe I've watched too many movies to know. I may take more walks on the beach and see if I stumble upon anything."

Marc moved to the chair next to me, placing his warm hands on my shoulders. "Tabby may have thought the same thing. Please don't go alone. Call me, and I'll join you."

"You live twenty minutes away, and it's not fair to disturb your plans. Sunny will protect me."

My German shepherd barked and looked back and forth at us. I rubbed her head. "It's okay."

Marc said, "I barely have time to work on my boats these days. Maybe I should look for a place on the island instead of living so far away."

I laughed. "You're my boyfriend, not my bodyguard."

"As your boyfriend, I'll do whatever it takes to keep you safe." He wrapped his arms around me, pulling me close. "Another perk to dating you is we can kiss whenever we want."

His lips touched mine, and I forgot about finding Tabby's killer.

Chapter Forty-Two

SUNNY RODE SHOTGUN, with her head hanging out the window and her tongue lapping the cool breeze, after I completed my Monday morning dog walking schedule. We headed to Stay and Play.

The morning's humidity was a sure sign of spring, and azaleas had burst into bloom along River Road. The beautiful sight took the sting out of knowing Tabby's killer still roamed free.

I slowed the Highlander and turned onto Kennady Plantation's drive. When I rounded the main house, Ethan and Violet Seitz stood near the dog barn with Yoyo. Dylan was talking to them. A glance at the SUV's clock confirmed I wasn't late. I parked in the shade, and we hurried to meet them.

Sunny barked her greeting to the puppy but remained at my side.

"Good girl."

Dylan smiled. "Hey, boss. I showed them around the dog play areas."

"Great. Do you mind taking Sunny? She's had a full morning, so it's probably time for water and a nap."

He nodded. "Come on, Sunny. Let's go."

I turned to Yoyo and his owners. "How are y'all today? Have you practiced what we worked on?"

"I've been practicing with him because Ethan worked all weekend." She pointed a thumb at her husband.

"How'd it go, Violet?"

Yoyo jumped on me, and I put my palm out. "Sit."

The black lab puppy with big paws sat and rolled his eyes up to me.

"Good boy." I rubbed his back and slipped him a treat.

Violet groaned. "That was amazing. I wish he minded me like he does you."

"Give it time." I pointed to Yoyo. "This is a perfect example of puppy dog eyes. Don't give in to him."

Ethan chuckled. "Yeah, I've seen that expression before."

I continued working with Yoyo and explaining to his owners what they should do at home so we'd all be consistent. During one of our breaks, I quizzed Ethan about finding a patient's drug history.

"It's not uncommon for me to look up and find out if a customer is taking the same drug from another pharmacy. Although it has to be a controlled drug to pop up."

"Say a man takes hydrocodone. When you search, do you only see if he's filling it in South Carolina?"

"I can request other states. For instance, if you moved here from North Carolina, and I knew that, I'll definitely check both states."

"Is it required?"

"It's up to the pharmacist's discretion." Ethan ran a hand over his face. "Seems like you were asking me about gabapentin last time we spoke. It's only a controlled drug in Kentucky and a few other states so far. It won't show up on a report. Before you ask, the only way I'd know if you took it was if you were dumb enough to have your insurance pay for it one place and you brought me another prescription. If I bill your insurance for the same thing, they'll reject, which tells me you filled it recently."

Yoyo bounded over to us from the water bowl and jumped on Ethan.

"Tell him to sit, Ethan." We continued the lesson, and I even extended the time at no extra cost. Ethan had been nice to answer my questions, and I wanted to return his kindness.

After they left, I headed to the dog barn and pulled an icy Coke from the retro refrigerator. We'd moved it from an old storage building on the plantation and painted it teal. It provided a pop of color and kept soft drinks super cold.

I texted Wade and David from my office, and soon my ring tone played.

"Hi, Wade. Thanks for calling." I propped my feet on the desk.

"What's up?"

"I was just talking to Ethan Seitz about checking a person's drug history. Can you find out if Danny's taking controlled drugs or gabapentin in Georgia?"

"Why?" His tone was gruff.

"Suppose Tabby stumbled into the middle of some kind of drug scheme. Say, smuggling?" I held my breath, waiting for his reply.

"If we have drug trafficking, we're going to need the Coast Guard, DEA, and maybe FBI to help us put a stop to it."

"That's a lot of people to bother for a hunch." I placed the cold bottle against my forehead.

"I believe it's more than a hunch, but we need to continue gathering evidence before we act. I plan to share this information with David. To make a case, we need to do this the right way. Be smart, Andi Grace, and be patient."

"I will. Thanks, Wade." I disconnected and sipped on my Coke.

Danny couldn't be involved with drug smugglers. I'd go as far as believing he'd gotten hooked on pain killers. Doctor shopping? Maybe. I'd seen him on the beach the day Leroy and I had gone for a walk. He'd attacked me again in the pier parking lot. Why? Did it go back to the fact I'd inherited Peter's plantation? Or something else?

Tabby died on the beach, and most of the clues revolved around her walking routine. A quick check of my schedule assured me I had time to run to the pier. I'd reexamine the area where we found her body and hope it triggered something.

In less than an hour, Sunny and I strolled onto the pier after texting Marc about my plan. He'd asked so nicely. How could I refuse to keep him updated?

White clouds drifted by in the blue sky, and a breeze tousled my hair. I secured it with an elastic hair tie and lifted my face to the sun.

"Andi Grace, how are you?"

I opened my eyes to see Ike Gage. "Hi, Ike. I'm good. How about you?" Did he feel as awkward as I did?

He propped his forearms on the pier's wood rail. "I'm not catching much today, but you can't beat the weather."

"Amen to that. How long are you staying in Heyward Beach?"

"It depends. I'm considering moving here." He nudged his hat back, revealing more of his face.

"Because of Lacey Jane?" At my feet, Sunny stretched out in a sunbeam.

"Yes. I've got a lot of lost time to make up for." He stared toward the beach. "How do you feel about me spending time with your sister?"

"I'm good with it as long as you don't break her heart."

"That'll never happen. She's my only child, and I loved your mother. So much so that I honored her desire to stay with her family."

"I appreciate that." I wouldn't judge him for his relationship with my mother over twenty years ago.

"I was sorry to hear about the fire."

"It was arson." A reflection from the sand caught my eye.

Ike straightened and turned toward me. "Andi Grace, I'm not your father and won't pretend to be, but I'm concerned for your safety."

"I don't plan to put Lacey Jane in danger."

He stood taller. "You need to protect yourself as well. Have you considered that the person who stole my truck and T-boned your sister may have done so in order to get you to quit investigating Tabby's murder?"

I shivered.

"Think about it. A person broke into my truck, hot-wired it, and hit the vehicle your sister was riding in. It's a small town, and I hardly think it's a coincidence. If she'd been hurt worse, you wouldn't have time to investigate."

"You make a good point. Let me see what I can find out." I pulled my phone out of my shorts' pocket and texted Wade, David, and Marc. **Did you catch the person who stole Ike Gage's truck?**

Sunny's tail swished through the air and landed back on the pier. She never opened her eyes, and I smiled. "She naps more than she used to."

Ike slid on aviator sunglasses. "She seems like a good dog."

"She's the best."

He nodded. "Who's good with engines or motors around here?"

"My mechanic is in Georgetown, but he also pastors a small church. His name is Robert Durgan, and I can't imagine he'd hot-wire your truck. He and my dad were friends, and for years he only charged me for parts. You'll learn that in Heyward Beach we believe in looking out for our friends." I lifted my chin. No way I'd let him suspect Robert.

"Who else can you think of?"

"Marc works on boats, but he focuses more on the wood, if that makes sense. Kayaks are one of his specialties, and they don't have motors."

"We're not going to consider your boyfriend. Who deals with boat repairs?"

How much had Lacey Jane told Ike? "Josh Tecco. He's the owner of HOSE, and he can fix all kinds of water crafts."

"Heyward Outdoor Sports Establishment? I met Josh the other day."

"Really?"

"Yeah, when I move here, I might want to buy a fishing boat. Tecco is older than you."

"By at least ten years. He used to be kinda wild, but I assumed he settled down when he started his business."

"Interesting." Ike returned to leaning on the rail.

We stood on the pier over the beach, not the water. The reflection caught my eye again. "Do you see that?"

He squinted. "The shiny object?"

"That's the one. I'm going to see what it is." I snapped my fingers. "Come, Sunny."

"Hold on. Let me put my gear in the back of my truck, and I'll go with you."

I walked with him to the parking lot and matched his brisk stride. Either my ankle had healed, or I was too distracted to notice the pain. "Did you get a new truck?"

"Sure did. Mine was officially totaled. I'd put close to three hundred thousand miles on it."

I nodded. "It's like losing a friend."

"You got that right." After stowing his gear in the truck bed, Ike touched my elbow, and the three of us headed to the beach entrance. "Lacey Jane said your SUV was destroyed in the fire."

"The fire was a warning for me to quit looking into Tabby's murder." I plowed through the thick loose sand until I reached the firmer area of the beach.

Ike said, "If your sister had been seriously injured in the wreck, I imagine you would've remained at her bedside."

"Without a doubt. We're a small family, and we stick together. I've always believed that one day we'll all get married and our family will grow. You've been a surprise."

Ike carried himself in an authoritative manner. He slowed his stride. "Andi Grace, I appreciate how you've taken care of Lacey Jane for all the years since your parents died."

I stopped and swallowed hard. "I've helped raise her since the day she was born. I knew there were problems between my parents, and I may have had childish suspicions, but I never knew for sure if one of them had been unfaithful until the day I met you."

"How'd you figure it out?"

I could imagine soldiers under his command shivering in their boots if they got sideways with the retired marine. "The resemblance is undeniable. I like to figure out mysteries and puzzles, and it didn't take long to decide you were here to find your daughter."

"Some people would've prevented me from taking action."

I nodded at the truth of his words. "I tend to believe Lacey Jane has a big enough heart to love us and to love you. If you can add joy to her life, I'm supportive. But if you bring her misery, watch out. You'll see me on full protective detail."

He met my gaze. "I believe you, but I have no intention of hurting Lacey Jane."

"Good enough. Now let's find the shiny object."

Together we moved with slow determined steps, looking at the sand for whatever we'd spotted from the pier. Sunny walked with her ears perked up and surveyed the beach.

"I believe this is what you spotted." Ike squatted and pointed to a small mound of sand.

Sunny circled and stopped beside me.

My heart picked up its tempo and I joined the retired marine. Half-covered by sand was a pair of high-powered binoculars. I reached for a shell and shoveled until the object was visible. "Look. A return address label."

"It's faded. I'm not sure I can make out the name without my readers."

I found the camera app on my phone and snapped pictures from different angles and zoomed in on the label. "It's hard to tell for sure, but it almost looks like Texas is part of the address."

"Is that a good thing?"

"Tabby was from Texas. I'm going to call the sheriff. If you don't want to be involved, I understand."

"Not the way I roll. I gave the cop my statement when that attorney came after you in the parking lot, and I'll tell the authorities about our find today." He stood and offered his hand to help me up.

Wade didn't answer, so I left a message. "I'm going to call Deputy Wayne."

"The young man who's interested in Lacey Jane?" His stance relaxed.

"Yes. Have you met him?"

"As a matter of fact, I have. He seems decent, and he's definitely smitten with your sister."

David's voice came through my phone and I held up my hand to let Ike know. "This is Deputy Wayne."

"Hey, it's Andi Grace. I'm on the beach with Ike Gage, and we've found something I think could be linked to Tabby's murder."

"Where exactly?"

"North of the pier."

"On the way."

I laughed. "He's not very chatty when it comes to work."

Ike smiled. "I can respect that."

"Andi Grace." A masculine voice called out.

Dread filled me at the sound of Danny's voice. Thank goodness Ike was with me. "I can't believe this. If he's involved with Tabby's murder, he's going to know we found a clue."

"No problem." Ike kicked sand over our evidence, making it invisible by the time Danny joined us.

Chapter Forty-Three

"ANDI GRACE, WHAT a beautiful day for a walk on the beach." Danny oozed charm when he greeted me. He smiled, and his eyes sparkled. He turned to Ike, and the two men chatted about the weather. Danny wore athletic shorts and a University of Georgia sweatshirt.

Sunny shifted into attack mode, with a soft, low growl rumbling from her chest.

My brain swirled. Hannah was onto something with the many moods of Danny. Why wasn't he at work? What would he think if David showed up? I sent a quick text to David to warn him of Danny's appearance. "Sorry to be rude. I get a lot of messages from dog owners and just needed to check." Each word was true.

"Being a dog walker suits you, Andi Grace."

His continual use of my name grated on my nerves. "Thanks. Are you campaigning today?"

"Not officially, but I'm always on the campaign trail. How do you two know each other?"

Ike removed his sunglasses and glared at Danny. "We bumped into each other. When Andi Grace mentioned taking a walk on the beach, I tagged along. You know, in case she needed protection from unprovoked attacks in the parking lot. You probably don't remember, but despite Officer Patterson's resistance to taking my statement, I was a witness to your attack on Andi Grace the other day."

My heart flipped. I wanted to cheer, and I couldn't wait to tell Lacey Jane what Ike had done.

Danny narrowed his eyes. "You're not remembering correctly. Her dog attacked me."

"I saw you grab her by the shirt, at which point her dog bit you."

"Hey, there. Everything all right?" David arrived, wearing his official uniform.

Danny's smile returned. "We're just having a conversation, Deputy Wayne. What are you doing here?"

"Some days I walk on the beach instead of eating during my lunch break. I'm always alert for trouble, though, whether I'm on the clock or not." He reached over and stroked Sunny's head. "Last time I saw the three of you together was at this very pier."

"Since when did it become a crime to have a conversation?" Danny's nostrils flared, making me suspicious he struggled to hold himself together.

"No crime, but I think I'll hang out with y'all. No need to risk an altercation that could be prevented."

"Don't worry. I'm leaving." Danny jogged toward the pier.

Ike said, "How about I follow him and you show the deputy what we found?"

"Sounds like a plan. Hey, Ike, how did you know Danny would show up when you offered to walk down here with me?"

"Experience dealing with enemies." He turned and left me with Sunny and David.

"For what it's worth, Ike approves of you as Lacey Jane's boyfriend." Uh oh. Had my sister shared with David about her relationship to Ike? And even worse, were they serious enough to say they were in a relationship? When would I learn to keep my big fat mouth shut?

"I appreciate you telling me, and yes I know he's her biological father. What do you need to show me?" David showed no signs of stress about me calling him Lacey Jane's boyfriend.

"We think we may have stumbled onto Tabby's binoculars." I got on my knees and explained why we buried the evidence when we spotted Danny.

David slipped on gloves and pulled out a large evidence bag from his pocket. "Let me. Why do you think these belong to Tabby?"

"Leroy Peck told me Tabby had put her return address label on her binoculars so nobody would steal them. This pair has one of those stickers." I inched back, and Sunny lay beside me. Getting sand in the Highlander later only concerned me a smidgen.

It didn't take long to find the binoculars, and David secured them into the bag. "We'll see if a lab tech can read the address clearly."

"Texas was the only clear word to me. You know what that means, don't you?"

He stood and rolled his eyes. "Tabby's from Texas."

"Correctomundo. Have you had time to talk to Wade about drug smuggling?" I hopped to my feet, and we walked slowly toward the beach exit with Sunny.

He sighed. "Yeah, it seems far-fetched but not impossible for our little town. Recently, a smuggling ring for expensive toothbrushes was discovered in Georgia. It's a crazy world."

"Why not just make your own toothbrush and sell it?"

"Yeah, I don't get it. Regardless, smuggling drugs is a lucrative business. Dangerous, but lucrative."

"We know Danny was probably on pain killers in Georgia after his accident. What's your gut instinct about him? Is he a drug addict or smuggler or dealer?" I asked.

"I wish we knew. He wouldn't be the first person to start dealing in order to support his addiction."

"Do you think Officer Patterson is involved?"

"We run in different circles, but I hope not. It's never good when an officer of the law goes bad."

We stopped in the middle of the parking lot.

"I'm heading to Phyllis Mays's house to walk her dogs."

"Keep your eyes open for danger, and by danger, I mean Danny."

"Yes, sir." My phone vibrated with a text from Marc.

David stood by his department vehicle. "You go first." No chance Danny or anybody else would try to come after me as long as the deputy stood watch. I hopped into the Highlander and headed home to drop Sunny off for a nap. I didn't want to wear the poor thing out, and we'd had a full day of walking already.

After getting her situated in the new house, I texted Marc. Heading over to take care of Captain and Pumpkin for Phyllis. I'll call you later.

On the drive, I couldn't shake off the disturbing thoughts of Danny. He'd been smart enough to get into law school and graduate. It was understandable he might get hooked on pain killers. Lots of people did. The issue was getting off them. But while never easy, it was doable.

Even if he was hooked, why become a dealer? If you weren't tracked for taking gabapentin in South Carolina, it should be easy enough to get medicine. Of course, if he was hooked on controlled narcotics, it'd be a different story. If a stranger approached Phyllis for her gabapentin, was there a drug ring?

My stumbling block was why would Danny bother? Was getting involved a way for Danny to get stronger drugs? Maybe he needed money for his campaign.

I parked in Phyllis's driveway and retrieved my supplies of treats, toys, and plastic bags. She'd asked me to wear the dogs out before her bunko group met at her house that night. I wanted to do a good job after irritating her over the medicine.

When I opened the door, Captain and Pumpkin appeared and jumped on me with happy barks. "Why aren't you two in your crates? Down." I gave them the hand signal, and both shepherds obeyed. "Good job." Each one got a treat, and we went to the backyard.

The dogs raced each other around the perimeter of the yard before dividing up to do their business. I threw two balls, and off they went. We continued playing catch until Pumpkin lay at my feet panting. "Are you thirsty?"

I filled the big outdoor water bowl, and left both dogs lapping it up.

Inside the house, I filled the other dog bowls.

The sound of footsteps sent chills racing up my spine. "Phyllis?"

"I'm afraid not."

My heart lurched at the sight of Danny's mother pointing a gun at me.

Chapter Forty-Four

"MRS. NICHOLS, WHAT'S going on?" My voice wobbled as much as my knees.

"I decided to take matters into my own hands." A curl had slipped out of her perfect bun, but her face showed no emotion. None.

"How'd you get inside? I'm sure I locked the door."

"Phyllis gave me a spare key for emergencies." Her nostrils flared. "Although I doubt she ever imagined this kind of quandary. You were warned, yet you continued to pursue my son."

"If you're afraid I want to date Danny, I don't. That was over long ago." I licked my dry lips.

"I'm well aware. All those years ago, Danny would've stayed in a relationship with you if I hadn't convinced him what a leech you would be. My family would've ended up raising your brother and sister. The expense was too much to consider, and I believed Danny could do much better than the likes of you. He needs a wife with good social standing."

Pressure spun around my skull. She'd convinced Danny to dump me when my parents died. It didn't matter. I was far better off without him. "We managed just fine without your money."

"Yet, you were able to convince my brother to leave you nearly all he owned." Her eyes narrowed to crinkled slits.

"We both know why Peter left his estate to me." I managed to keep my voice low and calm, not wanting to stir her wrath.

Mrs. Nichols snorted. "Let's go."

"I can't leave the dogs outside. They might run away."

"You're not going to trick me. I know there's a fence." She held the gun in front of her body and moved closer.

I backed away. "Seriously, we can't just leave them outside. Please. You've been here before and know the dogs. They won't hurt you. I just need to put them in their kennels, then I'll leave with you."

"No!" Her hand shook. "I'm not weak like the other killers you caught. We're leaving right this second. Where are your keys?"

"My pocket." I pointed to the front right pocket of my denim shorts.

"Okay, here's how we're going to do this. We'll walk out to your vehicle. You're going to drive. I'm going to hold the gun in my purse." She picked up her cute Vera Bradley hipster bag and crossed it over her body. Right shoulder to left hip. "If you make any sudden moves, I'll shoot you."

How could such a perky pretty bag be used to conceal a deadly weapon? "Yes, ma'am."

I walked to the front door as slow as possible. "Why did you kill Tabby?"

"She was gathering evidence against Danny and the boys."

"What boys?"

"Josh and Ian."

So I'd been right about that much. How'd I miss the fact Mrs. Nichols was the killer? "Are they all involved in smuggling drugs?"

"Andi Grace, you always were too inquisitive for your own good." She shoved me. "Walk faster."

I stumbled, caught myself on a sturdy, distressed table in the foyer, and managed to pull my phone from my pocket. Not wanting her to spot the device, I held it in my hand opposite of Mrs. Nichols. David and Marc were aware I was coming to Phyllis's house to walk her dogs. It made sense to alert them, but how?

Mrs. Nichols opened the front door. "No funny business. No screaming or trying to run away. I'll shoot you first then come back and shoot Captain and Pumpkin."

"That's a low blow. How can you threaten two innocent dogs?" This was bad. No, worse than bad. Terrible.

"Face it, Andi Grace. I know your weaknesses." She nudged me with the gun. "Go."

I walked slow, glancing in both directions. Nobody appeared to be outside checking their mail, getting into their car, or mowing their lawn. Drat.

We reached the driver's side of the Highlander first. "Should I unlock it?"

"Yes." A vein appeared in her forehead.

I pulled the keys out of my pocket as Mrs. Nichols walked around the front and stopped at the passenger door.

I pushed the lock button.

She tried the handle. "Quit fooling around."

"I'm not used to this SUV yet. My Suburban was destroyed in the house fire. Danny admitted he started the fire. Was he protecting you?"

"He's always been such a good son. Now open the doors."

I pressed the correct button then dropped the keys on the concrete driveway while she got into the passenger seat. I knelt down, swiped my phone open, and hit the text button. My last conversation with Marc opened. I mashed the button to call him. Straight to voice mail, so that's what I'd work with. I whispered, "Marc, I'm at Phyllis's house. Leslie Nichols is here with a gun, and we're leaving in my Highlander. Track me. Find me. Please." Sweat popped out on my face. Standing, I pretended to fool with the door handle, hoping somebody would drive by, preferably a cop.

Mrs. Nichols leaned over and opened the door from the inside. "You're every bit as incompetent as I'd imagined. Get inside!"

I glanced around one more time. Not a soul appeared, so I'd have to try to get a confession from Mrs. Nichols and hope my phone picked up her words.

I got into the vehicle and pulled on the seat belt while dropping the phone under the driver's seat. *Please, God, let it pick up our voices.*

I reversed out of the driveway. "Where to?"

She seemed at a loss, and she hadn't removed her purse. She pulled the gun out with her right hand and rested her left arm on the console. "Let's go to Peter's plantation. Seems fitting, don't you think?"

The plantation could work in my favor. I knew people there. They'd rescue me if they realized I was in danger. "Okay."

The drive was a good twenty minutes from Phyllis's house. Very few people knew about the Highlander I was driving because the Suburban had been my SUV for years.

Ahead of us the stoplight turned yellow, and I eased my foot onto the brake.

"Don't do anything stupid."

"Like what? You're holding a gun on me." My pulse throbbed in my neck.

"That's correct, and you might want to be a little more respectful." She squinted her eyes and the gun bobbed up and down.

Mrs. Nichols planned to kill me. My goal was not to die today. Once again, we were in conflict. I prayed for wisdom. This situation required more than counting in French.

Traffic whizzed by going north and south.

"Are you part of the drug smuggling operation?"

"No." She pointed to the green light. "Go."

I turned left and drove in the slow lane. "Why'd Danny get involved?"

"Hurting his neck changed him." She sniffed. "You know he's not the first person to get hooked on prescription pain killers. Nobody warned us. First it was oxy. Then hydrocodone."

"That's not as strong as oxycodone, so he was making progress." I glanced at the woman holding a gun on me.

"Not exactly. One of the clinics suggested he add gabapentin with the goal of coming off the hydrocodone. Again, he was successful." A prideful tone filled her voice.

He couldn't have been completely successful or else we wouldn't be in this situation. "So what happened?"

"He learned ways to abuse the gabapentin. Take more than prescribed or mix it with booze." She pinched the bridge of her nose.

"How did he get involved with the smugglers?" Cars whizzed past us in the fast lane.

"It became easier than getting multiple prescriptions."

"Danny shared this with you?" My voice squeaked.

Silence.

I worked to keep my voice even. "You two have always been close. I bet he shares everything with you."

Mrs. Nichols sat straighter in her seat. "We are close, and I wanted to do something nice for him. He's so busy with the election and his career. One day I went to his house to run a load of laundry and tidy up."

"Very nice." Gag. Danny was a grown man with no wife or kids to take care of. Why couldn't he wash his own clothes? Plus, I bet most of what he owned went to the dry cleaner.

I switched on the blinker and turned onto River Road. "What happened? Did you find his stash?" Like I'd stumbled onto Phyllis's pills?

"Yes, and he chose that particular moment to come home."

"You confronted him." Pine trees lined the two-lane road.

"I wouldn't call it a confrontation. We had a discussion."

Yeah, right. I gripped the steering wheel. There was never much traffic on this two-lane road. There'd be people at the plantation, but I hated to put their lives at risk. The clock was ticking on my ability to escape. "Why is Josh Tecco involved?"

"Business is down, and selling drugs keeps him afloat. They're counterfeit, which makes it very profitable."

"What about Officer Patterson?"

"Greed. Pure and simple. He wants money."

"Who stole the truck and T-boned my sister?"

"Josh did that. Danny tried to convince the others to leave your sister out of it, but they believed going after your loved ones would stop you. That's something we have in common, Andi Grace. We'll both do anything necessary to protect our family."

I'd never intentionally kill a person to protect my siblings, but I didn't argue. No need to waste time antagonizing Mrs. Nichols. I needed to plan my escape. The closer I got to Kennady Plantation, the faster my heart thundered.

If I died today, would Marc realize how much I loved him? What about Nate and Lacey Jane?

When Marc returned to practicing law, he fixed his phone to accept long messages. If a client had been arrested and only had one call to make, he didn't want them to get cut off mid-communication. I had time and hoped we could be heard.

"Mrs. Nichols, with you pointing your gun at me, I'm forced to look back on my life. What Danny and I had was puppy love."

"Naturally." She rolled her eyes like I was an idiot. "That's why I didn't want him to give up his life's ambitions for you."

In the distance, a large vehicle drove in the other lane toward us. "You did the right thing to break us up. I love my brother and sister too much not to have stayed home with them. I'm in love with Marc Williams. It's a deep and eternal love. If you kill me today, would you tell him?"

She cleared her throat. "Don't be an idiot. If I share your declaration of love, he'll know I murdered you."

That idea bombed if our voices didn't pick up on Marc's phone, but the SUV in the other lane continued heading toward us. No more bad ideas. I wrenched the steering wheel to the left and slammed my foot on the brake.

Mrs. Nichols screamed.

The Highlander spun.

The other vehicle honked, and brakes squealed.

Bang. The gun went off.

Chapter Forty-Five

THE WINDSHIELD exploded, and glass rained down on me. I closed my eyes until my Highlander came to a stop in the middle of River Road.

The big shiny black SUV ground to a stop mere inches from us.

Mrs. Nichols lay draped over the console. One hand held the gun, and her other hand rubbed her head.

I released my seatbelt and bolted out of the vehicle before she regained her wits.

"Lady, have you lost your mind?" A deep voice growled from the bigger vehicle.

"Run, she's got a gun! Please, call the sheriff. Tell him Andi Grace is in trouble." I dashed into the woods lining River Road and ran toward Kennady Plantation.

Azaleas, dogwoods and Bradford pear trees bloomed. I stepped on wild yellow daffodils in my haste to get to the main house before Mrs. Nichols pursued me.

Forsythia branches slapped my face and tugged my hair, bringing tears to my eyes. I angled toward the clearing near the river. I'd walked the path many times, but today I ran for my life.

Pain in my ankle and a stitch in my side slowed my attempt to escape. Coming to a complete stop was out of the question. Mrs. Nichols had a gun, and the man in the other vehicle might have decided I was a complete flake. He could be siding with Danny's mother. She'd fooled many good people over the years.

I reached the trail along the river and glanced over my shoulder. Nobody in sight, but I kept running as fast as possible.

I didn't slow as I neared the main house. This would be the most obvious place Mrs. Nichols would look. But where could I hide? One of the decrepit barns? Stay and Play? The sound of tires rumbling along the long driveway in the woods on my property spurred me to run to the dog barn.

"Whoa, whoa, whoa. Where's the fire?" Griffin called out from the old kitchen.

"Call Wade. If Danny's mom comes here, you never saw me. She's got a gun." I leaned over, hands on knees, and gulped in air. I couldn't think clearly. "I should get back to the house to protect Juliet."

"Not without me." Griffin pulled out his phone and ran with me to the back door of the main house. "Wade, it's Griffin Reed. We need you at the plantation. Andi Grace is with me."

The sound of a vehicle grew louder and closer. From the corner of the house, I caught a glimpse of the black vehicle driving to the front door. "Duck."

Griffin dropped to his knees. "Wade said a man tried to call 911 a few minutes ago but got cut off. The operator got River Road and your name but nothing more. The sheriff and Deputy Wayne are heading here now."

Gasping for air, I met his gaze. "We need to stall. Take Juliet and our guests to safety."

"What are you going to do?"

"If Mrs. Nichols is in the SUV, I'll talk to her."

"Andi Grace, I'm not sure what's happening." He fisted his hands and moved right then left as if he didn't know which way to go.

"We don't have time to discuss it. Be careful and save your sister." In a crouched position, I hustled around the side of the house and hid behind a large bush to assess the situation.

Mrs. Nichols sat in the passenger seat of the idling SUV, wearing a seatbelt this time. She pointed a gun at the beefy driver, who wore a faded ball cap. If he got hurt, it'd be my fault.

I stepped into the open with my hands held up in surrender. "Mrs. Nichols, I'm here. Don't hurt that man. I'm the one you want."

She stepped out of the passenger side and shuffled in my direction. Her steps weren't even, but the gun was pointed at me.

A dog's bark sent shivers up my spine. Chubb.

Where was he? I'd take a bullet before letting Mrs. Nichols shoot Marc's golden retriever.

Woof!

Mrs. Nichols looked around. "Call your dog off, Andi Grace."

"It's not my dog. Sunny's at home." *Please, Chubb. Don't come this way.*

She blinked, and her body listed toward the right. She stumbled.

Had she hit her head hard enough to get a concussion? I'd been able to escape, but I didn't believe she'd passed out.

The man driving the SUV opened his door quietly, keeping his gaze on Mrs. Nichols.

Not wanting anyone else to get hurt, I tried to wave him off without alerting the gun-toting crazed woman who stood in front of the stranger's vehicle.

He opened his back door. What was he up to?

Mrs. Nichols took another unsteady step.

The barking grew louder.

"Chubb," Marc's voice echoed through the surrounding woods.

No, no, no. Why wasn't Marc at the courthouse? He had no clue what he was walking into. If I didn't take some action, Mrs. Nichols could hurt a whole lot of people.

I zoomed my attention onto Mrs. Nichols.

Her gaze met mine, and she blinked. Slow. As if she couldn't focus. The gun lowered.

I sprinted to the woman and knocked the weapon out of her hand. It dropped to the ground with a dull thump.

"Oh no, you don't." Mrs. Nichols raked her fingernails down my face then elbowed me in the chest before searching for the gun.

A baby's cry froze me in my tracks.

Chubb's barking continued.

My head jerked up.

The driver of the SUV cradled a toddler in his arms and ran away from us.

I dove toward Mrs. Nichols in my version of a diving Hurricanrana, a move I'd seen often when watching wrestling with Nate. I didn't have the same momentum as if I'd sprung off the top rope, but I got the jump on Mrs. Nichols, landing on her back and pulling her arm toward me.

"*Umph.*" She twisted under me.

Holding my knees tight around her ribs prevented her from turning over.

Chubb barked furiously and appeared by my side.

"Good boy."

He kept his gaze on Mrs. Nichols and growled.

Footsteps pounded on the ground. "Andi Grace."

"Over here."

"Get off me." Danny's mom virtually growled.

"No, ma'am." My legs quivered from the stress of constraining her movements.

Marc appeared. "Are you okay?"

My nose tingled. "Yes. I tried to call you. Can you get the gun?"

He picked it up. "What's going on?"

"Mrs. Nichols killed Tabby."

Griffin approached us with cautious steps. "It looks like y'all are okay. Juliet and the others are safe."

Wee-oww-Wee-oww! A siren wailed, and Marc aimed the weapon at my captive. "That should be Wade and David."

Mrs. Nichols wiggled. "This is a big misunderstanding, gentlemen. Andi Grace is mistaken."

"No way. I'm clear on what happened." I glanced at Griffin. "The man who drove the SUV has a child. Would you check on them? Maybe Juliet can feed them, just don't let them leave. Once the sheriff and authorities arrive, they'll want to question the driver."

"Which way did they go?"

"Look around the side of the house. Maybe the back."

Griffin started running as the sheriff department vehicles appeared. He glimpsed at us over his shoulder. "Hey, don't let them shoot me."

"Don't worry." My words lacked strength, and I needed somebody to restrain Mrs. Nichols before I fell out.

Marc waved both arms in the air and signaled for Wade to come to us. David followed behind his boss, and soon they had Mrs. Nichols in handcuffs confined in the back of an official vehicle.

Chubb quit growling but remained alert at my side.

"Andi Grace, I'm glad you're okay." Wade unloaded the gun and inserted it into an evidence bag.

"No lecture?" Maybe I had a head injury, too.

One side of his mouth quirked up. "Would it do any good?"

Marc slipped his arm around my shoulders. "Wade may not want to complain, but you and I need to have a conversation."

More sirens wailed in the distance.

"Oh, no. I left my Highlander in the middle of the road."

Wade nodded. "Yes, you did. Our techs need to examine the scene and your vehicle as well. They'll gather evidence, but you'll eventually get it back."

The glass would need to be replaced, but I could deal with that problem another day. I leaned against Marc. "Wade, Mrs. Nichols killed Tabby. Danny is involved with smuggling gabapentin into our area. I don't know where it's coming from, but he's working with Ian Patterson. Josh Tecco's involved, too. This SUV belongs to a man. He drove Mrs. Nichols here, but I'm pretty sure it's because she threatened him with her gun. Oh, he's got a baby or toddler with him. I sent Griffin to find the two of them."

Marc said, "Take a breath. Wade's going to get every detail, but maybe we can continue this conversation inside."

Griffin rounded the corner of the house and joined us with the stranger and child. Juliet opened the front door. An ambulance pulled behind the SUV and stopped. Pandemonium reached a new high.

Dylan appeared with a dog leash. "I heard Chubb barking. Do you want me to take him to the dog barn?"

"That'd be great. Be sure to give him plenty of treats because he deserves it." I knelt beside Chubb and hugged him. "You did a good job protecting me, boy."

Marc rubbed his dog's head. "Yes, you did. Steak dinner for you tonight."

"Come with me, Chubb." Dylan attached the leash to his collar and the two walked to the quiet barn.

Wade talked to his deputies while an EMT spoke to the man and his son. Juliet wrung her hands and stood on the front porch, watching over all the activity.

Marc reached out, and we held hands and looked into each other's eyes. "Let's go inside."

"Sounds good." I needed to sit before my shaky legs gave out.

We sat on the couch in the library, and he ran his hands over my face. His jaw tightened. "She hurt you."

"I'm not going to complain about a few scratches that sting. It could've been so much worse."

His gray-eyed gaze met mine, and his hands dropped to my shoulders. "You shave years off my life each time you try to catch a killer."

"I can't explain why it keeps happening." I sighed. "How'd you get here?"

"Funny thing. The client I met this morning is pregnant and got sick on me, so I came home to change clothes. I'm so sorry I missed your call."

"How'd you know I was in danger?"

"I listened to your message when I took Chubb for a little walk. Somehow, he must've sensed you were in trouble. I followed, and voila, you were in danger."

"Nice way to add French into our conversation, but I had the upper hand by the time you arrived."

He nodded. "You sure did, but I wish I'd gotten to you sooner."

"It probably worked best this way. We've got a recording of Mrs.

Nichols's confession. You didn't erase it, did you?"

"No." He broke into a smile.

"Did you hear everything I said?" My face grew warm. Had he listened to my bold declaration of love?

"Pretty sure I did. Right up to the gunshot. I heard it on the phone and in real life."

"Oh, I guess that was creepy." I shivered.

"You have no idea. I almost threw up, and I don't have morning sickness."

I laughed at his attempt to lighten the mood.

"Seriously, Andi Grace, I heard you say you love me." His fingers tightened on my shoulders. "I love you."

"Really?"

"Yes, and I think we should do something about it." He dropped to his knee and held my hands in his. "Andi Grace, will you marry me?"

Air swooshed out of my lungs. Marc had been nothing but kind and loving to me once we got over the initial shock of meeting when we discovered our first dead body.

"Looks like you need some convincing. Good thing I'm an attorney. Andi Grace, I fell hard for you the first morning we met. Before meeting you, I was content with my solitary life building boats in my little shed on the river. You're usually one step ahead of me. For instance, you hired me to be your attorney so you could tell me what you'd found at the crime scene when Peter was killed. Because of you, I rediscovered my desire to be an attorney and help others. You push me to be a better person, without even realizing what you're doing. I love you and don't want to miss out on living another day without you. Please say you'll marry me."

Wade cleared his throat. "Put the man out of his misery. Say yes and let me conduct my questioning."

My face grew downright hot, but I ignored Wade and faced Marc. "Yes. Yes. Yes. I'll marry you, Marc. Nothing could make me happier."

He leapt to his spot on the couch and kissed me until Wade tapped our shoulders.

"Break it up you two. We've got questions for you to answer right now. You've got the rest of your lives to enjoy the mushy stuff." He smiled. "By the way, congratulations!"

Marc gave me a quick kiss. "I guess we better follow him."

"Yeah, I'd hate to get arrested on the best day of my life."

Chapter Forty-Six

APRIL FOOL'S DAY had never my favorite day because I'd fallen victim to many pranks during my lifetime. Sunny and I spent extra time with all of the dogs on my schedule. They could be trusted not to trick me. After my last appointment, Sunny and I headed to the house. Tabby's house, officially, but each day it seemed more like home.

Susan had been pushing me to make an offer, but I'd been dragging my feet because of Marc's proposal. Where would we live? I feared asking him in case he wanted to back out of the spur-of-the-moment proposal. He'd never given me a ring, so were we truly engaged?

I grabbed the mail and headed inside. "Do you need water?" I filled Sunny's bowl and sorted the mail while my German shepherd lapped the bowl dry.

I sat at the table and kicked off my cross-trainers and toed off my socks. An official-looking letter caught my attention. I ripped open the envelope and scanned the pages. "Girl, we've got another offer from Susan, and it's better than the first one. We have ten days to accept or move out."

My phone rang and Wade's name appeared. "Good morning, Sheriff Stone."

"Morning, Andi Grace. I wanted to update you on the drug smuggling ring."

"Shoot. Why was Danny after me?"

"Two reasons. They thought if you found the body, you might have the missing cash. You've also developed a reputation for catching killers, and they wanted to scare you away from the situation."

"Mrs. Nichols said Danny changed once he started taking drugs, but I still don't get why he'd resort to smuggling when he could get the medicine legally."

"He needed the money for his campaign, and the guys made a huge profit with the counterfeit gabapentin."

Sunny whined and paced near the back door.

"Thanks for the update, Wade."

"Have a good day."

"You too." I hung up and looked at Sunny. "What's wrong with you, girl? Do you need to go out again?" I opened the door.

Sunny barked and raced outside to where Chubb stood at edge of the porch. "Hey, boy. Where'd you come from?"

The two dogs nosed each other. Chubb wore a thick black collar with a small box attached to it. Had Marc dropped off his dog to respond to some kind of emergency?

Barefoot, I walked onto the cool patio. "Chubb, sit."

He and Sunny both sat, panting.

I reached for the little white box with a red ribbon tied around it. "Where's your master?"

Marc's distinct footsteps sounded from the kitchen.

I spun around, prepared to react to some kind of joke or trick.

Marc filled the doorway, wearing a black tuxedo and dressy shoes. "Hey, there."

Ooh la la. I glanced at my bargain T-shirt and shorts I'd bought at a local consignment shop. I was clean but plain. "You look so handsome. Where are you going?"

"Right there." He stepped onto the deck and closed the distance between us. "The first time I proposed was spontaneous."

"Oh, Marc. It was beautiful. I couldn't have asked for anything more." My knees shook.

"You deserve better. I stand here asking you to marry me. Open the box." His dimple appeared.

My hands trembled as I tugged on the red ribbon, tore the white paper, and slipped out a white velvet box. "Oh, Marc."

He took the jewelry box from my hands and opened it with a flourish. "Andi Grace, will you marry me?"

"Yes." I'd told him so the first time he proposed. He'd grown up without a lot of love. "I didn't need a fancy ring to marry you."

"It belonged to my mother. I had to get to the bank in Charleston to retrieve it from the safe deposit box, then I took it to the local jewelry shop to polish it."

Three diamonds sparkled. The biggest in the middle and two smaller ones surrounding it. "It's stunning."

"Besides the sentimental factor, I also thought it was practical enough for you to wear every day when walking the dogs."

"I love it almost as much as I love you."

He lifted the gold diamond ring from where it was nestled in silk and slid it onto my finger. "Perfect fit."

I stood on tiptoes and spent the next few minutes kissing my future husband. "Just one question. Make that two."

Marc laughed. "I expect life will never be boring with you, Andi Grace. What's on your mind?"

"Where will we live? Susan's pushing me for an answer about buying Tabby's place." I hesitated. "You're a boat guy, so if you want to live at your place, I'm willing."

"You're an island girl, and I think we should make Susan an offer on this place. What's the second question?"

"How soon can we get married?"

The dogs barked and ran in circles around the yard. "As soon as possible."

"I like the sound of that." I ran my hands down his lapels. "How about I clean up and we go out to celebrate?"

"I already made plans with Kylie to take over your appointments for the rest of the day. Let the celebrating begin."

His lips touched mine and fireworks exploded through my veins. No longer would April first be my least favorite day of the year. It'd skyrocketed right up to best day ever.

The End

Acknowledgements

Once again I must acknowledge my family who've encouraged me on my writing journey. Thanks!

My critique group has also been a huge help to me as they've listened to my dreams and fears. Thanks Connie Queen, Rhonda Starnes, Sharee Stover, and Sherrinda Ketchersid. You all are amazing!

Thanks to Dawn Dowdle who had faith in me. Also thanks to Debra Dixon and Alexandra Christle for helping me make *Bag of Bones* a better story.

About the Author

JACKIE LAYTON spent most of her life in Kentucky working as a pharmacist and raising her family. But she always dreamed of living on a beach and writing full-time. When she and her husband finally moved to coastal South Carolina, a change of jobs allowed Jackie more time to write. She loves her life in the Low Country. Walks on the beach and collecting shells are a few of her new hobbies she enjoys when not writing.

Bag of Bones is the third book in Jackie's Low Country Dog Walker Mystery series. Jackie also enjoys hearing from readers. Be sure to follow her on Facebook and her website:

jackielaytoncozyauthor.com